---- ★ ----

My memory of the night before was in sharp focus. The band, the lights, Vera touching her hair and tilting her head like a young girl. "Matt was right, Vera was meeting someone," I said. "She was kind of giggly about it—you know how she is. Was."

"She loved men."

"She really seemed to, didn't she?" I said. "Anyway, she said the man she was meeting was 'an officer and a gentleman.'"

Diane shuddered. "If he's the one who killed her, I'm afraid she was wrong. He wasn't a gentleman at all."

---- ★ ----

Celebration
IN
Purple Sage

BARBARA
BURNETT
SMITH

WORLDWIDE.

TORONTO • NEW YORK • LONDON
AMSTERDAM • PARIS • SYDNEY • HAMBURG
STOCKHOLM • ATHENS • TOKYO • MILAN
MADRID • WARSAW • BUDAPEST • AUCKLAND

For my adorable husband, Gary,
who is teaching me that all of life is a celebration.
With love and gratitude.

CELEBRATION IN PURPLE SAGE

A Worldwide Mystery/January 1998

First published by St. Martin's Press, Incorporated.

ISBN 0-373-26261-2

Printed in U.S.A.

ACKNOWLEDGMENTS

Special thanks to Librarian Extraordinaire,
Sandra Borders, who helped me track down musical
information; to author Polly Whitney for the same
reason; and to Deputy Laura Leeds of the McCulloch
County Sheriffs department, who filled me in on jails. I
admit I twisted the information given to me, but I hope I
will be forgiven since it was to make the story better. I
would also like to thank my friend/reader/editor
Caroline Young Petrequin.

Camp John Seybold is as fictional as the town of Purple Sage. However, POW camps to hold German prisoners did exist during World War II. I tried to portray them accurately in *Celebration*, and to share a few of the stories I've been told about them.

I named the camp John Seybold for a young boy of fifteen who went off to fight another war— the Civil War. He was lucky enough to come back and tell about it. It was lucky for me, too, since he became my great-great-grandfather.

—*Barbara*

ONE

"YOU LOOK LIKE A PI from the mean streets of Purple Sage."

I had been staring at my reflection in the full-length mirror and now I swung around to face my husband. Matt was lounging in the doorway, an old paperback in one hand.

"I beg your pardon," I said.

"You know, sweetheart," he said, doing a very bad imitation of Humphrey Bogart, "you look like a PI. Private investigator. A dick."

"You're reading Raymond Chandler again."

"Better. I'm reading Thomas B. Dewey. Much more prolific and, some say, more innovative. I agree; Chandler just got better press."

"Another blow for the press." I turned back to the mirror and groaned at my reflection. I was wearing a pair of gray trousers that had just the tiniest navy blue pinstripe, and a soft white shirt with the sleeves rolled up. I had thought it was jaunty, absolutely the perfect thing, but Matt was right: I looked like a private eye. "Okay," I said, beginning to unbutton the blouse, "so what do you suggest I wear?"

"Anything."

"Like what 'anything'? Name names. Colors, sizes, pieces of apparel," I demanded.

"Jolie, it doesn't matter, it's just my parents—it's not like the King and Queen of England are arriving."

"There is no King of England, and besides, your mother is far more important. She's never been crazy about me, and this time, well...you know," I said.

He knew. His mother was very nice to me in a I-wonder-why-he-married-you? kind of way. She much preferred the lovely Cecily. Cecily Wyatt, as in Matt's ex-wife. From England, with the charming accent. The alcoholic who couldn't hack life on a ranch, or life anywhere at all if it was too near Purple Sage, which is the small town where we live. We. Matt and I and my fifteen-year-old son, Jeremy.

What his mother doesn't know, and what I hope she never finds out, is that Matt and I aren't technically married, anymore. We had separated almost a year earlier and the divorce came through just as we got back together. We hadn't bothered to legalize the relationship again, but now that didn't seem wise. Especially since many of Edith's views on life and morality are a reflection of her fundamentalist Bible Belt education. That's not a bad thing, but sometimes rigid.

I sank down on the bed. "I can't take it anymore," I said dramatically, burying my face in my hands.

Matt, adorable as only Matt can be, opened my closet. "Here," he said, pulling out a pair of practically brand-new jeans. "Wear these. You've had them ever since we got married and I've never seen them on you."

"I can't get my rear end in them."

"Then why don't you throw them away?" he asked in that perfectly rational voice he uses. It sometimes gives me an entirely new perspective on life, and it sometimes gives me homicidal urges.

"Because someday I'm going to lose five pounds," I said, holding back a scream. "What else?"

He looked through the closet. "Okay, here. This dress looks great on you."

I groaned. It was a flowered sundress that looked like it came straight out of the fifties. "Who would wear a stupid thing like that?"

"You did. You bought it for that party at—"

I leaped off the bed and snatched the dress out of his hand. "Matt, I know I bought the dress. I know *when* I bought the dress. And I even know *why* I bought the damn dress. That does not mean that I am going to wear the frigging dress now."

Matt stepped back into the doorway. His voice came out calmly and reasonably, although I suspect it was an effort. He smiled as he said, "Now you're *acting* like a dick." He left.

My adorable husband does not talk like that unless pressured. At least not around me, and while I'll admit I've been less than even-keeled lately, it told me very clearly that he wasn't feeling all that casual about our impending guests either.

I threw the dress to the bottom of the closet and threw myself back on the bed. Life was not as it should be on this planet. It should be easy. I was an adult. I had a teenaged son; I had a wonderful husband; I had a mediocre part-time job, and now I was going to have a visit from my mother-in-law and it was scaring the hell out of me. And it wasn't just her. It was Cecily, too. And everyone else who'd ever lived in Purple Sage. Somehow Purple Sage seemed to be the beginning and the end of all my problems.

Purple Sage had been formed one hundred years ago this month, and to commemorate that event a Centennial Celebration was planned. There would be parades, speeches by officials, and a football game with teams composed of former players from the Purple Sage High School graduating classes of '65 through '85. There would also be a picnic in the park, which could be attended by as many as ten to fifteen thousand people. Obviously not all residents, since Purple Sage only has a population of a little over five thousand.

So where were all these people coming from? Everywhere. According to the news stories I had been reading on the air as part of my duties with KSGE Radio, they were coming from as far away as Africa (a missionary and his wife, class of '59). They were also arriving from Alaska (fisherman, class of '72) and Orlando, Florida (retired, Mr. and Mrs. William Wyatt, Jr., class of '42). And they were flying in from Dover, England (Cecily Wyatt, no class at all).

In anticipation of this great event, I had worked myself into some kind of nervous frenzy, which is not my regular style. During said frenzy, I had gutted our house, which just happens to be Matt's parents' old house that we now live in.

When I had married Matt a little over three years before, we had moved into "his" house. Had I realized that it had been his mother's for almost twenty years and still contained some of her junk, I probably would have suggested other accommodations. As it was, Matt's parents had been gone for several years, and the house was on the ranch, so I said fine and that was that. However, over the three years I had lived there, I had come to dislike portions of the place intensely. Like the den, which was Early American. I detest Early American. There were built-in bookshelves with little wire fronts and ugly curlicues that collected dust. And a beige carpet.

Knowing that Edith Wyatt was at that very moment driving in from the airport in San Antonio made me very aware that there were no longer any Early American curlicues in the den. Or anywhere in the house. The bookshelves had been stripped down to bare wood, the doors and all fancy trim removed, and everything had been restained a pale white with the tiniest tinge of pink. The bookshelves looked wonderful; they matched the three-foot-wide love seats in front of the windows. The windows were new, too. They flanked the new, very large, white rock fireplace.

The beige carpet was gone as well, replaced with a soft, rust-colored tile. And there were other colors that weren't anything like the dark blues and beiges Edith had left behind. Like a deep watery green, and a muted rust with some peach thrown in, and even some aqua. And the furniture was all new. It was also all mine, with no ruffles, no calico, and no maple.

And I hadn't stopped with the den, or even the downstairs. I had redecorated the entire house until it was just the way I'd always wanted a house to be. And just the way Matt said he'd wanted a house. He'd said he loved it. That I was a genius at decorating and he'd never seen anything so wonderful.

The man was such a liar.

I picked up the phone and hardly waited for Diane Atwood to get out a hello before I said, "You've got to help me."

"Help you? With what? Everything is done. I can't believe we got it all done in two months' time, either. My God, Jolie, there are workmen in town who, at this very moment, would be putting out contracts on us if they weren't busy greeting long-lost old buddies."

"I know that," I said. "It's a miracle that we got it finished, and you were wonderful to help so much. I can never thank you enough—really, you were great.''

"You're welcome. So, what's the problem?''

I paused, then said, "I think we screwed up big time. I think Matt's mom is going to hate it. She may be right—I think we overdid it.''

"We did not—''

"It looks like something out of a magazine. You know, forced. Like we tried too hard. Oh, hell, it makes me look like a phony. Even the plants—they're too new. Too symmetrical. She'll know I didn't raise them to look like that.''

"Jolie, you have lost your mind.''

"That's another possibility.'' I had been twisting the phone cord around my hand and I looked down to discover that I had cut off all circulation to my index finger and it was a throbbing purple. I released the cord and untangled myself. Then I said, "It's all just too perfect. What am I going to do?''

"Then clutter it up, for God's sake. I'll send over Randy. He and Jeremy should be able to trash the place in five minutes.'' Randy is Diane's son and Jeremy's best friend.

"And,'' I said, ignoring her offer, "I don't have a clue what to wear, either.''

"I thought you were going to wear your new trousers.''

"I was, but Matt said I looked like a private dick. And he was right. Much too, too...something, for just sitting around the house in the afternoon waiting for company.''

"Okay, then your dark green jeans and that striped shirt.''

"I already tried that. I matched the furniture.''

Diane let out a sigh and said, "Look, go to your closet and get those wheat-colored slacks—''

"They're old.''

"Nobody knows that but you. Wear them with that white Liz Claiborne T-shirt and the gold and green vest that Matt gave you.''

As she spoke I could see the outfit forming in my mind. It was perfect. "Thank you,'' I said humbly. "I don't know what I would have done without you.''

"You would have greeted Edith and Will stark naked. Aren't they supposed to be there soon?"

"Any minute. Their plane arrived in San Antonio at one-twenty. Allowing fifteen minutes to get their bags and ten to rent their car…" I'd done the math a hundred times. "And then the drive—they could be here momentarily. With Cecily."

"I know that part."

I took a breath. "Please, Diane, please, come over. And bring Trey and Randy. Maybe Edith won't notice anything with all of you here. Maybe she won't even see me."

"She'll see you. You'll be fine—perfect. Just like the house."

"Shoes!" I said quickly. "What shoes am I going to wear?"

"That's a decision only you can make. Good-bye." She hung up the phone.

I took a deep breath. I could handle this. I would be a charming and gracious hostess and I would make Edith, and even Cecily, like me if I had to kill them to accomplish it. Not only that, I would do it all with style and panache. I rolled over, sat up, and did some more deep breathing.

I heard a snorting sound behind me and turned to find my son, Jeremy, standing in the doorway in the exact position that Matt had been in. It's eerie. Even though Jeremy is just Matt's adopted son, and has only been that for three years, he's becoming more like Matt every day.

"How long have you been there?" I asked as I rose from the bed and put the phone back on the bedside table.

"Too long, Mom." He glanced at my bed, which I had rumpled during my conversation with Diane. "You told me I wasn't allowed to get on my bedspread, so how come you got on yours?"

"Because, I'm going to fix mine," I said, straightening the comforter and refluffing the pillows until they were perfect. "See?"

Jeremy watched me the whole time, shaking his head.

"What?" I demanded.

"I want you to know something," he said. "After I move out, and you come to visit me, I am not going to get all hyper like you do."

"You're never going to move out." I headed for the closet. "Not 'til you're over thirty. Maybe forty." I opened the door. "Now, please go away. I have to get dressed."

"Yes, Mother. Certainly, Mother. Anything else I can do for you, Mother? How would you like me to behave for company?"

"Act natural!"

He headed for the hallway, muttering to himself, "Wish I'd thought of that."

Less than a minute later Jeremy shouted up the stairs, "Hey, a car just turned off the highway. I think they're here!"

TWO

I THREW ON CLOTHES, raced down the stairs and out the front door, just in time to meet everyone on the front porch.

"Well, there she is," said Will, Matt's father, catching me up in a vigorous hug. He looked just the same as I remembered: about five ten, a little grizzled and very grayed, but with a twinkle lurking behind his dark eyes. He reminded me of a shorter, wizened version of Matt, with a mischievousness that was catching. "Thought you weren't even going to come out and say hello," he went on. "Heard you were on the radio nowadays and I just figured you got too good for us."

"Not hardly," I said, hugging him back. "I'm still way behind you—just running to catch up." I grinned and he laughed. Matt was also grinning, as was Jeremy. It was not a normal situation.

"You're looking real fine, Jolie. I always said Matt had good taste in women. Got that from me—" Will stopped speaking. He stopped grinning at the same time. Maybe because I wasn't the only one of Matt's women around at that particular moment.

I stepped away from Will and there she was. Cecily. In every picture I'd ever seen, Cecily had been like a waif: slender, refined, and almost ethereal in her beauty. Now I was seeing the woman in the flesh, and while she had changed over the years, it hadn't been for the worse. She and I were close to the same height—I'm five three and she looked to be about five five—and near the same weight, which is one hundred and fifteen. But there were differences. Her long pink shorts fit over her slender hips without a hint of a bulge and her white cotton blouse was sleeveless. That was the big difference—no one had seen my upper arms in a good five years. That was when they began to look like my mother's, which is another strike against heredity. Cecily had no such problems. Her arms were lightly muscled, like a gamesmistress's.

Her skin was still the creamy English kind that you always read about in books. I glanced down at her hands—they were smooth and elegant with perfect nails, naturally perfect, even without polish. The cuticles looked like they spent their lives in hot oil.

Edith had told us that Cecily had stopped drinking a few years before, and it was obvious that being on the wagon agreed with Matt's ex.

I took a breath, stepped forward, and forced myself to smile. "You must be Cecily." It was a gesture borrowed from Katharine Hepburn in *Philadelphia Story*.

As Cecily moved toward me, her creamy brown hair swung forward. It was cut in a bob that hung just an inch below her jawline. It made her look both gaminlike and sophisticated at the same time. "How do you do? And you must be Jolie; I've heard so much about you." The look on her face told me that she was sizing me up, but you couldn't hear it in her voice, which was a sweet lilt with an English accent.

"Yes, I'm Jolie, and isn't it nice that we finally get to meet," I said, realizing I had an accent of my own. It was more of the Katharine Hepburn stuff and I knew I had to stop it, but I wasn't sure how. "It's so lovely that you could come for the Celebration. There must be hundreds of people who are dying to see you again.''

"Here's that sausage.'' Matt's mother came swinging through the white picket gate and up the front walk, holding out a package wrapped in butcher paper. "Jolie. There you are.'' She gave me a quick hug. "We stopped in Fredericksburg and when I saw Elgin sausage I just knew I had to have some, but it can't sit out in this sun too long. So, how are you?''

"I'm wonderful, Edith. Come inside—you're right, it's too hot to be standing out here.''

"The house looks different. You expanded the windows, didn't you?'' Edith asked as she stepped over the threshold. Three paces inside the door she stopped dead still, and her mouth flew open. Everyone sort of bumped up behind her as she stood, unmoving, unspeaking, staring at the new living room. For a moment there was only silence, everyone taking in what I had done. Then Edith made a sound. It was a lot like a whimper.

"I guess it seems different from the way it used to be," I said, scooting around Edith, only to discover that huge tears were moving soundlessly down her cheeks. "Oh, no. You must hate it. I—"

Cecily nudged me out of the way, putting an arm around Edith. "Mumsie, it's just the shock—not what you were expecting and all. Here, come and sit down.''

Edith is a big woman, five eight and still in good solid shape. The delicate Cecily moved her like a tug might move a tanker. "Look at this lovely new chair; why don't you sit in it?'' Cecily was saying gently as she eased her down into a teal recliner. "That long drive and all this heat would do anybody in. I'll bet Mattie's got something cold for you to drink.''

I just stood there, stunned, as everyone began scurrying. Jeremy shot out of the room saying something about getting Edith a cool washcloth. *Mattie* went for lemonade. Will said he needed a bathroom and started for the hall before he turned back to me. "Is it still this way, Jolie?''

"Yes, of course."

He moved on, leaving only the three of us women in the room. Edith had dug a tissue out of her purse and was wiping her eyes and blowing her nose. Cecily was patting her hand and still making excuses. I moved closer and made a few of my own.

"I guess we should have told you," I said, "but I, I mean we, just decided to do the remodeling sort of on a whim. No, I don't mean that, but the house seemed so much more functional in the plans. I mean, brighter, and more open, not dark like it was. No, I, I—"

"It is brighter." Edith blew her nose again, although the evidence of the tears was still visible. "It's all right, Jolie. It's very bright. It's very pretty. It fits you. It's just that I don't like surprises—not this kind, anyway. Guess I'm just too old for them."

"It's so completely different," Cecily added, still patting Edith's shoulder. "It must have been the shock that got to you, Mums. It *is* surprising."

Edith nodded. "I just expected to walk in and find my old home. You know, just the way it's always been, only I came in the door and..." A sob escaped and her body heaved with it. The tears started rolling again.

Welcome home.

EVENTUALLY THE FIRST crisis was behind us. Everyone was seated in the living room; Edith, who was still the focal point, was on the recliner. Cecily was perched daintily on the arm of her chair. Had it been Jeremy sitting there I would have told him to get off so he wouldn't break it; the thought of saying something to Cecily actually crossed my mind. It was ungracious, and I knew it, so I sat curled up on a window seat feeling like an outcast. Matt and his dad had taken the couch and the love seat respectively, while Jeremy was on the hearth.

Instead of discussing the renovation of the house, which was obviously uppermost on everyone's minds, we said mundane things. "How was your flight?" "Isn't it hot outside? Of course, this is August in Texas.'' ''What will be happening during the Celebration?''

I still wasn't breathing easy, because there was another surprise yet to come, and when it did, things could get even worse. Matt and I hadn't said a word about it to his parents, but then he had told me that his mother *loved* surprises. He honestly believed that to be true based on a party he and his sister had given her and Will for their twenty-fifth wedding anniversary. So now the surprise was on us, and he hadn't looked directly at me since his parents had arrived. I kept wondering if he was also concerned about how to break our next bombshell, or whether he was simply enjoying the visit with his folks. And Cecily.

''It's such a Texas event, this Centennial Celebration,'' Cecily was saying. ''What is happening first?''

''Tonight,'' Jeremy said, ''there's a picnic in the park and then a dance. We're all going, but you know about that.''

''How many people are they expectin' for this shindig? The whole Celebration?'' Will asked, looking at his son.

Matt nodded toward Jeremy. ''We've been taking bets on that very thing. What was your latest estimate, Jeremy?''

''Twenty-two thousand, four hundred people.''

''He figured it out scientifically,'' Matt said, with some pride in his voice. ''Tell them how.''

Jeremy began explaining. ''Well, there are around five thousand people in Purple Sage, and almost twelve thousand in the county. Assuming that for every four people you have a house, I figure that over eighty percent of them will have company.'' His eyes moved from Will to Edith to Cecily, probably to judge better how his theory was going over. ''That's the starting point.'' He went on to factor in motel rooms, camping spaces, and even motor homes. Eventually he took a breath and finished up with, ''When I added in the day visitors I got a grand total of twenty-two thousand, four hundred and forty. Give or take a few. And that's a cumulative total for all six days.''

Cecily's light brown eyes glowed with admiration. She clapped her hands together and said, ''Aren't you the clever one, Jeremy! Can the rest of us get in on the wagering or is it closed?''

''It's not anything official,'' he said modestly.

''Oh, but it should be! We'll each ante up a bit of cash and the one who comes closest wins the pot,'' Cecily said. ''Surely the *Tribune* will have some sort of official figure when the Celebration is over. Come on, it will be great fun.''

Will grinned at Cecily. ''It isn't exactly the lottery, but I reckon it wouldn't hurt my conscience too much to take a few dollars off you.''

''It's not going to bother your conscience at all,'' she responded, ''because it's not going to happen. I'm going to win the pot, or our brilliant Jeremy will.''

She had just met him and already he was *our Jeremy.* And he appeared delighted by it. I had the fleeting and uncharitable thought that I should get her to share his orthodontic bills.

Cecily turned to Jeremy. ''Can you find paper and pencil so we can make this official? I wouldn't want anyone trying to cheat us.''

Jeremy practically flew out of the room and was back in seconds, passing around pencils and sheets of paper. Matt wrote down a figure quickly and handed it back to Jeremy. ''I'll stand pat with the number I had.''

''Ooh, aren't we confident?'' Cecily asked.

Matt cocked his head. ''There are times when we should be.''

By this time Jeremy had given Will and Edith their papers and pencils and was now standing in front of me. The doorbell rang. ''I'll get it,'' he said, unceremoniously dumping the things in my lap and heading for the front door.

''Maybe it's Diane and Trey,'' I said, sounding wistful. I glanced over at Edith and tried for a little more spirit. ''I invited them, but she didn't think they could make it.''

Jeremy had already flung open the door. ''Hey, Mac, come on in.''

Mac Donelly is the sheriff of Wilmot County and a semi-hero around our house. Jeremy thinks he hung the moon, or at least lent a hand when it was going up. At that moment,

Mac's smile looked strained. He was dressed in his standard-issue khaki pants, short-sleeved khaki shirt, boots, and western hat. As he stepped into the room, his hand went to the brim of his hat automatically and pulled it off, holding it in front of him.

"Thanks, Jeremy."

"You want something to drink, Mac?"

"No, thanks," Mac said. "Howdy, Jolie. Miz Wyatt." He nodded at Edith, then glanced around the room. A real grin stretched across his face when he spotted Matt's dad. He stepped forward and shook hands with him. "Will, you old cuss. Guess they'll let anybody back for the Celebration if they let you in town."

"I can't believe you're still here, Mac Donelly. Figured they'd've sniffed you out long ago and shipped you out of town on a rail. Can't be much for a sheriff to do around here, anyway."

Mac grinned. "Just keepin' Jolie out of trouble is a full-time job. Jeremy sometimes needs a bit of keepin', too."

"I'm over that, honest," Jeremy said.

"I'm glad to hear it," Mac said, with a fond glance at Jeremy.

We'd had more than our share of troubles in the past six months, but Mac had always been there to help, both in his official capacity and as a friend. There weren't many people I'd rather have on my side than him.

Will sat down again and pointed to the couch where Matt was. "Sit down and visit a spell," he said to Mac.

Mac shook his head. "Sorry, don't have the time. I'm afraid I'm bringing some bad news. Matt, a half-ton came tearin' along the highway and ended up stoppin' real close to here, but not before it tore up maybe a quarter mile of your fence."

"Was anybody hurt?" Matt asked.

"No, they were lucky. The most damage was done to your property, the fence and all. The real problem is that there must be fifty head of cattle wandering down the highway. I've got Wiley up there tendin' to traffic, but he can't do much alone with all that livestock. It was city kids in the truck and they were mostly worried about their equipment—they've got some kind of band.''

Matt was up instantly. ''The band wouldn't be Carl and the Cattle Drovers?''

''Yep, that's the name.''

''That's the band for the picnic tonight. Jeremy, why don't you saddle a couple of horses while I drive the pickup out to the road?''

''I can help,'' Cecily said, jumping up. ''Let me get some jeans.'' She flew out the front door like a kid about to go on a big adventure.

In the meantime, Jeremy smacked his forehead. ''Uh-oh. Uh, Matt, I—uh—forgot something. I was supposed to tell you that Mrs. Meece called. About one o'clock.''

Vera Meece was the chairwoman (who hated the term *chair-person*) of the Celebration. Matt was on the steering committee, a position he took because he believes in giving back to the community. In this case he assumed it would mean some decision making, some fund-raising, and a great deal of delegating. Mrs. Meece assumed that he, along with all the others on the steering committee, had taken the job because they wanted to be her personal drones. Needless to say, the mismatched expectations caused more than a problem or two.

Besides chairing the entire Celebration Committee, Vera Meece had also taken on Camp John Seybold as her personal project for the event. The camp had been created during the 1940s to house German prisoners of war. Although it had been dismantled at the end of World War II, it was a part of the history of Purple Sage, and Vera wanted to make sure the site, and the men who had lived there, were properly remembered.

''What did she want this time?'' Matt asked. My normally devil-may-care husband sounded almost downtrodden, a reflection of just how many problems there had been with Mrs. Meece over the Celebration.

''She said that the tables weren't set up right at the pavilion for tonight, so 'you and Trey had better go see to it.' Those were her exact words. Oh, and she said the band hadn't arrived from San Angelo, either, but I guess that's solved. The big thing was that I was supposed to have you call her. First thing."

Matt patted Jeremy on the shoulder. "It's not a problem. You get the horses and I'll worry about what to do with Mrs. Meece."

"I could kill her for you," I offered. "Being a mystery writer and all."

"No thanks, I'd rather do it myself," Matt said, patting his pockets, a sure sign that he was looking for his keys. "In fact, if she keeps it up I *will* do it myself. Cheerfully. Gleefully. With great zeal and"—he headed for the mantel and began searching under and around the potted ivy—"right after I deal with these cattle."

"I'm coming too," Will said.

"I don't think so," Edith said. "You didn't tell Matt about your fall off the roof."

"What roof?" Matt asked, stopping his search.

"It wasn't all that bad—" Will started to say but Edith cut him off.

"No, it wasn't. You could've killed yourself and you were real lucky you didn't. But what would Dr. Feinman say about you trying to ride a horse? Or rounding up cattle? He wasn't too keen on you riding in a car for two and a half hours, so I figure he'd call this a real bad idea. And I'd agree with him. Bart can help. And Jolie. Let them handle it."

Bart is the foreman of the ranch, but he was in Austin picking up some relatives for the Celebration. As for me, I'm a city kid. I can drive a pickup, and do so willingly, but while I like horses, I like them best when I'm on level ground beside them. I don't have any idea how to saddle them, and when I ride I prefer it to be in a pen or an enclosed ring where they can't get away from me. Matt didn't explain any of that but merely said, "It's not a problem; Jeremy and I can manage."

"I've called for a deputy," Mac said, "but I'm afraid he won't be much good. Sure hasn't been good at much else."

Cecily raced in the front door, jeans, boots, and socks in her arms. "I'll get changed," she said, hurrying toward the downstairs guest bath. "And then I'll help you saddle the horses, Jeremy."

"And while y'all are gone," Edith added, "we'll bring everything in from the car and start unpacking."

My stomach sank. Now I had to tell her and I didn't know where to begin.

It was in the midst of this chaos that the doorbell rang. Now who? I stepped to the door and pulled it open just ahead of Matt, who had finally found his keys, and the sheriff, who was on his way out.

There on our front porch was a man I'd never seen before. He was about six feet tall with curly brown, salt-and-pepper hair, and when he looked at me with his pale blue eyes, I wondered if lightning had come from a clear summer sky.

"Yes?"

"Hello," he said, his smile dimming even the brilliance of the sun. "I'm Howard. Howard Bremerton." His accent was English and I decided that someone must have called Central Casting—the U.K. branch—and requested a gorgeous stranger.

He tilted his head and held out his hand. "You must be Jolie, and I'm Cecily's friend. Didn't she tell you I was coming?"

THREE

CENTRAL CASTING hadn't sent him. No, indeed. Instead the lovely Cecily had gone to Central Casting herself and picked the most charming, most appealing, and most sexy male she could find as an accoutrement for the trip.

"Uh, Howard. No she hasn't mentioned you, yet. But let me introduce my husband, Matt." I reached back without looking, put my hand on Matt's arm, and pulled him forward. When he hung back I turned around to see why. That's when I discovered that I had a grip on the sheriff's arm, not my husband's. Holding back an "oops," I turned to my other side and discovered Matt, who was either thoroughly amused or intensely annoyed—his look didn't give me a clue as to which.

There was only one thing for me to do, and I did it. I fell back into the Katharine Hepburn routine. "This is Matt Wyatt, my husband. Formerly Cecily's husband."

I could almost feel the testosterone level in the room rise as Matt and Howard shook hands.

"Glad to meet you," Matt said.

"I've been looking forward to this," Howard added.

Either the man was demented or he was playing Clark Gable to my Katharine Hepburn.

I finished the introductions. "And this is the sheriff of Wilmot County, Mac Donelly." They shook hands as well.

Mac stuck his hat back on his head as he said, "Well, I'd best be gettin' out to the highway and see about that mess."

"There are cows everywhere," Howard volunteered. "I assume they're yours?" he asked Matt.

"Unfortunately."

"I do ride—perhaps I could help?"

And then Cecily was there. While she only has an inch or two on me, those inches are in her legs—they make her look lean in a way that most women can only envy. Her jeans fit as if they were custom-made for her, then worn to a faded and ragged perfection.

"Howard, you're here." She kissed him on the cheek. "You've met everyone?"

"Not your in-laws, yet."

Ex-in-laws, I wanted to point out.

Arm in arm they glided into the room; Cecily did the final introductions, then whisked Howard out the back door with Jeremy also in tow. On the way she called over her shoulder, "We'll meet you at the highway, Matthew."

I was beginning to think this was a woman who did not share well with other boys and girls. Or perhaps it was more accurate to say she didn't share boys well with other girls.

Mac Donelly left the same time as Cecily, while Matt hesitated, looking first at his parents, then at me. "Maybe I should help you explain first...."

Yes, he should have. In fact, he shouldn't have been *helping*. He should have been doing all the explaining himself; after all, these were his parents. Unfortunately, there were cattle strewn along the highway, probably wandering halfway to Purple Sage by now, and someone had to stop them before they got any farther. Or caused additional accidents.

"Go," I said. "I'll explain things."

"I have a better idea—let's leave it until tomorrow."

"No," I said, somewhat emphatically. I'm a devotee of the if-it's-going-to-be-unpleasant-let's-get-it-over-with school of life. I didn't want to continue worrying about this. "It won't be a problem," I added optimistically.

Matt kissed me quickly. "You're wonderful."

"Keep that in mind—I have a feeling I'm going to need to hear it often." As soon as I finished he was gone, leaving me with Edith and Will. I turned around and smiled at them brightly. They in turn watched me with puzzled looks; obviously they knew something was up, and, being the patient type, they both were willing to wait for me to explain.

"It might be easier if you just followed me," I said. I snatched the keys to my almost brand-new Intrepid off the mantel. "You see, we have a present for you—"

"And it can't wait 'til we unpack?" Edith asked.

"Not really. We, Matt and I, came up with this brilliant idea to make you feel more comfortable when you're here. So you can stay longer. And we know how you like your privacy—and having your things around. I mean, we all do. I certainly do. And anyway, I didn't know that you didn't like surprises, or we would have told you, only now that I know..." I sounded just like Jeremy, talking in circles to avoid saying what was going to come out eventually. I took a deep breath and let it out. "I think my first instinct was right; would you just come with me?"

Wary, but game, they followed me to the front, where our vehicles were parked.

"You want to drive, Jolie?" Will asked.

"Um, let's take two cars." I got in mine and started off. A glance in the rearview mirror told me that they were still with me, their rented Taurus bouncing a little on the ruts as we headed for the highway. Once there I could see the traffic jam and the cattle, about a mile down the road on our left. I turned right, then right again, toward Purple Sage.

Maybe I should have been rehearsing what to say, but my brain was overloaded and I was just grateful for the moments of respite.

On both sides of the highway was ranch land. The right side was our land, the Hammond place, which we had bought just a few months before. You couldn't see much beyond the barbed wire and cedar post fence because of the trees, and below them the algerita, a squatty, spreading, prickly-leaved bush that reminded me of a pale blue-white holly. The scenery wasn't as pretty as it is most of the year. Normally there was a lot of green, but in August, much of it had turned a dull gold, faded from too much heat. Only the live oak trees still flourished, their small leaves a deep dark green, along with the mesquites and their light, feathery foliage.

After almost six miles, we turned off the Farm to Market Road and traveled for another half mile along a bumpy ribbon of caliche that sent up a white cloud of dust behind us. I thought of it as Hammond Lane. A few hundred yards and we turned right inside the gate and then veered left. I stopped the car at a wire fence surrounding a small, older but immaculate, wood frame house. With its incredibly green yard and flowering bushes, it looked like an oasis in the ranch country. It wasn't by accident that it appeared that way; the Hammond place has its own well and I'd made the trip over there every other day for the past month, watering, weeding, and trimming to make sure everything would look its best when Will and Edith arrived. We'd worked on the inside of the house, too, but I was afraid no matter what we'd done, it hadn't been enough. At least not under the circumstances.

Will and Edith pulled up behind me and got out of the car, a fine white dust from the caliche road showering us. I swung open the wire gate. "It's this way." My mouth was so dry I couldn't even tell them that it was supposed to be a surprise and we really hoped they liked it. Instead I mutely led them up the walk and onto the cement front porch. Two tubs of bright red petunias flanked the walkway.

"In here," I said, opening the door and letting them enter. "It's for you."

The air conditioner was pouring cool air out into the square, old-fashioned, living room, which contained all their furniture—the things I'd cleared out of my house. Edith's heavy oak table with six chairs stood at the far end of the room, its surface gleaming like ice. Will's favorite blue recliner was angled toward a new TV, and their couch rested on the edge of the braided rug that had been in our home. I'd put new, creamy lace curtains on the windows, along with new shades to keep out the heat and the cold. We'd furnished it with all their beloved things—even their kitchen utensils and bedclothes. There were groceries in the kitchen, and fresh soaps in the two old-fashioned baths. We'd even had a telephone installed. It had been a labor of love to give them a real home here, so that they could come and go as they pleased, and stay as long as they wanted. But I couldn't seem to say any of those things.

Will and Edith stood a moment in the doorway, giving their eyes a chance to adjust to the indoors after the bright sunlight. Both blinked several times, and, moving only their eyes, began to look around the room. No one said a word—not me, not either of them.

Finally Edith looked at me.

Then, for the second time since I had known her, she burst into tears.

AT FIRST I had thought Edith was touched by all the work we'd done, but several hours later, I wasn't sure of anything. As she'd wiped away the tears she'd said, "You went to so much trouble. Just—" She'd stopped herself to blow her nose.

Will had put his arm around me, given me a squeeze, and said we'd done a real fine job. That recliner sure looked good to him, and here we'd gotten them a new TV with a remote and all.

On the surface, things were fine, except that as we brought in the luggage and I told them about some of the things we'd done to get the house ready, Edith got quieter and quieter. Finally she said she had a headache, and probably the best thing would be for her to lie down for a while before the picnic. It would have been impolite to stay, so I made my excuses and left. I *had* urged Will to come with me, but he said he needed to stretch his back.

After the great cattle fiasco had ended, Cecily and Howard had taken their rented car over to see the Hammond place and they hadn't come back. Cecily called a half hour later to say she would be staying with Will and Edith.

"It's fine," Matt said, staring at our image in the bathroom mirror as I got ready for the picnic.

I put down the eyelash curler and shook my head. "It isn't fine. Your mother hates the house and she hates me. Worse, she wishes you were still married to Cecily and she wishes I were dead."

Matt stared at me distractedly for a minute before he said, "Well, as long as I don't agree with her, and her wishes don't come true, then I guess we're okay."

He scooted out of the room just ahead of the hairbrush I threw at him.

FOUR

THE PAVILION in the park, usually just a drab cement square, was festooned with colored lights and surrounded by redwood tables gaily draped with red, white, and blue tablecloths. Families had come and paid five dollars a table for the privilege of picnicking on them. Now almost everyone had finished eating and the sun was setting behind us, adding its own luster of colors to the summer evening. The rise and fall of laughter and talk, the greeting of old friends and introducing of new, was drowned out by music.

Sawdust had been strewn on the pavilion to make the surface better for dancing, and a built-up stage at one end held the band. Carl and the Cattle Drovers had enticed people away from their conversations with a fast-stepping polka and now were playing the "Cotton-Eyed Joe." It seemed most of the crowd was up circling the floor in the traditional dance that went with the song. Even the littlest members of the group, some as young as two or three, were out on the floor. More than one little girl was dancing in her daddy's arms; a little boy was hopping alongside his older sister, hanging onto her belt to keep up.

This is one of the reasons I love living in Purple Sage. Families blend into other families to form a community. It's like a Greek wedding or a Mexican birthday—everyone is welcome. I would have been dancing myself, but at the moment Matt had gone off to try and call Mrs. Meece for about the fifth time. Calling didn't seem that important to me, since it left me playing hostess to Howard and Cecily. Even Jeremy had abandoned me. Not that I would have found that unusual under normal conditions—after all he was a teenager, and as such had a moral responsibility to eschew the company of his mother as often as possible. However, these were not normal conditions. I needed him.

"It's so...so..." Howard seemed stunned by everything around him, too awed for words.

"So down-home folksy? Rural? Backwoodsy?" Cecily asked, with just a hint of irony in her lovely lilting voice.

"No, no, that's not how it strikes me. So authentic."

Cecily laughed. "Oh, Purple Sage-ites are authentic, all right. What do you think, Jolie?"

"I think Howard is right; they are a very genuine group of people. Caring and real."

"What an interesting way to put it." She was laughing at me under her breath.

I looked around for someone else to talk to, someone to

wave over to our table, but everyone was either talking or dancing, some doing both at the same time. I didn't even have Will and Edith for buffers since they were busy table-hopping.

I had always considered my mother-in-law the stolid pioneer type. Her mother had come to Texas in a covered wagon, and Edith had spent her early years in a log cabin. She really *had* walked three miles to school, carrying her lunch, a piece of sausage and a biscuit, in a tin bucket. In the first years of her marriage she had tended cattle just like her husband, riding, roping, branding, and doing whatever else had to be done. She'd had two miscarriages before Matt's older sister, Priscilla, was born, and then eventually Matt. This was not a woman who was new to sorrow or hardship. When she and Will had retired to Florida five years before, they deserved the rest.

While I didn't feel particularly close to Edith, I admired her. I always suspected that if our relationship wasn't good the fault was mine. And now I'd really botched it. Instead of thinking the Hammond house was their own little getaway, I was pretty sure Edith saw it as a place I had sent her, where she'd be away from her son. When Matt, Jeremy, and I had arrived at five-thirty to get them for the picnic, Edith insisted that the four of them ride in their own car. After all, seven people in one vehicle was just too many...and Will had fallen off that roof, so he might get tired and need to come back early. We ended up taking all three cars. It was all very civil and polite, and I felt like the biggest species of sewer rat known to mankind.

"I'm surprised you aren't table-hopping," I said to Cecily, speaking at just under a yell to be heard over Carl and the Cattle Drovers, who must have cranked up the amplifiers. "Don't you know a lot of these people? You must be dying to talk to them." And no one was going to approach our table with both of us seated together. Most of my friends had smiled or waved, and then they'd spotted Cecily. After that they didn't come any closer, and I could hardly blame them.

"I'm perfectly content just to sit and watch for the moment," Cecily said. Her eyes scanned the crowd, then widened. "I can't believe it!" she practically shrieked to be heard over the music. "Oh, my God, it really is, isn't it? Elizabeth Street. Oh, Howard, look quickly, you mustn't miss this."

I looked too and discovered that it was indeed Liz Street. I should explain that while Liz grew up in Purple Sage, she had moved to New York and become fashion editor for a large daily newspaper. Even though she's been back a good ten years, the experience warped her in ways that may never be cured. Liz is definitely eccentric and her appearance has sometimes even been described as psychedelic. She has salt and pepper hair that sort of frizzes its way down to her waist, when it isn't hidden under something like a cloche or a turban. Tonight her hair was in two pigtails, one over each shoulder. And while denim is still popular, Liz had pushed the envelope a bit too far. She was wearing a pale blue denim skirt and matching blouse with silver studs all over both. Even in the August heat, her boots were buckskin, as was her vest, and she had what looked to be an honest-to-God powder horn slung over her shoulder as an added accessory. She was busy talking to some others across the way, flipping her braids periodically for emphasis.

Howard stared for a few minutes, then turned to Cecily, speaking loudly, "In Purple Sage would she be called a fashion plate?"

"A fashion victim, is more likely," Cecily said. "It would take emergency treatment to bring her around to normal again." The two of them laughed heartily.

Liz Street is not my best friend, but she is in my writers' group and I like her. She's at least not boring, certainly not predictable, and never catty.

"We should explain," I said, leaning over the table to speak to Howard, "that Liz was very involved in the fashion industry in New York, and of course Europe, for many years. She thinks clothes should be either rigidly functional, for work and such, or more like costumes." I smiled. "She has such a streak of whimsy."

Cecily watched me silently just long enough to let me know that she wasn't buying it for a minute. Howard had gone back to people watching. I got up and began packing up the remains of our picnic, which had consisted of baked ham, kaiser rolls from the bakery, fruit salad, and ice tea.

"So who can I talk to about the POW camp?" Howard asked, his eyes still focused on the dancers, who had slowed their pace to a schottische, a traditional dance done to "Put Your Little Foot."

"I haven't the slightest idea," Cecily said. "Didn't you talk to someone when you went out to the camp this afternoon?"

"No. I didn't."

"So where were you all that time?"

"I wasn't gone all that long," Howard said, taking small quick sips of bottled water. His actions made me think he wasn't feeling quite as nonchalant as he wanted us to believe. "I probably wasn't but twenty minutes behind you."

"More like forty-five," Cecily said. "Oh, wait, of course—you got lost! I knew I shouldn't have let you out wandering on your own."

Howard finally pulled his attention back to Cecily. "It wasn't so bad as all that. After you drove off with Will and Edith, I decided to get the lay of the land, as it were. I drove around town a bit, filled our hired car with petrol, and started off. Unfortunately I must have taken a wrong turn. I was sure I was on the right lane, but I didn't see anything that looked like a camp. By the time I stopped to consult that map you'd drawn me, I was practically at the ranch. So I just drove on."

"Poor darling," Cecily said, patting his arm. Then she leaned toward me and added, "Howard could get lost in a tin can."

I couldn't think of any response, so I went back to something else they'd said. "Did you say you were looking for the POW camp?" I asked Howard. At the start of World War II the Allies suddenly found themselves with prisoners of war and someone in our government had come up with the idea of interning foreign prisoners in camps in the United States. Most of them were in rural America, and dozens were in Texas. One had been located about five miles outside of Purple

Sage. "Are we talking about the German POW camp? Camp John Seybold?"

"That's the one," Cecily said. "Howard is positively obsessed by it. That's why he came along on this trip; you see, he had an uncle who was interned here."

"Your uncle was a…a…" I couldn't bring myself to accuse his uncle of being a Nazi.

Howard saw where I was going and shook his head. "No, no, he wasn't a Nazi." He pronounced the word so that it rhymed with snazzy. "He was practically a youngster when the war started, just sixteen, but my mother's family—he was her brother—was living in Germany at the time. They were country people, and a bit removed from the real world. My grandfather was already dead and my grandmother didn't understand how serious Hitler's movement was until it had blown up into a war. She was planning on coming back to England but before she could do anything my uncle had been picked up and shipped off to fight. Poor Uncle Friedrich."

"Friedrich Bremerton was his name?"

"No, Linzer. Friedrich Linzer. Have you heard of him?"

"No, sorry," I said, putting the last of the fruit salad back in the cooler and closing the lid.

"So what exactly is out at the camp?" Howard asked, cleaning a serving spoon with a napkin and handing both to me.

"Well, there's an exhibit that Mrs. Meece is putting together; we did a story on it at the radio station. She's collected some artifacts and memorabilia from the forties that will be on display. Oh, and she's contacted people who used to work there. They're even expecting some of the former prisoners to come back for a visit. Isn't that something?"

"Actually, I'm not a bit surprised. From my uncle's letters it was really the best place to spend the war. He had a far better time than the rest of the family."

"You're kidding!" I sat down next to Howard. My throat was getting sore from shouting over the music, and it was hard to hear. "How can you have a good time in a prison camp?"

Howard laughed. "It sounds queer, I know, but you have

to realize that in Europe rationing was in effect and there were horrible shortages. Plus, of course, there was the constant threat of bombs and death.'' His tone grew somber. ''People queued for hours to get a winter coat, or a pair of shoes. Food was in short demand, and during the winter months people froze in the bombed out buildings. My mother and grandmother can tell some incredible stories.''

''They were in Germany the whole time?''

''No, no. They escaped in nineteen forty-two to Belgium, and after the war they came back to England. That's where grandfather was from originally. The family's quite a mix.''

''My father was Polish,'' I said, my tone matching his. ''Second generation American, but I remember him talking about cousins who were still living in Krakow. When I was little I kept thinking, I have relatives who are Communists. That was during the cold war of the fifties, and I thought the whole thing was like a horrible dark secret! I was afraid that if the government found out they'd ship us all back to Poland—or at least my father. I couldn't even ask my parents about it because I worried someone would overhear. Spies, you know.''

Howard watched me for a moment, his head tipped to the side. Then he said, ''Must have been a big burden for a little girl.''

''Funny,'' I said. ''I hadn't thought about that in twenty years.'' I smiled at Howard. ''Isn't it interesting how our minds work?''

He was looking into my eyes. ''Absolutely fascinating.''

I realized that our conversation was taking place on two different levels, and I wasn't comfortable with at least one of those. I straightened up, reached for the pitcher of tea, and in doing so brushed my hand against my glass. It went over and I ended up with a lap full of watery tea and ice.

Cecily saw what had happened and, while Howard jumped for a napkin, she started to laugh. ''Now how are we going to explain that to everyone?''

''We won't have to,'' Howard said, handing me several

heavy linen napkins. Picnic or not, I had still brought out all the heavy artillery. "In this heat you'll be dry in no time."

I shook the ice out onto the ground and dabbed at my wheat-colored pants. The whole front seemed to be wet. The only good part was that the color was light enough that it wasn't too noticeable as long as I stayed seated. "Guess I'll just have to sit here," I said.

"Howard and I will stay with you," Cecily offered as she moved closer and patted my leg. "We don't have anyplace to go or anything to do."

Howard, who was standing near the edge of the table, leaned forward. "Actually, Cecee, I do. Jolie, who did you say was in charge of the POW camp? A Mrs. Meeks?"

"Meece. Vera Meece. She's the head of the Celebration Committee."

"And she knows all about Camp John Seybold?"

"As much as anybody," I said, still dabbing at my pants. "It's her personal pet project. She wants to install a permanent museum, or exhibit of some kind, when the Celebration is over." I put down the napkin. "Her family was involved in the camp—I think her mom worked out there, but I'm not sure. Anyway, she's spent a lot of time getting the camp ready for display."

"Then she's just the person I need to meet. Is she here?" Howard asked, peering through the crowd as if he might recognize her.

I shook my head. "No. Matt was trying to call her. I'll bet she's out at the camp. She's got an office set up there with the exhibit."

"Then I think I should motor out and see her."

"But it's almost dark," Cecily said. "How can you possibly expect to find the place now?"

"Oh, that's not going to be a problem. I think I know where I went wrong." Howard was up, already fishing the keys out of his pocket. "I showed Matt your map before we ate and he added a few landmarks, new, I'm sure, since you lived in Purple Sage. I shouldn't have any trouble now. I won't be gone but an hour.'' He flashed her a smile. ''You don't really mind, do you, Cecily?''

Cecily seemed on the verge of pouting, and I didn't doubt for a second that it would be very effective in helping her get her own way. After a moment's hesitation she stopped, looked at Howard, and smiled. ''How can I deny you anything? Go on. Just don't be too late; I don't want to be stuck here all night.''

''Oh, if everyone leaves early I'm sure you can get a ride.''

''I'm sure I can.'' She reached for his sleeve and pulled him toward her, kissing him quickly on the lips. ''Don't get lost this time. Sheriff Donelly has better things to do than keep bailing out the Wyatts.''

Like they were all part of the Wyatt group. And, damn, I suppose they were.

''Don't worry about me; I'll be fine.'' Howard gave us a quick wave and said *''Ciao!''* before he hurried off.

Cecily and I settled back down at the table and I focused my attention on the dancers. I spotted Diane and Trey Atwood, our best friends. Apparently they'd arrived late, but they were making up for lost time, doing a two-step with lots of spins and twirls. Jeremy was at a table on the other side of the pavilion with a crowd of teenagers. Several of the boys were wearing straw Stetson hats that looked too big for their growing bodies. The girls didn't seem to mind, though, as they crowded around, laughing and talking.

''Finally, there's Mattie,'' Cecily said, pointing.

He was crossing the pavilion, but as I watched he stopped, said something to his mother, and then whisked her onto the dance floor. They moved to the music with quick synchronized steps. Matt made another comment and Edith started to smile. She nodded and then they were twirling around with the rhythm of people who'd danced all their lives.

''Isn't she something?'' Cecily asked.

I could only nod and say, ''She really is.''

''And she and Matt have always been so close. But, then I suppose it was inevitable that they should grow apart at some point. It's just so sad for her.''

Cecily was ignoring the fact that it was Edith and Will who'd moved off to Florida, and anytime you put that many miles between people there's bound to be some loss of closeness. Intimating that it was my fault seemed unfair, but before I could think of anything to say in response my attention was caught by another woman. She was about Edith's age, but she was shorter and softer looking. Her blondish gray hair was curled into a style that reminded me of the forties, and she was wearing a dress; she was one of the few women who was. The first thing that always struck me about Vera Meece was her femininity, although after hearing Matt talk about her, I had to assume it was only skin deep. According to Matt, Mrs. Meece could swear like a sailor and make demands like a slave driver. Which made me a little nervous since she seemed to be heading directly for me.

FIVE

"JOLIE, AREN'T YOU looking lovely this evening," Vera said, her words syrupy with a southern accent. "I feel terrible, having to bother you when you have company and all, but you know how those pesky details can get away from you, if you don't just check them right, straight off the list." She glanced at the band, then turned back to me with a smile. "It's so nice to know that the band arrived safely. And on time. I can't tell you how I worried about that, especially when I asked Jeremy to have Matt call, and he didn't. But then I should have known that Matt would see to it that everything got handled. He's so efficient."

Had I not been standing there, watching her face and looking directly into her eyes, I would have assumed she was being more than a little sarcastic. But no, not Vera, at least not visibly so. Somehow she had perfected the art of making unsubtle demands and sugarcoating her criticism in a way that seemed perfectly innocent. It's one of those southern-belle maneuvers that few women truly master. Thank God.

"The band had a slight accident, practically in front of our house, no less," I said. "Matt would have called, but it was something of an emergency, fixing the fence and getting the cattle back in—"

Vera was holding up one hand in a graceful but somehow imperious manner. Her voice was as gently understanding as before. "Oh, now, Jolie, you don't have to explain to me. I know how busy an important man like Matt is. Running that big ranch and all the other businesses he has."

"Yes, only he really has been trying to call you ever since we got here." I stopped when I heard Cecily snickering beside me. I followed her gaze, and Vera's now, as well, to see Matt in the middle of the dance floor doing some very fancy maneuvering with his mother on one arm and my friend Diane on the other. Matt was laughing at something that Diane must have said, because he shook his head at her, then swung his mother and somehow managed to link all their arms before they began to two-step side by side. They didn't look a bit businesslike. I turned back to Vera. "Well, he was trying to call. Guess he just got pulled into the festivities."

"I do understand. It just would have been so nice if he had reached me, and saved me the trip out here and all. It's a good twenty minutes, not that I mind." Vera Meece had never had children and I began to think it was a real shame. Her kids could have kept Oprah in business for years with all the guilt trips she could lay on them.

"Let me get Matt—"

"Oh, Jolie, no!" Her hand was on my arm and gripping like the claw of a lobster. "I wouldn't think of disrupting him. As long as he has everything running smoothly, and I'm sure he has, then there's no need. I'm headed home now. I've been working until almost midnight every night for the past several weeks and, as much as I feel it's important to give back to one's community, I must admit it is just the tiniest bit wearing. I'm going to eat a bite and then freshen up before I go back out to the camp." She leaned forward and whispered in my ear. "Then I'm having a visit from a gentleman caller. Actually, a gentleman and an officer."

"Then you aren't going to be at the POW camp for an hour or so?" Cecily asked, joining the conversation for the first time.

"No, dear, I'm not."

"Well, bloody hell."

"Excuse me?"

Cecily stuck out her hand and shook with Vera. "We haven't met, or at least if we have it appears neither of us remembers. I'm Cecily Wyatt. I have a friend who is dying to see the camp and to talk with someone about it. He's actually on his way out there to find you. He left not more than five minutes ago."

"But I'm not there."

"Yes, and it appears you're not going to be."

I looked over at Vera. "Howard Bremerton is from England, but his uncle was interned here in the camp. Howard's pretty excited about actually seeing the place."

"Oh, really?"

"Yes," Cecily said. "Only the problem is that Howard is what you might call geographically challenged. He can hardly find his way out of his flat some days."

"You say he's on his way to the camp now?" Vera asked, appearing just a touch annoyed by this unexpected turn. When Cecily and I both nodded she said, "Then I suppose I don't have a choice but to go right back."

"Oh, no, don't bother...." I said.

"I consider it my civic duty. After all, those men were family. I practically grew up at the camp, and this is my way of paying them back. I suppose I must hurry on. Good night to you both." She started off, then swung back around. "Oh, and Jolie, you tell Matt that if he doesn't mind, after the dance he can just bring me the money we collected tonight. I'll be at the POW camp. Bye, y'all."

"Bye," Cecily echoed, duplicating the southern accent. When Vera was out of sight Cecily turned to me. "Well, I believe that takes care of duty, and Howard, too, leaving us perfectly free to do as we like.''

"Okay, so what would you like?" I didn't use the word we; I suspected Cecily didn't give a damn what I liked.

"It's time for some fun," she said. "Don't you think so?"

She responded to my hesitant nod with a malicious little grin as she stood up and eyed the dance floor. She reminded me of some very beautiful predator looking for a victim. And she found one rather quickly. Diane's husband, Trey, was standing alone only a few feet away, and Cecily snagged him immediately.

Trey is only a fair dancer, but that didn't seem to bother Cecily. She had him spinning her in circles within minutes. Or perhaps she was just twirling around Trey. Whichever, their dancing garnered some attention. It was hard not to watch a woman so lovely, and so graceful. Her movements were quick and lively, yet there was a flow that almost made her steps seem choreographed. With each turn her soft brown hair would gleam in the light as it swirled out.

When the dance was finished she kissed Trey on the cheek and turned him loose, obviously looking for her next partner. There was no hesitation on her part: She went straight to Matt's side. Next thing I knew she was dancing with my husband to the song "Easy Come, Easy Go."

I know that some religions find dancing sinful; a friend once said they must think dancing is a whole lot more fun than it is. However, as Matt and Cecily moved in synchronized rhythm to the music I reconsidered that point of view. Matt twirled Cecily out, his hand firmly grasping hers. She swung away, then back toward him; as she leaned into him her soft brown hair brushed his face, her head resting for just a moment on his shoulder. Matt's dark eyes, so striking against his light hair, were watching Cecily as she twirled out again. This time she spun only once, then grabbed the belt loop at the back of Matt's jeans and glided alongside him. For several seconds, their booted feet moved in perfect unison as they danced side by side. Then they were facing each other again, their hands touching on one side, while Cecily's other arm came to rest on Matt's shoulder. That's the standard form for western dancing and there was no way I could object without looking like a jealous wife. That's one thing I refuse to be, so I tapped my foot to the music, and smiled, pretending to have a wonderful time. It didn't take me long to realize that no one was noticing me at all; everyone's attention was focused on the dancers.

Two songs later, when Matt looked at me and held out a hand in invitation, I acted as if I hadn't seen him and waved to Diane on the other side of the floor. His invitation to dance felt like an afterthought, and that's another thing I refuse to be.

AT TEN O'CLOCK the party was still going strong, but our small group was fading fast. Will and Edith were tired from traveling, and Cecily claimed exhaustion from all the dancing. I have to admit, she had been dancing. A lot. She switched partners often enough to give the impression she'd been elected prom queen for the night.

I was tired and cranky, with no excuses that I cared to offer. Deep down I knew that much of it was jealousy. I had no reason to be jealous, at least none that I knew of. Matt had certainly never expressed any great sorrow over the absence of Cecily in his life, and since her return he had behaved like a good host and nothing more. If he hadn't danced with Cecily, I probably would have wondered why. Yet every time I looked at her I wished our country had broken all ties with England after the Revolutionary War. And kept them broken.

Sometimes I think there is an unwritten rule that second wives have to be jealous of first wives. I've seen it many times in my friends. The irony is that most first wives would prefer having postbirth hemorrhoids to having their ex-husbands back. Still, second wives continue to suffer with periodic jealousy. In part it may be that second wives never really know what their husband's first marriage was like. During those years did he laugh a lot? Did the two of them fight? What were their little inside jokes? And what was the real cause of the divorce? Knowing those intimate details about Matt and Cecily would certainly be cruel and unusual punishment, but they comprise a part of my husband that I can't know. Maybe that's what it all boils down to, and that particular night I seemed to be seething with it.

I did have some legitimate reasons for wanting to go home early. I had been putting in extra long days to get both houses ready, and I had to work in the morning. Even though I was only part time at the radio station my hours started early, and I needed every second of sleep possible if I was going to survive the rest of the Celebration.

We would have left by unanimous consent except that Howard had not returned from the POW camp.

"He's probably just having a great time," I said, stacking the remaining plastic cups so we could throw them away. Everything else was packed up and ready to go. When you're not dancing you have time for such things. "Vera is more than likely explaining each and every exhibit in detail. And Howard's loving it." Then I remembered Vera's comment about an officer and a gentleman and wondered if I was way off base.

Cecily added, "Either that or he's roaming the countryside, halfway to Mexico by now. That's only four hundred miles or so off course. Howard could manage it."

Matt glanced unobtrusively at his parents. They both looked exhausted, sitting on the bench, their bodies slumped back against the table. It was rare to see them like that.

"Why don't we just go?" I suggested. "Howard has a car; he can make it back on his own."

"I think I should run and check on him, just to make sure," Matt said. "Besides, I have to take the receipts to Vera Meece. You can ride home with Mother and Daddy. I'll round up Jeremy."

Will moved faster than he had all day. He jumped up and reached down to pull Edith to her feet. "That's a good idea."

"I don't mind waiting for you," I said to Matt.

"There's no need; you have to work in the morning."

Will was already holding the picnic basket. He nodded his head in my direction. "Come along, young lady, we won't make you walk. Even though it's not much more than ten, maybe fifteen miles."

So we loaded the picnic things into Matt's Explorer, extracted Jeremy from his crowd of friends, and then all of us but Matt climbed into Will's car for the trip home. As Cecily closed the back door, Edith rolled down her window and called out to Matt, who was parked beside us, "Now you'll come over for breakfast in the morning, won't you?"

Matt turned from the open door of the Explorer. "Tell me what time and I'll be there."

"Anytime after seven. It'll just be bacon and eggs and grits. No pancakes until I do some grocery shopping."

Matt laughed. "Mother, whatever you fix, it will be a treat for me. I only have a hot breakfast on Sundays when we eat at the country club."

As we drove off, Cecily, who was on the other side of Jeremy, said softly, "I think breakfast is Matt's favorite meal."

I work in the mornings so I rarely eat breakfast with him and I wouldn't know about that.

THE WOMAN staring back at me from the mirror the next morning had round mascara circles under her eyes, a film on her teeth, and hair that looked like Lyle Lovett's on a bad day, only a lot longer. It was me; I shuddered.

I heard a sound from the bedroom behind me and turned to see Matt, just fresh from bed, looking slightly rumpled and thoroughly adorable. I consider it more proof that God is not a woman. She wouldn't do this to us.

"Jolie?"

I closed the bathroom door fast. "Be out in a minute, Matt."

I used the hand towel and some water to get rid of the mascara, brushed my teeth, and then pulled my hair up into a ponytail. I'd love to say I looked all dewy like a young girl, but in truth I looked like a thirty-nine-year-old woman without her makeup.

"Good morning," I said, opening the door.

Matt was already dressed in a yellow knit golf shirt and jeans. He was just putting on his boots. Even his hair looked combed—he'd probably run his fingers through it. "Hi, sweetie," he said, standing up and kissing me on the end of my nose.

"You're already going?"

"Just let me brush my teeth and I'll be out of your way."

I looked at the clock—just after seven. "But it's early."

"Early by your standards, maybe, but I'll bet my mother's been up for over an hour."

"Your mom's not the only one over there. What about Cecily and Howard?"

"They're probably still on UK time. Even without it, Cecily would be up. She thinks the best part of the day is dawn; you know, when you can walk through grass that still has dew on it."

"Oh." That's one of those things I never wanted to know.

"At least she used to think that. Then, later in our marriage, I guess she didn't like mornings at all," he said, his tone rueful. "She didn't like evenings, or afternoons, either."

We both knew it was because she'd been drinking, but Matt hadn't said such a thing out loud since he'd first told me the story almost four years ago. I suppose he thought if he didn't talk about it, it hadn't really existed. Maybe it was his way of overcoming residual guilt about Cecily's alcoholism and his proximity to it.

I slid my arm through his. "People change for lots of reasons," I said. "It's not really anyone's fault."

"Oh, I know." He said it quickly, as if he'd shut the words out before they could touch him. Then he stepped into the bathroom and closed the door.

I smoothed the comforter on our bed. Matt had made it, but

I added that little touch that made me feel righteous or something. Then I pulled out clothes for the day. Dark green jeans, a white shirt with handkerchief detailing on the short sleeves and collar, and a pair of green suede loafers. Casual, but not too casual; chic, but not in a pushy sense, and who gave a damn anyway?

My insecurity stemmed from events that happened long before I even knew Matt Wyatt existed. It went back to my first husband, who was also Jeremy's real father. Amazing how a marriage that lasted less than two years could leave such a stain on my psyche, but it did. I still fought those "less than" feelings, and having Cecily around made them pop out like chicken pox.

I didn't know a lot about the marriage between Matt and Cecily. Matt had been young, Cecily even younger, and it had only lasted five years. I'd never pried for details and Matt hadn't volunteered them. He'd been wary when his mother had announced that Cecily was coming for the Celebration. Old sins coming back, I suppose. When I'd asked him flat-out how he felt about it, Matt had been candid, saying, "I don't really know her anymore."

My fear was that he'd get to know her, and as much as I didn't want to feel that way, I couldn't shake it.

By that time Matt was back. "When you get off work why don't you stop by the Hammond house?" he said.

"You think you'll still be there?"

"Probably. I'll call if we go anyplace."

Jeremy appeared in the doorway. "Can I go with you?" he asked Matt. His hair was combed and he was wearing clean, untorn, untattered clothes. I was convinced he was developing a crush on Cecily. Either that or a miracle had occurred during the night that I had missed.

"Sure," Matt said to Jeremy, not commenting on the clothes. "But I'm leaving now."

"That's okay; I'm ready."

With a final wave Matt and Jeremy were gone, and I was running late, so I did one of those all-inclusive grooming things that meant I showered, dressed and did a slipshod job on both makeup and hair in less than ten minutes. Then I headed for the radio station. All the while I was thinking of Cecily and comparing myself to her. That's a very bad way to start the day.

THE KSGE BUILDING is shaped like a horseshoe. The right-hand side has a big open office space where the two salespeople and our traffic person work. Beyond that are a closet, coffee room, bathroom, and the owner's office. That whole side is gorgeous with wainscoting, Ralph Lauren-looking wallpaper, wooden desks, and a plushy hunter green carpet. On the left side of the horseshoe, the side where I work, there are a production room, news booth, control room, and, finally, two offices; the first serves as the CD library and jocks' lounge, while the other is the news office. It contains two back-to-back desks, many battered gray filing cabinets, and a news and weather wire. I've been told that during the remodeling of the building the funds ran out somewhere in the middle, which is why we don't have any of the niceties on our side. Instead we have mostly glass and soundboard that I suppose was white once upon a time. We also have a tritone shag carpet in shades of orange left over from the fifties.

We do have our own door with a push-button security lock, which I used to enter the building. By that time I had resolved to put Cecily and all the Wyatts out of my head, at least for the day.

As I arrived at the news booth I found that F. Rory Stone, our young news director, was already on the air doing the 8 a.m. newscast. Rory glanced up and saw me. With a tip of his head he gestured toward our office. I nodded back and went to search my desk, rightly assuming he'd left me a note. I found it taped to the computer screen. *J—something's up at the SO. Find out what.* He had scribbled a *please* at the end, to fool me into thinking he was trainable.

The note piqued my curiosity. Since I had connections at the sheriff's office, primarily the sheriff himself, it would be easy enough to satisfy. All I had to do was get past Trina, the early morning dispatcher, so I could talk with Mac Donelly. I called the number I knew by heart, and waited for Trina to come on the line. Trina wasn't the one who picked up the phone. It was Wiley Pierce, a young deputy.

"Wiley, hi. This is Jolie Wyatt at K-SAGE. Is Mac around?".

"No. Why'd you ask that?"

Interesting response. "Because I wanted to talk to him."

"Oh. He's not available. He won't be here today. Not at all. Not today."

"I see." My curiosity was now thoroughly aroused. "So, will he be back tomorrow?"

There was a long pause before Wiley said, "I don't reckon I could say."

"Then maybe I could reach him at another number? Maybe go see him?"

"Nope. You can't call and you can't go see him, either." Wiley stopped and there was an even longer pause.

While I waited, I tried to figure out where Mac might be. He wouldn't leave town, not with the Celebration about to start. Because of the visitors we'd need every available law enforcement officer to cover the events. Which meant that Mac must be somewhere close. Wiley had almost made it sound like Mac was being held against his will. That was absurd. Mac wouldn't be in the jail. The only other forced imprisonment I could think of was the hospital.

"Wiley, is he okay? Did something happen to him?"

"Well, it's like this," Wiley replied in a maddeningly slow drawl. "It's serious official business and I can't say."

My jaw felt stiff. "Is-he-okay?"

"I don't know what you're—"

"Yes you do. Where is Mac?"

"Miz Wyatt, this is off the record, you understand. Ain't nobody supposed to know anything yet—"

"Wiley!"

He let out a sigh. "You can't say nothing, but..." He took a breath before he said, "We had us another shooting in Wilmot County. A shooting, and a murder, too."

SIX

"OH MY GOD! Is Mac—?"

"No, ma'am! Don't even be thinkin' like that. Mac's fine. Well, he had some bullets in him, but he's had surgery and they say he's *gonna* be fine. He just ain't around. Not around at all. He isn't even close to Purple Sage...."

I heard the lie, but something else was more important. "You said there was a murder, too. Who was it?"

"It was Miz Vera Meece. She was shot out at the POW camp same time as Mac, only she wasn't as lucky."

Vera Meece was dead. Shot and killed at the POW camp. The same camp where Matt had gone last night to deliver the receipts from the dance. I shuddered, envisioning my husband in the dark night, walking up to the small, army-green building that Vera had managed to get erected for her artifacts. That vision was replaced by another as I remembered Vera during our interview at her museum. Her face had been aglow, her voice sweet and southern as she pointed to the items being displayed in a glass case.

"Now this is a first-aid pouch that our men carried in the field." It was of heavy canvas, the color dark green, the bandages and scissors laid beside it. "There were actually dozens of different kinds and sizes of first-aid kits, and they were assigned to the soldiers based on their jobs. This is the Carlisle model."

I had nodded, not quite seeing the charm in the implements that men took to war but recognizing that Vera was bringing back to life some fascinating part of her own history. Modern-day archaeology.

"And this," she had said, her voice filled with pride as she pointed to the gun on the wall, "is the OM1 carbine with a bayonet lug. See? It was the most popular rifle carried. There was also the Springfield, but it was heavier, so this one was much preferred. You see, Jolie, fighting men rarely got enough sleep, and they fought long hours and had to walk long distances, too. Nutritious food was difficult to obtain, so after a while they didn't have the strength to be carrying heavy guns. Of course, the OM1 didn't have the firepower of the Springfield, and my daddy said that a lot of men died because of this gun.''

This gun. "Wiley," I said, grounding myself in the present by pulling a yellow pad toward me. "What were they shot with? Do you know?"

"We believe it was a rifle from the display that Miz Meece was so proud of. Only it's missing so we can't be sure. It was the OM1 carbine.''

With a bayonet lug. "What time were they shot?" I wrote the word *time,* but the real reason I had to know was because of Matt and all the ''what if''s that were careening around in my head: What if Matt had been there? What if he'd been shot instead of the sheriff? He hadn't carried a gun, or a police radio....

"We can't say for sure because the sheriff hasn't been able to talk much yet. But he called for help 'bout eleven-thirty and said he'd been passed out for a while. Coulda been earlier, I guess. Why'd you ask?"

"My husband went out to the camp last night, after the dance. He had to give the receipts to Vera.'' I stopped writing and felt another shock wave. "I just talked to Vera last night. She was on her way home, except she went back to the camp to meet Howard.''

"Who?"

"A guest of ours.'' I took a breath. Time to be professional again. "Wiley, I need to get some information, so I can write a story.''

"Can't do that, Miz Wyatt.'' He began giving me all the reasons why that was impossible just as our news director, Rory Stone, came into the office and put the news copy in the wire basket. Once Rory was seated at his desk across from me, I slid my yellow legal pad toward him. The scribbled notes told the story. Rory's hazel eyes widened and he looked up to mouth in disbelief, "The sheriff? Shot?"

I nodded as Wiley ran down: "...so you see that no one knows about the sheriff and we got to make sure that the lid stays tight on this."

"Wiley," I said. "I do understand your concern, but even as we speak, everyone at the country club and the Sage Cafe is talking about what happened last night. And if they aren't now, they will be by noon."

"It's just not so—"

"Don't you think Mrs. Meece's neighbors will notice she's not home? That she hasn't been home? And what about the people who stop by the POW camp? Not to mention the neighbors of the funeral home?" Jackson's funeral home ran the only two ambulances in town. Everett Dayton and Lily Braden had homes across the street from Jackson's, and those two could be relied upon to know each time the ambulances left the garage. Within an hour they knew why the ambulance had left, and within two hours Everett was usually holding court at the Sage Cafe.

"Miz Wyatt, we can't add fuel to the rumors. To protect the sheriff." After a slight pause he added, "Although I've talked to him and he didn't see nothing, and he's not in Wilmot County, anyway."

"Wiley, if I were you I'd let Trina handle the rest of the inquiries; you're not a very good liar."

I heard a long, shaky sigh. I had almost forgotten that Wiley was still new at all this, and while Mac believed that Wiley had good people instincts, and would someday be a fine law enforcement officer, I didn't think that someday had arrived.

"Here's what we'll do," I said, making eye contact with Rory, who quietly picked up his phone to listen in. "We'll air a bulletin," I said. "We'll give the information on Mrs. Meece's murder and then we'll add that Mac—"

"No story—it's already been decided."

Rory rolled his eyes as I asked Wiley, "Who decided this?"

"Me and Ed Presnell. We're in charge now."

Like when President Reagan had been shot and General

Haig said he was running the country. And just about as frightening. Wiley Pierce was merely young and inexperienced, but Ed Presnell was...well, as the dispatcher had once said, "His motherboard is missing some chips." Mac had inherited the guy when he took over the office and didn't have the heart to let him go. Instead Ed was relegated to doing a lot of paperwork, patrolling during the slack times, and was instructed to call for backup immediately should any real law enforcement work be required.

There was a third deputy, Linc Draper, who seemed to me more capable of holding the reins of the sheriff's office. I'd search him out later. In the meantime there was Wiley.

"Wiley, have you ever heard of the First Amendment rights of the press?" I asked. "It means you can't control the news—"

"But you can?"

"That's how it works, but don't worry, we won't do anything to jeopardize Mac Donelly. Wait just a second—"

"No, ma'am. No disrespect, but I'm hanging up." And he did so.

I looked at Rory as we replaced our phones. "Guess he told us," I said. "But I think I know how I can get some more information." I was already pulling my keys out of my purse.

"How?"

"By nefarious means," I said. "Don't air anything 'til I get back."

Rory, who is a good fifteen years younger than I am, shot me a look, but nodded. It made me hope he was mellowing. Or cared as much about the sheriff as the rest of the town.

Mac Donelly has always been reelected as much for his good deeds as anything else. Rather than arrest a minor, he'd been known to deliver the kid to his parents, with an appointment already scheduled with a counselor. I had seen that side of Mac personally when a friend of Jeremy's had been killed. Mac had been there to listen, to care, and to offer his strength. Not just to me, but to Jeremy as well. I haven't forgotten that, and I know Jeremy never will.

Mac was a good person, a quiet-spoken, great person, and I was very glad he was alive.

THE SIGN OUTSIDE the Wilmot County Hospital says MIRACLES HAPPEN HERE. I knew for a fact that it was true, because I'd spent a lot of time in that building. So much time that I could enter at night without disturbing the guard or the nurses; I could sneak a midnight snack from the kitchen without anyone being the wiser; and I knew the combination to the locker that held the clean towels—a very valuable commodity, for some bizarre reason. It was all knowledge that would probably be useful in the future. However, at that particular moment, I went in the front door and just acted normal. This "acting normal" is a wonderful phrase, and I've often wondered what it meant.

The two glass doors whisked open automatically as I stepped on the black matting, then a rush of cool air chilled me. The big, airy waiting room, with its almost unnaturally shiny, white vinyl flooring and blue-striped chairs, was empty except for two elderly women, one in a wheelchair. I nodded in their direction, waved at the young woman at the reception desk, and kept on going, just like I knew what I was doing.

Down the hall, past the nurses' station, then around the corner. There were only three halls of actual patient rooms; most of the doors were partially opened, allowing me to see inside. The first three rooms had their heavy drapes pulled back to let in the cleansing sunlight. Each was neat and pristine, waiting for the next person who needed some help to heal. Several more rooms had people in the beds, most of those had their drapes shut, and muted TV sounds filtered toward me. None of those people was Mac Donelly. I checked the entire hallway, then rounded a corner and started on the second.

Empty, empty, wrong person, empty, too dark to see. That was sufficient to make me stop and read the file in the acrylic holder by the door. Weaver. I didn't know of any Weavers in Purple Sage. The NO VISITORS sign was also unusual.

Cautiously I slid around the door and waited for my eyes to adjust. The drapes were open just an inch or so, and I could see the tall rolling tray that was used to serve meals. Silhouetted on it were a pitcher, a glass, and box of tissues. Also in the room were two straight-backed chairs, a functional white bedside stand, and the one luxury that each room contained: a recliner, big and overstuffed, with dozens of controls to change the position, to add massage, even alter the temperature of the chair. I knew those chairs well.

From the ceiling hung a white curtain that could be drawn around the bed, but this one was pushed back, giving me a view of a man. He was lying on his stomach and when I tiptoed forward I could clearly see that his hair was almost completely gray. As my eyes grew more accustomed to the darkness and I crept closer, I could see the ridge in his hair caused from wearing a hat. Even with his face turned away from me, I knew it was Mac. I wanted to reach out and touch him.

Instead I took a step backward and inadvertently bumped the tray. Mac's head came around more quickly than I would have expected. "Jolie?" he said, his voice a croak.

"Hi, Mac," I said softly. "How are you feeling?"

"Like shit."

"I'm sorry to hear that."

He tried to clear his throat, and ended up coughing harshly. By his pained expression, each cough must have hurt horribly.

"Would you like some water?"

"That'd be nice." He didn't move anything but his head, and that only an inch or so, while I poured fresh water and put the straw in his mouth. He drank several swallows, then closed his eyes for a second to signal that he was done. "That's better," he said. His voice was smoother now, but still soft, as if it were too much effort to speak any louder. "What're you doing here?" he asked.

"I just had to make sure that you were all right. You know, doubting Thomas."

I sat down on the recliner so he could see me without having to move. As his head once again touched down on the bed, he grunted slightly. "I'm fine," he said, "Just shot. Doesn't look like they killed me, though."

"But I think they tried. It's a good thing you're so tough."

"Yeah, me 'n' Arnold, we got a lot in common." His smile was more like a grimace.

I waited until he'd taken a few breaths. "Do you know who did this?" I asked.

He closed his eyes for a moment, then opened them again, his expression sad. "Don't know a thing, Jolie, except Vera Meece is dead. Damn. If I'd just—"

"Ifs don't count. Didn't you tell me that once?"

"I suppose I may have."

It was odd, having this conversation with Mac lying on a hospital bed.

Normally Mac was the source of strength regardless of the situation. As I had learned from experience, he could always be counted on. Now that strength was gone, drained away by bullets and surgery. His muscles were completely still except those needed to talk. The lines around his eyes and mouth were deep, harsh grooves, and his ruddy skin seemed parched and pale.

In the dim light I looked at his back, covered by a thin sheet, and I could make out lumps—no doubt bandages covering the bullet wounds. I realized how lucky he'd been.

I stood up. "Mac, I'd better go. If you need anything, though, I—"

"Not just yet, Jolie," he said. "Please, just sit a minute more." When I was back in the recliner, he said, "I got to know what's happening out there. I have responsibilities. The nurses just pat me on the head like my brain got damaged instead of my back; I can't just go to sleep and pretend like everything's all right."

"Sure you can, Mac. Nothing is happening in Purple Sage. Maybe when the Celebration starts tonight we'll have all kinds of things going on, but so far, nothing. I passed two cops on the way over and they looked bored." Everything within the city limits was the responsibility of the police department, rather than the sheriff's office, and that's where the bulk of the Celebration activity would take place.

"Who's minding the store, Jolie?" Mac asked, his voice growing softer, his eyes beginning to droop.

"I'm not sure, but I called your office earlier and everything was fine...." I let my voice trail off, hoping he'd gone to sleep.

He had one final comment. "Linc will be back later. Then I can relax."

As I watched, he slid off into sleep, his back rising and falling, little snorts of sound escaping every few breaths. Gently I pulled the sheet higher on his shoulders, and stole quietly from the room.

I only got as far as the hallway outside Mac's door.

SEVEN

A HAND COMING from the sleeve of a white coat grabbed me. I stifled a gasp.

"Why, Mrs. Wyatt, how are you?" It was Dr. Richard Baxter, a dear man who'd spent some of both his professional and personal time mending the wounds and curing the ills of the Wyatt family. He dropped my arm and pointed to the sign on Mac's door. The one that clearly stated NO VISITORS. "Guess you must have missed that," he said with an innocent smile.

I smacked my palm against my forehead. "Amazing. Would you look at that sign, and I didn't even see it. But I didn't go in that room, so I guess it doesn't matter."

He threw back his head and laughed, the sound filling the empty hallway. "Between you and Jeremy, Matt's life must be like a TV sitcom."

"Oh, right," I said. "But not *The Brady Bunch* this week." I grew serious. "Actually, I'm glad you showed up. I need a few minutes of your time."

"Okay. How about if I buy you a cup of coffee?" He gestured in the direction of the break room.

"Thanks, I appreciate the offer, but I'd prefer that we stay here." I was planted in front of Mac's door and while I'm not large or very dangerous looking, I could certainly be a temporary deterrent to anyone trying to get in. "How is he? The sheriff. Really." I asked.

Richard Baxter's face acquired the tired, but satisfied look I'd seen it wear a number of times, as if all the hours of worry, and tedious surgery, came back to him in a flash, then swiftly moved on. "He's doing much better. Believe it or not, none of the bullets hit anything major. He must have had an angel on his shoulder and, barring any unforeseen complications, he should be back to normal in a few weeks."

Some residual tension eased from my body and a great relief I hadn't expected hit me.

"Are you okay?" he asked.

I nodded. "Fine." When I had taken in a few breaths, and let out a little more tension, I said, "I heard that Vera Meece died."

"That's what I heard, too," he said with a shake of his head. "I don't know that firsthand, though; she never made it this far."

The sound of some visitors arriving caused both of us to look toward the end of the hall. Two elderly women nodded in our direction, one adding a pleasant "Good mornin'" before they entered a room.

Dr. Baxter shifted. "Well, if you won't drink our coffee, which is probably a wise decision on your part, I'm going to get myself—"

I stopped him. "Actually, there's something else I need to talk to you about."

"And that is…?"

"The safety of Mac Donelly. Richard, anyone could walk into his room. Anyone."

"That's the way most hospital rooms are, Jolie. Access and egress, and all that. The architects planned it that way."

"I don't think they took into consideration the fact that Mac was shot last night." I looked at him squarely. "Dr. Baxter, whoever shot Mac is still roaming around somewhere. They could stop by to finish the job.''

"Ah. From sitcom to a medical thriller.''

It did seem out of place; much too melodramatic for this quiet spot, but we live in that kind of world, and the melodrama had somehow found its way from urban streets to the gentler ones of Purple Sage.

"Richard,'' I said. "I'm really worried about this. Mac should have some protection and there doesn't seem to be any.''

Our conversation paused as three men walked toward us. They were obviously from the same family, of at least two different generations, and not anyone I had ever met before.

"Excuse me,'' the eldest of the three men said. "Can you tell me where we can find room four thirty-eight? Bessie Belle Tripp's room? The woman at the front desk gave us directions, but we don't seem to have followed them very well.''

Richard pointed the way, while I watched. The men were probably in for the Celebration, but we didn't know that for sure. They could be anyone, here for reasons that didn't include comforting the sick.

By the time Richard finished his conversation with them, I was more concerned than ever. "Those men are a perfect example,'' I said. "We don't have any idea who they are—what if one of them is the person who shot Mac? What if they have guns? All they have to do is ask for Mac and someone will eventually tell them where to find him. Maybe even you.''

Doc Baxter leaned against the wall and let out a long breath. "I'm sorry, Jolie, I guess I just didn't want to face the problem. The hell of it is, I can't do anything about it. We don't have the manpower to protect anyone. We're even short of Sunshine Rays and Gray Ladies, what with everyone busy with the Celebration. My big idea was to put a different name on his door chart, which we did—''

"It didn't fool me,'' I said. "So what about the sheriff's office? Couldn't they send a deputy?'' Even before he could answer, I had thought it through. "No, I guess not, since there's only three of them left.''

Dr. Baxter straightened up. "Look, the last thing I want is Mac getting shot here in my hospital. Or anywhere, for that matter, but I just don't see many options."

My mind was racing, moving as if down a series of paths that formed a maze, only I was seeing the end of each as well as the journey. "Why couldn't you send him somewhere? The problem is that if you use Jackson's Ambulance Service everyone in town will know within an hour. Could you get an out-of-town service? Send Mac to San Angelo or San Antonio? Maybe Austin—"

"I thought about that, but that much time in an ambulance wouldn't be good for him, not to mention the comfort factor."

Richard chewed his lower lip for a minute, then the worried look on his face was replaced by a quick flash of a smile. "I've got it! I know where we'll move the sheriff. Jolie, I'm glad you stopped by—this could be very good. You don't have to worry anymore." He pulled the chart from the acrylic holder and put it under his arm. "Thanks again."

"Wait a minute," I said. "Where are you going to take him?"

He opened his mouth to tell me, then stopped. "Maybe that's not something I should talk about."

"Like I'm not trustworthy?"

"As the saying goes, if you tell one person, it's the same as telling ten. And in Purple Sage, it's more like telling a hundred." He shook his head. "Besides, you found Mac once. If you really need him, I expect you can find him again."

As soon as the sound effect that announced a news bulletin began to fade, I pushed open the microphone switch and turned up the pot. *"There was a shooting last night in Wilmot County, leaving one person dead and another wounded.*

"Good morning, I'm Jolie Wyatt and this K-SAGE news bulletin is brought to you by Jackson's Funeral Home and Ambulance Service, home-owned- and -operated for over fifty years.

"Sometime between ten-thirty and eleven o'clock yesterday evening, Sheriff Mac Donelly and Vera Meece were shot near

Camp John Seybold on FM Four forty-four. According to un-official sources, Mrs. Meece had been shot twice in the chest, apparently killing her instantly, and Sheriff Donelly had three bullet wounds in his back. Dr. Richard Baxter performed emergency surgery at the Wilmot County Hospital and later the sheriff was transferred. His condition is considered stable.

"The sheriff told his deputies he heard no sound except that of the OM1 carbine rifle that was used in the incident and he did not see his attacker. The attack is currently under inves-tigation by the Sheriff's Department.

"Vera Meece, who died in the shooting, was the chair of the Centennial Celebration slated to begin early this evening in Purple Sage. The committee heads are meeting at eleven this morning at the Sage Country Club to plan a tribute to the woman who has given so much to make the event a success. It is believed that the Celebration will go on as planned."

I looked up at Dan, the disk jockey on the other side of the double glass, just to make sure that everything was okay. He nodded slightly and I continued. *"Tune to K-SAGE News at Noon for an update on this developing story, as well as all the news for Wilmot County. I'm Jolie Wyatt."* I pushed the button that started the Jackson's Funeral Home commercial, and switched off my microphone.

It was my last official duty before I could head home. Usu-ally that elicits a sigh of satisfaction from me, because WW Ranch seems worlds away from anywhere else. I can leave behind all the politics of Purple Sage and K-SAGE. The drive home gives me time to plan the rest of my day before I have lunch with Matt and Jeremy. Then I spend my afternoons writ-ing, or reading, or taking care of those zillions of details called life.

Today I wasn't all that enthused about leaving, in part be-cause Matt and Jeremy wouldn't be at the ranch when I got there. Jeremy was at the Hammond place with Cecily and the senior Wyatts, while Matt was probably on his way to the country club for the Celebration Committee meeting scheduled to start soon.

I hadn't a clue as to what I was expected to do. It was

obvious I wouldn't be cooking or entertaining guests, and I doubted that the group at the Hammond place would be thrilled to see me if I showed up on their doorstep. They wouldn't even need me to chauffeur them to the downtown parade that was going to kick off the Celebration.

I went down the hall to our office and left the bulletin on Rory's desk. After I buzzed the front desk to tell Michelle that I was leaving, I headed out the back door.

It was miserably hot outside, a dry heat that baked all of Wilmot County, so I had the air conditioner going full blast by the time I was navigating the square. It was then I realized that Purple Sage was no longer the quiet little town I had driven through earlier in the morning. The traffic around the square was so heavy it almost looked as if the parade had already started. A steady stream of vehicles, mostly mini vans, clogged the streets, and all of them seemed to be loaded to the headliners with families, suitcases, and even dogs. Some had camping gear stowed on top—obviously the unlucky ones who couldn't find hotel space. Some drivers were dawdling, gawking like the tourists they were at the changes around town. There was a near-miss accident in front of *Miz Priddys*, the artsy-craftsy store on the corner of the square.

The police were putting up barricades on the sidewalks for traffic control tonight. I spotted Andy Sawyer, the assistant chief of police, and waved. He raised a hand in salute and smiled before he went back to work. In the center of the square, booths had been erected under the huge pecan trees that surround our elegant three-story courthouse. In the still August air the enticing aroma of popcorn and hot dogs added to the festive mood. I might have stopped had there been anyplace to do that, but every single parking space was taken.

On impulse, I decided to see how the committee was coming along at the Sage Country Club.

The country club is not a posh place where only the rich congregate. It is, however, one of the nicer facilities in Purple Sage, with massive windows in the pink, native stone walls. The floors are tile and the decor is southwestern with lots of glass and stone and some attractive, light wood furniture.

The club offers most of Purple Sage's organized socializing. For example, they have dances twice a month with country bands. There are golf tournaments, poker nights, and swimming in the biggest pool in Wilmot County. This is also where you'll find the best, and practically the only, tennis courts around. My husband is a tennis fanatic, which is why we're members.

The main reason the Sage Country Club remains private is that in our county liquor-by-the-drink is illegal, except in membership-only establishments, which makes this a very popular place.

I parked in the lot, and noticed quite a few cars already there. Inside I discovered that Arielle, the young woman at the front desk, had a line of people in front of her, apparently joining for the week. That would be a nice little boost in revenue that would help repair some damage we'd had to the golf course earlier in the summer. I kept going through the dining room to the private conference and game rooms on the south side of the building. There were only two, but they came in handy for things like fiftieth wedding anniversaries and fortieth birthday parties when you didn't want to clean up your own home.

The door to the first of the rooms was open and when I peeked in I discovered the committee members already seated around the big oval table. Matt saw me come in and smiled as I slid into one of the chairs near the door. When he turned back to the group he was saying, "So, we've agreed that we should keep the POW camp open, since we've advertised it in all the mailings. Now what we need is someone to take charge of it. Do I have any volunteers?"

"What about you?" someone asked.

Matt shook his head. "If I'm taking over the chair's job, I think we can consider my boat loaded. And you can consider yourself lucky we didn't elect you."

There were a couple of laughs, some scooting around in the chairs as everyone eyed everyone else. Finally my friend Diane stood up. Diane is about five-seven and willowy, with deep brown hair and eyes, and she has the IQ of Einstein and

Edison put together. At least that's how I tell the story, and when we play Trivial Pursuit I always make sure we're on the same team. We win a lot.

Diane looked around the table before she said, "I'll probably hate myself for this in the morning, but... I'm willing to take on the POW camp for the duration of the Celebration." Spontaneous applause began and Diane offered a small bow before she added, "Now, I'm telling you up front that I'm not willing to spend the whole next week out there myself. What I'm offering to do is help recruit volunteers, show them what to do, and fill in where I have to. I might end up shortening the hours the exhibit is open, and we'll just have to consider that a fortune of war." Only a few of us groaned at her pun, and we did so softly, because she went right on. "But I will take charge of the thing and have it open at least some of the time every day of the Celebration."

Her suggestion was put to a vote by Matt, and unanimously accepted. I slipped out of the room to get a glass of ice tea, and by the time I got back a small disagreement had broken out.

Matt was arguing with our chief of police, Bill Tieman, who was standing with his chair pushed back from the table. Matt was saying, "Bill, I think that Mrs. Meece was a fine person, too."

"And don't forget that without her, we probably wouldn't even be having this Celebration." Bill's jowly face was red, and his belly, which was hanging over his belt buckle as usual, was jiggling with indignation. "So I just don't get how you people think we can go right on, without so much as a—"

"That's not what we're suggesting!" someone from the other side of the table said.

"We just believe that we can't make an announcement at every event or we'll kill the whole Celebration," Matt said, in what I thought was a reasonable enough voice. "People will start leaving if things become maudlin, so we—"

"I know what you want, Matthew Wyatt," Bill growled. "You want to have your big old party, with your drinking and your dancing, as if a woman of her saintly attributes hadn't been killed in cold blood. Well, I think that's heathen. Down-right heathen!'' Besides being police chief, Bill is also a member of a fundamentalist congregation that doesn't believe in drinking or dancing, smoking, swearing, or card playing. I'm not sure how they propagate: That's got to be forbidden, too, but somehow they manage.

Last spring, Bill tried his hand at politics. He ran for mayor against Diane's husband, Trey. Bill took to public life with the fervor of a traveling evangelist. Despite the fact that he lost the election, he seems to believe he is on some kind of mission to better Purple Sage. His idea of a fund-raiser is to get on the radio and preach to people about how they should donate their hard-earned money to his pet charities. I think it's ludicrous, as does most of the population of Purple Sage. Not only do we not like his choice of needy recipients, but Bill also hasn't grasped that people want something in return for their money. Sometimes a feeling of satisfaction is enough, but sometimes they want fun. That's probably against his creed, too.

Matt's handsome face was becoming flushed, but he kept his comments in check and held out his hands, palms up, in a gesture of invitation. ''My own belief is that sorrow is a private thing, Bill. We grieve alone, usually at home, not at a dance or a picnic, or on the courthouse lawn. The other side of that, though, is that we commemorate a life, or an accomplishment, in public. Now if you'll let me finish, what I'm suggesting is that we vote to take some of the proceeds from the Celebration and make a permanent exhibit. In honor of Mrs. Meece.''

''Too expensive,'' Buddy Wayne Hargis said. He's the ex-husband of reporter Rhonda Hargis from the Sage *Tribune*. She's a friend of mine, and in my writers' group, while Buddy Wayne is a hothead, and not close to anyone who works a real job. ''First we'd have to find someone to run the place,'' he said, with more vehemence than seemed necessary. ''Then we'd have to keep making money for repairs, and what's it all for? A bunch of foreigners we were fighting in a war that we had to haul home and put in prison. That's a crock of—''

Diane cut him off. "I think Matt's idea will work *if* we put the exhibit in the museum at the old jail. We can designate a special room; there are a couple of them downstairs that were part of the old sheriff's quarters and they aren't currently in use." Bill Tieman started to growl again, but Diane kept going. "And we'll do a special memorial plaque, dedicating it all to Mrs. Meece."

"Excellent idea," Matt said. "We'll form a committee to come up with more specific suggestions after the Celebration is over. So, let's end the discussion and vote. All in favor..."

The loud chorus of ayes was interrupted by a man coming through the door. His boots landed hard, and it seemed intentionally so, on the wood floor of the conference room.

"Excuse me!" Ed Presnell, his deputy's badge shining on the pocket of his khaki uniform, stepped up to the head of the table near Matt and said, "Could y'all hold it down? I got official business here."

His eyes darted around, his legs were spread, and his hand was poised above his gun.

"Ed," Matt said with a cordial nod. "We were just about to finish up here, if you could give us a minute."

"No sir," Ed said. "We don't have a minute. Now, are you Matthew Wyatt?"

Stupid question, and I might have rolled my eyes at its absurdity if I hadn't felt an uncomfortable tickle of premonition.

"Yes, as you know, Ed, I am Matt Wyatt."

"And I want the truth now, did you, or did you not, leave the dance last night to drive out to the POW camp? By yourself."

Matt took a breath. "Yes, as a matter of fact, I did."

Ed grabbed Matt's arms. In a reflex action Matt jerked away from Ed's grip, and Ed grabbed again, this time holding on more tightly. The second time Matt stood perfectly still, his expression alternating between mild annoyance and curiosity.

"I'm taking you in for questioning," Ed said. "Because you're a suspect in the murder of one Vera Louise Meece."

The group seated around the table appeared stunned as the

deputy pushed Matt toward the door. Matt is more cool-headed than most of us, and he was smart enough not to resist.

When Ed saw me, he stopped long enough to say, "Ma'am, if you have one of them high-priced defense lawyers, you might want to call him."

EIGHT

IT WAS DIANE who got me moving. "I think this is illegal," she snapped as she grabbed my arm. "Come on."

"You think I should call a lawyer?" I asked, racing to keep up with her. Once we were out of the building I spotted Ed Presnell's patrol car parked in a handicapped space. Matt was already in the back.

"Let Matt decide. That jerk!"

I was beside Ed before he could get into the driver's seat. "Ed, excuse me—"

"I don't have time for female tears, Miz Wyatt."

"This has nothing to do with tears," I said, never more dry-eyed in my life. "This has to do with the law, and what you can and can't do."

"I am taking a man in for questioning."

"Fine," Diane said. "We'll just follow you over and wait for Matt."

"I wouldn't even suggest that if I were you," Ed said. "Might hear some things that would upset you—it could get ugly."

I grabbed Ed's khaki-covered arm and jerked him around so fast that, as my mother would have said, his head should have been spinning. Then I said, "It damn well better not get ugly! Number one, answering questions in a murder investigation is strictly voluntary. Unless you either press charges or get a court order, Matt is doing this to help you. Got it?" At least I'd learned something useful from that Simpson trial.

"And number two, my husband is a gentle, kind, wonderful human being. I, on the other hand, am not a gentle—"

"Me, neither," Diane said. "And if you are in any way abusive, you will discover what real torture is all about."

Ed Presnell, never very quick, was stunned into complete silence and immobility. As well he should have been. In the meantime, I pulled open the back door of the county car to discover that Matt was laughing.

"This is not funny!"

"I know, honey," he said, the grin never quite leaving his face. "It's okay. I'll just go to the courthouse with Ed. Don't worry, when I get there the sheriff will take over."

Which is when I realized that Matt didn't have current information. No wonder he wasn't upset. "You haven't listened to the radio this morning, have you?"

"No. Should I have?"

"How'd you find out about Vera Meece?"

"Trey tracked me down at Mom's. But we didn't really get a chance to talk—"

I took a breath. "Matt, the sheriff is the one who found Vera's body. And then he was shot."

"Mac? Is he—?"

"He's in the hospital with three bullet wounds in his back, but he's okay. No. That's not quite right. I mean, he is okay, but I don't know where he is. I talked Dr. Baxter into hiding him, since the person who did the shooting is still on the loose."

Matt sank back into the seat of the car, his face grave. "Dear God."

"Do you want me to call Ellis Kramer?" He's Matt's attorney, the kind who handles land deals and wills. I wasn't sure how much criminal law he knew, but I couldn't think of anyone in Purple Sage who was any better versed on the subject.

"No," Matt said. "I don't think that's necessary. But would you and Diane drive my truck over to the courthouse so I can get home later? And keep the cellular so I can call you." He was beginning to look concerned.

"No problem."

"And don't say anything to my mother; you know how she'd worry."

I leaned into the car and gave him a quick kiss. "I'll handle everything, and if you're not home for dinner, I'm coming to get you."

"That I'd love to see."

As we'd talked, Ed had climbed into the driver's seat and started the engine. Now he turned around to me. "Miz Wyatt, we got to go, and you got to get out of the car."

"I'm going," I said. "But if you get overzealous, I assure you, you will be sorry." I stepped back from the car and Diane slammed the door so hard the vehicle was rocking as it pulled away.

"We probably shouldn't have threatened him," Diane offered.

"Frankly, my dear…" And for a moment I just stood there in the hot sun feeling bereft. A lunatic was running the world and my husband was still being civilized and cooperative. Worse, he was on the way to the courthouse, where the lunatic was going to question him. "I'm calling Ellis anyway," I said. "I don't like this."

"That's not a bad idea. Not that Matt can't take care of himself, but it never hurts to have someone spouting legalese." Diane slid an arm around me. "Come on. You can drive Matt's Explorer and call Ellis on the mobile at the same time. I'll follow you in my car. When we're finished, I'll drop you back here. Have you eaten?"

I shook my head. "I'm not hungry. And we don't have time."

"Maybe not, but I have the feeling you're going to need your strength." She was moving me toward Matt's car.

Diane and I both write. She does thrillers with a spy as her protagonist, and I write mysteries; so far we haven't sold anything, but we have agents, and we both have manuscripts out there in the black hole of publishing reserved for unheard-ofs. We both also take our writing, and the research, very seriously. We have books on poisons, guns, wounds, crime scenes, and evidence. We've taken seminars both on writing and on crime investigation. One in particular had been put on for writers by some ex-FBI agents. It had been a day filled with gory pictures and terms like *blow-back* and *lividity*—not exactly pleasant, but we'd learned a lot.

We'd learned that the first twenty-four hours of any investigation were crucial, and the longer an investigation took, the less likely it would ever be solved. That knowledge caused my worry.

"Do you realize that Vera was killed almost fourteen hours ago?" I said. "And nothing worthwhile is being done."

"We don't actually know what's being done."

"Sure we do. They arrested my husband."

"They're questioning Matt," Diane said. "That's all."

"He can't tell them anything. And he sure as hell didn't murder anyone," I said. "And besides that, if the murderer is someone who's just here for the Celebration, they'll be long gone in about five days. If they aren't already."

I HAD TO DRIVE AROUND the square six times before I found a parking space, and Diane found one just a few minutes later. They were on opposite sides of the courthouse, and while Diane walked over to meet me, I called Ellis Kramer. He assured me he would be there in minutes, and he sounded like he meant it.

"He's on his way," I told Diane as I folded the deposit slip I'd written Matt a mushy note on. After I wedged it in the steering wheel, I locked the Explorer. Normally that's not necessary in Purple Sage, but times are changing and it was apparent we needed to catch up with them. "Will you come with me?" I asked. We were already headed inside.

"You're planning on staying here? For how long?" Diane asked.

"As long as it takes."

We started up the staircase to the second floor. The inside of the courthouse needs remodeling, but the county commissioners haven't found the funds for that project yet. The floors are wood, once a dark brown and now worn to a paler shade.

The wooden doors have glass windows, with names painted in silver on each one. We went straight through the door marked SHERIFF'S OFFICE.

Loretta, the afternoon dispatcher, wasn't there. Instead, behind the scarred wooden counter, was the early morning part-timer, Trina, who is also the last known living Neanderthal on the planet. Trina can be exceedingly quick and articulate on the scanner, and I've seen her function like an efficient human with the sheriff, but that's not her style with me.

"Trina," I said. "Where's my husband, Matt?"

She looked at me as if I were a foreign species, one she found distasteful. "You can wait there." She pointed to two old straight-backed chairs that sat against the wall.

Diane took over. "We came with Matt Wyatt and Ed Presnell, only we had a little trouble finding a place to park. If you'll just point us in their direction, we won't take up any more of your time."

Trina looked purposefully at the chairs, then at us. "Wait."

I hadn't really expected to be ushered into an interrogation room, and even if I had been, I'm not sure what I would have said or done. This was a totally new experience for me.

Diane took my arm. "Why don't we just sit down while we wait for Ellis?"

"Sure." We sat and stared at the counter. Behind it were four doors. The one on the far left was to Mac's office; the door on the far right led to the deputies' office. I didn't know what the two center ones were.

I began to hear male voices, and after a minute or two I discovered they were coming from one of the center rooms behind the counter. Eventually I recognized Matt's voice, but I couldn't make out the words. I assumed he was using that nice even tone he does when everyone around him is under stress.

Diane tapped my arm and nodded toward the room. I nodded back. At least we'd found them. If we heard anything I didn't like, we could leap the counter and storm the door.

Waiting in that situation was almost intolerable. I paced, I sat, I paced some more. Finally the outside door opened and Ellis came in.

Ellis is about my age, but pretends to be part of the old guard of Purple Sage. His thinning hair helps, as do the old-fashioned glasses and conservatively cut suits he wears.

"Thank God," I said, jumping up.

He smiled. "That's a bit elevated even for me, but I'll take it." He shook my hand quickly while his other hand rested on his tie. Ties are his one idiosyncrasy, and this one was down-right odd; it was exceptionally narrow with piano keys down the front. "Diane, how are you?" he asked.

"Better than Jolie." She looked toward the interrogation room. "Can you get in there?"

"That's my job."

He appeared to be pretty good at it, too. After a brief discussion with Trina, he was allowed behind the counter. "You can go on home, Jolie," he said. "We've got this under control."

"Right," I said. But I wasn't going anyplace.

Once he went into the interrogation room I lurked near the counter, hoping to overhear what I could. It helped that Ellis had left the door ajar. First I heard the standard greetings among the men, then some questions from Ed, and some softer answers from Matt. I still wasn't catching more than a few words in every sentence.

Diane turned to me. "Look, Jolie, I have to go out to Camp Seybold now, and I think you should go with me. I could use some assistance, and we can look around. Maybe take some pictures if we see anything important. My camera's in the car and I've got scads of film."

"No thanks. I'll wait."

"But you can't do anything."

"I'm lending moral support to my husband."

Diane rolled her eyes. "He doesn't know you're here."

"He will if he needs me."

I went back to listening and Diane remained beside me. I heard Matt say, "...gave her the money then." As opposed to later? Earlier? I strained even harder to hear and could just make out Ed saying, "Start from the top."

Matt's words were clear and crisp, as if he was getting irritated. "I pulled up to the gravel parking area, and I didn't even have the door opened before I saw Vera running toward me. At first I thought something was wrong, but she said no, she was just in a hurry. Anyway, I gave her the bank bag, she said thank you and went back to the museum. I waited until she was inside, then I drove off."

"So you didn't even get out of your vehicle."

"I got out, but I didn't go much farther," Matt corrected.

"And you're trying to tell me you never went inside the headquarters."

"That's correct."

"That's a lie!" Ed was triumphant. "Your wife said you did! She told Wiley that this very mornin'. So you better start over, and you better start with the truth!"

"No." I jumped up, ran to the counter, and put my elbows on the old wood. "I was wrong." It was crazy; I was yelling at a door. "Ed," I said, trying to be loud enough but also to sound as calm as Matt usually does, "let me come explain." When there was no response, I said to Trina, "Damn it, let me in there."

By this time Diane was beside me at the counter and Ed was in the doorway. "Okay, Miz Wyatt, I heard that and I won't have you messin' with this investigation!"

Ellis came out, hurried around Ed, and headed toward me. "It's okay, Officer Presnell," Ellis was saying. "I'm sure Mrs. Wyatt didn't intend to be a disruption."

I was trying to see Matt, but he wasn't in my line of sight. All I could see was Ed, glaring across the expanse of the sheriff's office. "Maybe Miz Wyatt don't understand this is important police business. We got us an officer shot, and a woman dead, and her standin' out here shoutin' ain't helping things." His eyes were on Ellis, not me. I responded anyway.

"I'm sorry," I said. "What I told Wiley was that Matt was out there at the camp; I didn't say inside the building. I thought it could have been Matt who got shot, that's why I told him.

I was just worried, that's all." When Ed continued to glare in silence, I went on. "If you'll just let me talk to you..."

By this time Ellis was beside me, with an arm around my shoulders. "I appreciate what you're saying, Jolie, as does Officer Presnell," he said, walking me toward the outside door. "What you have to understand is that you're not helping."

"But Ed has faulty information. I was wrong; it's as simple as that."

I glanced over at Ed in time to see him step back inside the interrogation room and close the door sharply.

"I understand," Ellis said. He practically had me in the corner. "Jolie, I'm going to ask you to let me handle this. I think that's much wiser."

I lowered my voice. "Ed's being overzealous, and anyway, he's an id—"

Ellis cleared his throat loudly to drown out my words. When I stopped talking he said, "Jolie, you have to understand something. Can you just listen for a minute?" He waited. "Will you do that?"

I stood perfectly still. "I'm listening." He was going to explain a good ol' boy situation—I could sense it coming.

"Thank you." He straightened his shoulders and said, "Maybe Ed is being a bit overzealous, however, this is a unique situation for him. There has been a murder, and the shooting of a police officer. That adds an edge to things, because there is personal involvement. Surely you can see that."

"Ed has misinformation."

"You've made that very clear. We all heard you."

"And Ed didn't believe me!"

I'd never seen Ellis ruffled before, and he was only slightly so now, but he did draw a deep breath before he said, "Jolie, I know that you are concerned about your husband, but you can't help. Not now. The best thing you can do for Matt is leave." He scowled, his own irritation slipping out. "Jolie, the longer I stand around arguing with you, the longer Matt is stuck here. Let Ed interrogate him and get all the information he needs. It might actually help the investigation."

I felt a hand on my shoulder and turned to discover Diane. "He's right and you know it," she said. "You're just going to confuse the issue."

I could see their side of the argument, and I did recognize that I was being protective of Matt. What I couldn't tell is whether or not I was being overly protective. Jeremy would probably say I was.

"Okay." I shrugged off Diane's arm and took a few steps away so I had some breathing room. "I'll go. Ellis, I'm sure you'll have Matt out of here in no time."

"A couple of hours at most. And thank you, Jolie," he said, visibly relaxing. "I knew you'd understand."

I'd left my purse on the chair, and I walked over and picked it up. Once I had it in my hand I straightened up and said loudly, aiming my voice in the direction of the interrogation room, "I'm sure Ed will find the real murderer. And if he doesn't, I will."

As I CLIMBED into Diane's silver Mercedes, I said, "Okay, so I shouldn't have yelled. I have no couth."

"Very little. And I know how you feel, but logically, Ellis can do something useful that you can't. It's one of those legal things, so let it go." Diane pulled around the corner, which was not the way we should have headed.

"Where are you taking me?"

"I need a news story on KSGE asking for volunteers at the camp."

"Everyone's already so busy, you may not get any response."

"Don't say that; don't even think it. I'm hoping people will come out for Vera," Diane said, waiting for the unusual line of oncoming traffic to clear so she could pull into the radio station's parking lot. "Like a final thank-you or something. If not, this is going to be a long week."

We made it just in time to add Diane's request to the headline news at one-thirty. After that we picked up sandwiches at the Sage Cafe and headed for Camp John Seybold.

"Did Wiley say they'd called the DPS mobile lab?" Diane asked as we drove down Main past IdaMae Dorfman's bakery.

"He didn't say it, but I'm sure he did." Anything else was unthinkable. "You don't suppose he'd try to investigate a crime scene by himself?" I asked.

"Ed Presnell might, but Wiley knows better." She thought about it for a second as she fumbled with the paper wrapper on her sandwich. "No, thcy had to have called DPS. They know Mac will be back in charge eventually and he'd skin them for botching an important investigation like this."

I was already eating and she looked over at me. "A dry turkey sandwich with no chips, and no cookies? That's like penance. Aren't you going a little overboard?"

"You've seen Cecily," I said. "What would you be eating if she were Trey's ex and had flown several thousand miles to come back for a casual visit?"

"What was it he said in *Silence of the Lambs?* Her liver with a nice Chianti?"

I shuddered. "Not my cup of tea."

With the more pressing worries of Vera's murder and Matt's interrogation, I was no longer too concerned about Cecily. And I certainly wasn't foolish enough to think that it would make a difference to lose those five persistent pounds I'd gained when I quit smoking many years before. Still, eating a cookie would have felt like taunting fate, and I'm very much against that.

Diane started to take a bite of her sandwich, but paused just long enough to say, "Vera couldn't have been back in Purple Sage for more than what, eight months? Twelve maybe? But she sure took over the Celebration." Diane took a bite, chewed in thoughtful silence, then washed it down with tea sipped through a straw. After she replaced the white foam container in the cup holder between us, she negotiated a right turn that would take us to the camp. All the while she was still frowning, thoughtfully. "Isn't that odd?" she asked. "Vera leaves Purple Sage, comes back thirty years later, and in less than a year she's murdered."

"It's the Celebration part that worries me. I can't get past the thought that the killer leaves town on Sunday and gets away clean and free.''

"But why was she killed?" Diane asked, still on her own track. "It makes sense that Mac walked up on the murder, or Vera's body, and the killer was still there, probably hidden, but around. To get away he had to shoot Mac. That's logical, isn't it?"

"Conjecture, but logical."

"Okay, so that could be the reason Mac was shot, but it doesn't explain the motive behind Vera's killing. Do you think it was for money?"

"What money? The receipts from the dance?" I asked. Diane nodded and I went on. "Those were mostly local checks, and no one could cash them and get away with it. I'll bet there wasn't over a hundred dollars in hard currency."

"People have been killed for less."

"Isn't that the sad truth." We drove for a while in silence, then something occurred to me. "We don't even know that the money's missing. I'll ask Matt about it tonight."

"Good idea. Did I see you talking to Vera last night at the dance?"

"She was worried about the band—" I stopped, realizing again that it had been just last night that Vera Meece had come to the dance hunting for Matt. I stared over at Diane.

"What's wrong?" she asked.

"It was just last night," I said. "Vera Meece was alive last night. And then someone killed her."

Diane patted my hand. "Which just shows how you can't count on life. So go on. What did she say?"

My memory of the night before was in sharp focus. The band, the lights, Vera touching her hair and tilting her head like a young girl. "Matt was right, Vera was meeting someone," I said. "She was kind of giggly about it—you know how she is. Was."

"She loved men."

"She really seemed to, didn't she?" I said. "Anyway, she said the man she was meeting was 'an officer and a gentleman.'"

Diane shuddered. "If he's the one who killed her, I'm afraid she was wrong. He wasn't a gentleman at all."

NINE

THE POW CAMP is located northwest of Sage Lake. According to what Vera Meece had told me when we taped our radio interview, it has been a permanent fixture in Wilmot County since World War II. Yet, in truth, there's been nothing there, at least not as long as I've been in town. When the war ended and the camp closed, everything was either taken down or allowed to disintegrate as the vegetation reclaimed the land for its own. Now it's only a clearing with a couple of barely discernible roads, and a large, oblong, concrete slab in the middle of it.

During the war, however, it was the center of a great deal of activity. Some Purple Sage-ites worked there, but, more important, it was where local farmers went to find a ready source of labor. From the stories I've heard, the prisoners were invaluable replacements for the young men who were fighting overseas. They were paid for their efforts and, in turn, considered themselves contributing members of the Purple Sage community. Many of the men stayed in the United States when the war ended. Others took home fond memories of the place when they returned to their own villages in Germany.

The camp hasn't changed much since I first moved to Purple Sage four years ago. The main difference is a small building, off to the left, that Vera had erected. She'd done it with money she'd raised and some matching funds from the city, along with a fair amount of volunteer labor and materials. The headquarters, as she'd begun calling it, wasn't much, just a fifteen by fifteen box partitioned into two almost equal halves. The first half was the display section where visitors could view the artifacts; the back portion was an office where Mrs. Meece had stored every record of the camp that she could find. I had been amazed at how much that woman had dug up.

Surrounding the entire camp were live oak trees, like a natural fence around the open area. The large slab was still there in the center, as was the road circling it, which had been recently cleared of weeds.

Diane stopped the car on the gravel that served as a parking area. "Looks like we already have a visitor," I said. I recognized the other vehicle; it was the "hired car" that Howard Bremerton was driving.

Howard emerged from the vehicle as Diane shut off the engine of the Mercedes and reached for her purse. "That man is so good-looking," she said.

"I wouldn't mention that around Cecily—she seems to be the possessive type."

"You're only saying that because she was once possessive of your husband. When he was *her* husband."

"Was she really? Possessive, I mean."

"I'm not having this conversation, Jolie. Neither are you."

"I'm not sure Cecily's been possessive so much as critical. Was she critical of Matt, too?"

Diane ignored me completely as she touched the button that popped the trunk. "Come on, we have work to do." But before she opened her door, she had one more thing to say. "Do me a favor and stall Howard out here. I need to get those pictures before hordes of people come tramping through."

"That's not likely."

"You know what I mean. Just keep him occupied."

"No problem." We got out of the car, she took her huge camera bag from the trunk, and then I followed her toward the front of the building.

Howard was beaming at us. "Jolie! I've finally found the place!"

"Third time's the charm," I said.

"I was thinking it was rather clever of me." He looked around the clearing. "I'm positive I drove right past it at least twice. I may even have stopped nearby to check my map, but

I was expecting something more military. Guards and guns and walls and such. Very American and very imposing.''

"Sorry," I said. "What you see is what you get."

"Yes, small, quaint, much like Purple Sage itself." That was blather and we both knew it. He smiled at Diane. "I'm Howard Bremerton. You were at the dance last night."

"Right. I'm Diane Atwood. Nice to meet you," she said as another car pulled in off the road. Without waiting to see who it was, she added, "Well, if you'll excuse me, I'd better get busy." She went over and unlocked the door of the tiny exhibit building.

"I wonder who this is," I said to Howard, my hand resting lightly on his arm. It was the only thing I could think of to stop him from following Diane. He looked down at my hand, then back up into my eyes and smiled. I dropped my hand and turned away.

It was Liz Street who stepped out of her car. This morning she had skipped the overdone denim look she'd worn to the dance last night and was in a simpler ensemble: plaid walking shorts, a yellow short-sleeved blouse, brown shoes with fringe and little tassels, and yellow kneesocks. A Scottish golf pro came to mind.

"Hi, Liz."

"Hello, Jolie," she said, coming toward us. Around her waist was a furry purse of sorts that she was putting her keys in. It resembled a Scottish sporran. "I don't think we've met yet," she said, giving Howard a quick once-over. "I'm Liz Street and you're Cecily Wyatt's new beau. Isn't that right?"

Howard smiled and took the hand she had outstretched. He didn't kiss it, and he didn't shake it, but he did squeeze it gently and bring it close to his chest as if it were a rare privilege just to touch her. "I should hate going through life being known only as some possession of Cecily's." He smiled at Liz and for the first time I saw Liz Street soften as if she might, just might, go fluttery on us.

One of the worst things about moving to a small town like I did is that it's like coming late to class: You don't know all the history, so everyone tries to catch you up. I had made the mistake of not only listening to the stories, but also believing most of them. Like all history, the stories were biased. I'd been told that Liz Street was ditzy, but over the past four years I've learned it isn't so. Liz is in my writers' group, and while she writes very literary pieces that I don't particularly like, or even understand, I've come to like Liz.

I have my own theory about the way she dresses and behaves. I suspect that, at first, it was just a put-on to amuse the natives, or maybe to amuse herself. Now it's become a habit. I do know that underneath her bizarre clothing, Liz is a woman with few illusions, especially about men. Maybe because of her brilliant, but equally odd, husband.

Now she continued to watch Howard with a raised eyebrow, and he didn't disappoint her. "I'm Howard Bremerton," he said. "It's lovely to meet you, Liz. May I call you Liz?"

"Oh, you may."

It seemed to be getting hotter from the noonday sun pouring down on us. The only sounds besides our voices were faint rustlings in the distant trees. Probably birds trying to get more comfortable before their afternoon naps.

The small museum was silent, and I assumed Diane was still taking pictures. That meant I was still supposed to be stalling.

"So, Liz," I said, "what are you doing out here? You can't have come to volunteer."

"Actually, I have. I'm just distraught over what happened to Vera Meece. Absolutely distraught. And after all the work she did on the Celebration..."

Howard looked confused. "What is this?" Apparently none of the group at the Hammond place had listened to K-SAGE's news. I wondered if Will and Edith knew yet. Or Cecily.

"The woman who put together this exhibit, Vera Meece, was killed last night," Liz explained.

"Killed? How?"

"Jolie did the news story," Liz said. "She can explain better."

So for the third time I told someone about Vera's murder and the shooting of the sheriff. Only this time I had Liz helping with little punctuations of sound: a tiny gulp, a sigh, and a shudder with a hint of a groan. As far as I knew Vera Meece hadn't been her personal friend, so I wondered about Liz's connection to the camp.

"And now," Liz added, "we need people to help man the exhibit. I intend to do my part." There was a tiny tilt of her chin, as if she were Scarlett O'Hara and the Confederacy needed her. Even for Liz it was a bit much, and she may have sensed it. She turned to me and asked, "Is Diane here?"

"Yes, as a matter of fact, but…um…" I glanced at the building, wondering what excuse I could offer. When I couldn't think of one I said simply, "Can you wait just a minute?"

"I've allocated an hour before I have to be back to my editing. Albert can hardly do without me, you understand." She glanced at Howard. "Albert is my husband. A brilliant man, but like so many brilliant men he has little common sense."

"I see," Howard said. He seemed to come to some internal decision, then looked at me. "You know, I could certainly put in a few hours here and there to help out. I can't think we'll be all that busy. After all, this is Purple Sage, right? And what better way for me to learn about the camp?"

"And it has a fascinating history," Liz said.

"I would expect no less and I should love to hear it. Perhaps you can answer one question for me first, though. Where are all the buildings? Surely the men didn't sleep on the ground?"

"Let me give you a tour of the original camp," Liz offered, sliding her arm through his. "If you're going to work here, it will be useful."

She began to walk, and I followed along looking at the ground, attempting to spot some telltale signs of what had gone on the night before. Even in the glaring afternoon sun my stomach became queasy at the thought. It would have been different for Mac out here. There was only one outdoor light that I had noticed, and it was on the headquarters building. The night would have been dark, and the spot was isolated.

Especially to Mac, wounded, in pain, and very much on his own.

I focused on the dirt, pale in the blinding sun. Only a month or so before, Vera had convinced the county to bring out a grader and clear the entire area of unwanted foliage. The few plants that were present now were fast-growing weeds that had sprung up, only to turn dry and brittle from the summer's heat. It had rained two days ago, but the water was gone, and the ground was already too hard and unyielding to take our footprints.

"Now this," Liz said, stopping at the concrete slab, "was the administration building. Behind it were the barracks for the men; there were four of them in all, but two were broken up and hauled away, although I can't imagine why. The other two were behind those trees." She pointed to the back perimeter. "There was a time when this area was completely cleared; the purpose was to prevent escapes. As if the men had anywhere to go. At any rate, it's been fifty years and luckily trees do grow back."

"What kind of buildings were here?" Howard asked.

"Some were wood, or stucco. This one was a tin building, but the tin was taken away, too. Oh, and the German officers had small individual tents. They weren't required to work, so to pass the time, a few had gardens." She led us across the slab and down the right side, between the trees. A ramshackle building, its windows now just holes in the rotting wood, was tucked away back there. We didn't go closer because of all the heavy brush. I suppose we could have, but I wasn't willing to risk snakes, or spend several hours picking tiny burrs out of my socks. Neither, apparently, were the other two.

I did notice a narrow path off to our left, and I caught myself wondering where it could possibly go.

"This was the cook house," Liz said, pointing to the overgrown structure. "Behind it were two other buildings for the guards and their families. They fell down years ago."

"You're quite impressively knowledgeable," Howard said. "Thank you."

"How many men lived here?" Howard asked.

"Something under two thousand; a plethora, when you consider that Purple Sage had only three thousand souls at the time. My father told me that the good citizens of PS were stunned when the train pulled up at the station in town and hordes of young, handsome, blond men started filing out. I imagine it was like that old Volkswagen commercial where people just kept coming and coming. He said they marched through town to the camp, with the residents standing on the sidewalks, watching with their mouths agape."

"Must have been easily entertained," Howard said.

I was about to ask Liz how she knew all this when I heard Diane call to us. "Wouldn't y'all like to come in where it's cooler?" she said from the steps of the exhibit building. The "y'all" was a sure sign of stress, but the others didn't know her well enough to realize that. "I've got the air conditioner going, and I found some soft drinks," she finished.

As we turned around and walked toward her, I could hear the rattle of a window unit. The cool would be welcome, because, as they say in the South, I was beginning to glow. Like crazy.

By hurrying I reached Diane ahead of the others. "What's up?" I asked in a whisper.

She shook her head and said softly, "It feels hopeless. So many questions."

"Such as?"

"Like how did our murderer get out here, and leave, without Mac seeing his car?"

I thought about it for a second. "You're right, that's a very good question."

"There are more, too." But Howard and Liz had caught up with us.

"Liz," Diane said, putting on her brightest welcoming smile, "nice to see you. Are you here to volunteer?"

"Actually, I am."

"That's wonderful. There's a schedule on the display case inside; Vera had already arranged for a few volunteers, but feel free to fill in as many of the vacant time slots as you want. And don't worry about being greedy."

"Spoken," Howard said, "like a truly generous woman."

Liz was already on her way up the steps. "In a community like Purple Sage, one's responsibility to her fellows is far more apparent than in a large and impervious city." She went inside, closing the door.

"Well, I guess that means I, too, should pull my weight," Howard said. He saluted, started up the steps, and stopped. "Are you coming?"

"Not yet," I said. "I have to get something out of Diane's car."

"Very good." Then he was gone.

Diane knew there was nothing of mine in her car since my purse was slung over my shoulder and I was carrying my ice tea. She said, "I got some pictures of the room and all. Nothing looked unusual, but I didn't think it would hurt."

"Is that where Vera was killed?"

She shivered slightly. "I don't know. You don't either?"

"No. I've looked around out here, but nothing jumped out at me."

"And aren't you glad?" Diane said.

I gave her the obligatory smile. "Wiley did say that Mac crawled to his car," I said. "Maybe he was shot in that area." Diane and I moved closer together, then walked slowly toward the road, our eyes focused on the ground.

As we moved to the parking area, I realized again that Vera had been a very smart woman, and this whole camp proved it. For example, she'd had gravel donated to form a spot where people could park without the worry of the soft white caliche mud that can be messy in any kind of rain. Mud that could keep visitors away—but not at Vera's camp.

Diane and I looked over the gravel carefully, even checking under all three of the cars. As I moved to the edge I discovered some rocks that were discolored. "Think this was blood?" I asked.

Diane moved the gravel around with the toe of her loafer until we could see the caliche underneath. Normally the clay-like substance is almost white, but this was dark brown. "They did a good job of rinsing this down," she said. "But this must have been where Mac's car was. I don't think Vera would have been here, though; you wouldn't shoot someone this close to the road.''

I moved away from the spot. Why wasn't someone official here, doing something useful? I felt so frustrated. "We just don't know enough.''

"Can you talk to Mac?''

I shook my head. "How? Dr. Baxter moved him," I said.

"You can find him, if you really want to.''

"I guess." I looked at my watch.

"Are you okay?" she asked.

"I don't know what I am. I guess mostly I'm worried about Matt and that bozo at the sheriff's office.''

"That's the one thing you don't have to concern yourself with." We wandered toward the small building. "Matt's fine, Jolie. You heard Ellis. Besides, realistically, what can happen? This is Purple Sage, and the Wyatts are well known and well respected." She was interrupted by yet another car pulling onto the gravel.

I turned around to watch it park. "Popular place," I said.

I recognized this vehicle; it was an old white Lincoln Continental that lumbered self-importantly around town. It always seemed to be going slower than the speed limit, and usually it was right smack in front of me when I was late for something.

The door opened and Bill Tieman heaved himself out.

"Good afternoon, Chief," Diane said.

He nodded at each of us in turn. "Miz Wyatt, Miz Atwood. I've come to volunteer some of my time.''

"Why, thank you," Diane said. She sounded genuinely surprised.

"It's the least I can do for Vera. This was real important to her.''

"There's a schedule inside. Just fill in any slots that are convenient for you.''

As he clumped up the steps to the door, Diane said to me, "At least we're drawing some volunteers." She narrowed her eyes. "But this is not the crowd I expected.''

TEN

THE WALLS didn't shout of murder and the display cases didn't bleat about the treachery they had witnessed. In fact, after looking around, I suspected there had been no treachery in the little building at all. It was plain and simple, just as I remembered, decorated completely in beige.

"This place is impossible," Liz said. "I mean really, I don't do beige. You can't intend to leave it this way. Diane, you should do something."

Diane gave her a quick smile. "I'm glad you brought that up, because that's exactly what I had in mind."

"Excellent. Dreariness is a visual dirge."

The first thing anyone would see as they came in the door was a large glass case with all of the items in it arranged unimaginatively. At right angles to it sat another, smaller, case, and on the wall behind it were some additional things from Vera's collection. Two khaki-covered water bladders with black pourers hung on long green straps; there were two fiber helmets; there was a web belt with a canteen; and in the center yawned an empty space with only three hooks to show that something had once hung there. I knew what it had been: an OM1 carbine rifle. With bayonet lug.

Other than that there was little in the room and nothing more on the walls.

Bill Tieman harrumphed. "This is the way Vera wanted the headquarters to look, and it should be left exactly as it is."

"I don't think that's right," Diane said, her tone gentle but firm. "I'm pretty sure Vera wasn't finished in here. A rug is rolled up in the office, and there's a box of pictures she apparently intended to hang. I'm going to try and get all that done this afternoon."

The last word is something that Bill Tieman cherishes, and

he certainly wasn't about to give it to Diane. "If you put a rug on the floor and someone slips, you could have a lawsuit on your hands. Are you aware of that?" he demanded. "That's foolishness, pure and simple. I suppose hanging pictures won't hurt any, if that's what Vera wanted."

"Then," Diane said, "to make sure we get this right, you'll want to stay and help. And we do appreciate—"

"Miz Atwood, we have a major function going on in Purple Sage. As the chief of police I don't have time for hanging pictures." He hitched up his uniform khaki pants, but they still didn't come up over his belly. "I will be here for the two hours on Sunday that I put down on that sheet, but that's the limit of what I can give. Now, if you ladies will excuse..." As he turned, he spotted Howard standing near a display case. "I'm sorry, I should have said, ladies and gentleman. Now, if you will excuse me, I have duties." He clumped out the door.

I rolled my eyes at Diane, who was trying not to smile. Since Diane's husband, Trey, had beaten Bill out of the running for mayor in the primary election a few months earlier, the Atwoods weren't his favorites. Trey would take office in November and become Bill's boss. I was almost positive Trey wouldn't consider abusing his position of power over Bill, but I could still hope.

Diane turned to Liz. "Well, Liz, at least you can add your—"

"I'm so sorry, Diane," she said, already pulling her car keys out of her furry purse. "I simply must get back and work with Albert on his latest paper. The geniuses of the world can be such a trial to the rest of us mortals." She stopped in front of Howard on her way out. "Good-bye, Mr. Bremerton. I look forward to seeing you again when we have more time to visit." Then she, too, was gone.

"Well, hell," Diane said. "What about you, Howard? You're staying, aren't you?"

"I should love to, I really should, but I've promised Cecily and Jeremy that I would go riding with them. And since I'm the one with the car, I had best hurry and retrieve them." He smiled at both of us, charming as ever. "I shall see you both soon."

After Howard was gone, I said, "Three up, three out."

"Well, at least you're not leaving me."

"I probably would if I had my car."

"Which you don't. And you don't have anyplace else to be." She was very firm about that.

"Okay. Then maybe I'm glad they're gone," I said. "Especially Bill. He's such a sermonizer. And Liz would just want to do something totally unacceptable anyway." I walked back into the office and looked around. There was an old battered wooden desk, a braided rug on the floor, an apartment-size refrigerator in the corner, and a closet that was partially open, giving me a view of the edge of two boxes, one containing cleaning supplies. There may have been more in the closet, but I didn't investigate. "So," I said, returning to Diane. "What do you think? Was Vera killed in here?"

"If she was, I'm going to hire Wiley and Ed to clean my house. There's not a trace of anything. At least none that I found." She looked around the room, her hands on her hips. "Well, shall we get to work?"

"Do I have a choice?"

"Not much."

At her direction, I began emptying the display cases.

"When you've got everything out, let's redo the display with more pizzazz," Diane said.

"What kind of pizzazz?"

"You'll think of something. In the meantime, I'm going to spend a little time in the office. I want to see what's in the closet. And the desk."

"Now that's a fair division of labor." But I went to work, trying to figure out how I was going to add pizzazz to a display of army items. It was a far better train of thought than wondering where my husband was, and what was happening to him.

"Hey, listen to this!" Diane called from the office. There was a click, and a whirring sound, and finally came the sadly seductive World War II song "Harbor Lights." The quality was tinny, and there were some of the crackles and pops common to old records, yet the melody itself was haunting.

"Where in the world?" I stepped back into the office and Diane was standing over an old wind-up record player. It wasn't fancy, just a plain wood box, lacquered and polished, with a small hole where a metal crank was inserted. The lid was up and I could see the old-fashioned seventy-eight record spinning on the turntable.

We listened in silence to the music.

> *"I longed to hold you close,*
> *and kiss you just once more...*
> *"But you were on the ship,*
> *and I was on the shore...."*

When the record player wound down, the last strains of the song drifted away and I looked at Diane. "Incredible."

"Isn't it?"

"But I thought that was a hit in the fifties."

She lifted the record off and looked at the label. "The copyright date is nineteen thirty-seven, but I seem to remember Sammy Kaye made the song a hit in the early fifties. It must have been a remake, or re-release or whatever. Isn't that right?" The woman is a font of information.

"Beats me."

She still had a dreamy look in her eyes as she said, "I used to love the old black-and-white movies. That whole era was so romantic."

"Tragic."

"Yes, but it was so much bigger than the people who lived through it. Don't you remember the quote from Franklin Delano Roosevelt? 'This generation has a rendezvous with destiny.' It gives me chills." She rubbed her arms. "And they had songs and movies to bolster everyone's moral. Maybe that's why people rallied for their country. Dancing with soldiers at canteens. We didn't have anything like that in Menard."

"Or anyplace during the Vietnam War," I said, recognizing so clearly the differences in the ways people responded to the two wars.

"Police action; not a war."

"Bullshit. Soldiers kill people, it's a war and I don't care what the politicians called it."

Diane nodded sadly. "Maybe we just have a romanticized version of World War Two because we weren't there. Maybe if we'd lived through it, we'd feel the same way as we do about Vietnam." She gestured toward the boxes. "There are more records; why don't you pick something out?"

I sat down on the floor and went through the boxes gently, careful not to rip the brittle paper sleeves that covered the heavy black records.

"You were right about one thing—they had great music," I said. "'String of Pearls.' 'As Time Goes By.' 'Don't Get Around Much Anymore.'"

I stood up, stretching quickly to get the kinks out of my knees. "Here, try this one," I said, handing Diane 'Sentimental Journey' and heading to the display cases out front.

I worked to the beat and when the song wound down, literally, Diane turned it off. "I'll be back," she said, taking her camera outside for some additional photos.

I got gravel from the parking area and spread it carefully over the bottom of each glass case before repositioning the artifacts. Then I replaced the cards that labeled each item.

I was just finishing when Diane returned. "So what's next?" I asked her.

"The braided rug."

Together we moved it from the office to the center of the display room. It was in shades of blues, pinks, and greens, probably not authentic for a POW camp, but it added some desperately needed color and it would help deaden the sound. In the closet Diane had found two straight-backed chairs dating to camp days that some community-minded soul had donated; we brought those out and arranged them, along with a small wooden table for the visitors' book.

Last, Diane dragged two cardboard boxes from the back

room. Each was filled with old black-and-white photos that someone, probably Vera, had matted and framed. While I began sorting through the pictures, Diane made another trip to the office and returned with a hammer and a sack of nails.

"Let's not start looking at the pictures now," I said, "or we'll be here all night. Let's just stay focused and get them all hung."

She stepped around me to the far wall and gestured with the hammer. "How about up here?"

"Good idea," I said. "But no rows. We'll do an interesting hodgepodge."

"All the remodeling and redecorating we've done this summer and that's the best word you can think of to use?"

"I'm a writer; words are my life," I said. "Hodgepodge is two words."

"Actually, it's only one."

I marked the places for the nail holes, while Diane did the actual hammering. I couldn't help but remember my previous visit to the camp, when Vera had been alive.

"Diane," I said, "I just realized something. There were a lot more boxes in the office the last time I was here. A lot."

"How many is that?"

"I didn't count them, but I think there were at least five or six. And everything in them was neat. Militarily neat, not just thrown in like these pictures were." The pictures had been in such a jumble that one or two had broken glass.

"So maybe someone went through this box looking for something," Diane said as she hammered a nail into the wall with three solid smacks. "Now, that's an interesting thought. I wonder who it was and what they were looking for?"

"No idea." I handed over another nail. "And where are the other things that Vera collected?" I asked. "When I was here to interview her, I was amazed at the kinds of things people had donated. Actually, I was most amazed that anyone would keep the stuff in the first place. She had a box half full of old clothing, once worn by the POWs. She had old letters, too, and even a cookbook. Did you see any of these things in the office?"

"No, but they could be at Vera's house. Or maybe Ed and Wiley took them. For evidence."

Which reminded me, again, that my husband had been hauled off by a sheriff's deputy. I looked at my watch.

"Jolie, relax," Diane said. "Matt is fine." Diane is not only bright, she also knows me very well.

I shook my head. "I'd just feel better if someone else were in charge of things at the sheriff's office. Anyone." And then I remembered what the sheriff had told me earlier. "Diane, Linc Draper should be back in town by now!"

"Ah, the voice of reason."

The third deputy, the one with solid police experience and lots of common sense, was due *later*. I looked at my watch; surely this was later. I could feel my stress level lowering. Matt's interrogation had probably been finished up by Linc Draper, and he was most likely on his way home. Or to the Hammond house.

"We could have been out of here sooner," I said, hurrying now, "if our dear volunteers had stayed to help."

"You can't have it both ways, Jolie. Either Liz Street and Bill Tieman are royal pains in the butt and would have been in our way, or they should have stayed. When they left you said you were glad. So, which is it?"

"Both. Neither. Hell, I don't know. Here, let me have the hammer." She gave it to me and I whacked a few nails, but it wasn't enough action to alleviate my antsy mood. "Okay, I can understand why Bill had to leave; he's got a town filled to the brim with people and he should be doing something useful. God knows why I expect that, he's never done anything useful in the past, but I'm an optimist—I still have hope. And as for Liz, I guess I really don't want her mucking around with this place." I stopped to watch Diane spray the window with cleaner and wipe it down. "Oh, wait, I forgot to tell you what's really strange."

"What?"

"Liz gave Howard and me a tour of the camp. And, Diane, this woman knew her stuff. She told us what the buildings used to look like and which one was where. I was very impressed.''

''What's strange about that?''

''How does she know so much? The camp closed before Liz was even born. Or if she was born back then, she was just a baby. So how did she pick up the information? Prenatal osmosis?''

I hung the last of the pictures and Diane stood back to view the room. Above the rattle of the window unit she said, ''It looks much better, doesn't it?''

''Better, but do you think Vera would have liked the way we've arranged the place?''

''She wouldn't have done it this way,'' Diane said as she twitched a picture into horizontal perfection. ''But I think she would agree that it's attractive.''

''In other words, she'd like it about as much as Edith liked what we did to my house.''

''I think you're in overload,'' Diane said. She turned me around to look at the room. ''I'm going to bring that big fern of mine and hang it in the corner. And I think the table needs something, but not now. Let's just put everything away and call it a day. At least it's ready to open to the public tomorrow.'' She began gathering stray nails. ''You know, Liz could have read a book on the camp.'' She frowned. ''Oh, but there aren't any; I remember because Randy wanted to do a paper on it one time and we couldn't find any information.''

''You see my point?''

''Well, she could have talked to someone.'' Diane paused. ''Actually, that is weird.''

''Yes, it is.'' I began carrying things back to the little office, talking as I went. ''But you know who can tell us a lot about the camp? And about Liz? IdaMae.'' IdaMae Dorfman is probably close to the same age as Purple Sage, and she remembers everything she's ever heard. She also owns the bakery and makes the best cream pies in the world.

''Oh, damn, we forgot something,'' Diane said as I returned. ''Any idea what we ought to do about that spot?''

I followed her glance. Above the large glass case was the

wall display with the rifle missing. Every time I looked at that spot I thought of Vera. And Mac.

"I don't think we should worry about it right now," I said.

ELEVEN

WE WERE PICKING UP OUR purses, ready to go, when the door opened, temporarily blinding me with the brilliance of the outside light. All I could see were two silhouettes. As they moved into the room a wave of heat came with them, and when the door closed, the silhouettes filled in. I found myself facing a couple in what I would guess to be their late sixties, maybe early seventies.

"Hello," Diane said. "Welcome to Camp John Seybold."

"Hello." The woman smiled. Her white hair was thin, but permed into a fuzzy halo that framed her cheerful face. She was wearing a blue and white flowered shirt tucked into blue polyester pants. On her feet were athletic shoes, and over her arm was a large white purse. She wasn't a small woman, yet she seemed petite compared to the man beside her, who was at least six foot three. He was wearing baggy gray shorts, well-worn running shoes, a T-shirt touting the San Antonio Riverwalk, and a beige cotton hat that looked like something better saved for fishing.

She said, "I'm Minna Braune and this is my husband, Klaus."

"Nice to meet you," Diane said as we shook hands all around and told them our names. Then she asked, "Did you just drive in for the day?"

"That would be a big drive," Minna said with a laugh. "We have come from Raemlich, Germany." Her English was very good, with a gentle accent that turned Germany into "Churmany."

"Really! How long have you been here?" Diane asked.

"In this country? Three days. Klaus has a cousin we visited in San Antonio and then today we come here. We are hardly driving past the little sign that says Purple Sage before Klaus insists he must see the camp. He was so excited about this reunion and visiting your town again. I have heard of nothing else for months."

"But you get to come to America, which is such a burden for you." There was a glint of humor in her husband's eye. "My poor Minna, such a hardship."

She slapped his arm playfully. "Only the packing."

"It will be worth it all. This is a wonderful town," Klaus said, looking around the room. "Wonderful."

"You were only here for the end of the war," Minna said. "I still think maybe the people weren't so wonderful to the prisoners at first. My uncle said that."

"He was in Kentucky. It was different; you will see." He turned to us. "Are there many people coming in for the Celebration?"

"Thousands," Diane said, "although I don't have any idea how many are coming from the camp."

"And Vera Meece, where is she?" he asked. "She has sent us many letters about the Celebration."

Diane's face seemed to sag. She swallowed, looked at me, maybe for comfort, and then said, "I hate to tell you, but Vera isn't here." At our guests' puzzled expressions she said softly, as if the gentleness of her voice might break the shock, "I wish I knew a better way to say this, but I just don't. Vera Meece died last night."

Minna gasped and clutched at her husband's arm. "So, how did this happen? She was old? Sick? An accident of some kind?"

"No," Diane said. "She was murdered. Shot."

Minna said something to Klaus in German. He shook his head vehemently and responded, but I didn't understand the words. The actions were clearer; Minna was tugging at him, as if she wanted to leave right then. They exchanged a few more sentences, but he was as unmoving as the Statue of Liberty.

"No," he finally said in English. "It was just some bad person. There can be these kinds of people anywhere, even here." He slipped his wife's hand through his arm. "We should go to our hotel now. You will see, Minna, Purple Sage is a nice place."

"I'm sorry," Diane said, as if she were personally responsible. "Normally Purple Sage *is* a nice place. And very safe."

"I have heard about the guns in Texas," Minna said with a shake of her head. "We read about this, even in our country."

"Honestly, the reports are exaggerated."

"We will have some supper," Klaus said to his wife. To us he added, "We have been in Texas three days already, and while our watches know the time, our stomachs are never sure. We will eat and Minna will feel better."

As they started for the door, Diane rushed ahead to open it for them. She added, "And please come back tomorrow. We'll be open at ten."

"Good. We will be here."

THE TINY headquarters building was locked, and a carefully hand-lettered sign invited visitors to come back the next morning. The POW camp was as ready for the Celebration as we could make it.

"Straight to the country club for your car?" Diane asked as she started up the Mercedes.

"No, let's go into town. I want to see if Matt's okay."

"Jolie, he's fine. Ellis is there, Linc is there. Hell, Matt's probably not there. I'll bet he's already home."

"We don't even have to stop unless the Explorer is still parked at the courthouse," I said.

Despite her words, she backed out onto the highway and headed into Purple Sage. "In which case you will start an insurrection. A small, quiet, and perfectly tasteful one."

"With couth. After it's over you can take me to my car, I'll go find my son, round up my guests, and we'll all drive back into Purple Sage for the parade. What about you? Want to join us?"

"No thanks; I'm having pizza and a hot bath. Maybe I'll write."

"But you'll miss the parade."

"With any luck, I certainly will."

Diane turned off the highway onto South Main and it was like turning into a used-car lot. The street was jammed and nothing was moving.

"What in the world?" she said.

"Oh, brother. Look up there." A quarter of a mile ahead of us I could see a large float that was stopped dead in the middle of the street. Beside it was a minivan and the two seemed to be meshed. Not a good sign since we were still about two miles from the square.

"I'll try cutting over to Winchester," Diane said. She began maneuvering, and after a few minutes we were headed back the way we'd come. At the intersection with Winchester, Diane stopped and looked at the traffic, then at me. "Well? I can try it if you insist."

Traffic was being rerouted this way, and with all the visitors it was a solid wall of vehicles. It could take an hour to get to the court-house from this end of town.

"That's okay," I said. "Just drop me off at the country club."

"Yessir, boss."

All the delays were making me more anxious to be in my own car. My worry was lurking like a headache, ready to pounce if I made one wrong move.

"I took a bunch of pictures of the camp," Diane said. "There was something I meant to show you."

"Oh?"

She shook her head. "No, you can see the picture. Then decide for yourself if it means anything. I'll get the film developed overnight."

By the time Diane pulled into the country club parking lot and up next to my car, I really did have a headache. I was out of the Mercedes as soon as it stopped.

"Thanks for your help," Diane said. "Where are you headed now?"

"The courthouse."

"Jolie, you'll never get there in the traffic. Besides, Matt's probably picking up Jeremy and his parents."

She was right, I knew she was, and it was way too far to walk. I nodded, jumped into the Intrepid, and started the engine. "See you tomorrow."

There was no traffic going out toward the ranch, and I found myself pressing hard on the accelerator. I hit the horn to alert an ambling motorist that I was going around him, and then I passed him doing eighty.

Let the sheriff's deputies stop me for that, I thought.

I believe in hunches and premonitions. I think they are messages from our subconscious mind, which sees all, hears all, and knows a lot more than our conscious brains do. As I whipped along the highway I had the strongest feeling that Matt wasn't going to be at the Hammond place. By the time I was on the caliche of Hammond Lane, I was positive. I discovered my hunch was correct when I turned toward the yard gate. Either that or he was on foot, because the Explorer wasn't parked along the fence with the other two cars.

The thought crossed my mind to turn around and head out, back to town to see if I could find him, but that would have been an intolerable rudeness, not to mention another black mark on my soul in the eyes of the senior Wyatts. Instead I parked with a jerk and jumped out of the car, but I wasn't planning to stay long.

From the house came the sounds of talking and laughter.

I pulled open the wood-framed screen and tapped quickly on the front door itself. There was a pause in the conversation as Edith called, "Come on in."

Everyone was gathered around the dining room table, with sweating ice tea glasses in front of them, and an almost empty bowl of pretzels closest to Howard. There was also a recent copy of the Purple Sage *Tribune*.

"Oh, Jolie," Edith said.

"Matthew's not with you?" Cecily asked.

"No, I thought he might be here," I said, stopping in the middle of the room.

Will waved me toward the table. "Come on in and set a while, Jolie. We haven't seen Matt since just before dinner." Dinner is lunch in the country. "I reckon it's just taking a little longer than Matt thought it would to get that Celebration Committee straightened out."

"I'm sure you're right," I said, doing my best to match his smile. "But if Matt's not here, then I'd better round up Jeremy so we can all go to the parade." I looked at my watch for effect. I knew exactly what time it was. "It starts in thirty minutes."

"I think we'll take our cars and meet you there," Edith said.

"We don't want to miss the start of the parade," Cecily said, laying her hand on Howard's arm. "You'll love it, Howard. There will be the antique fire truck, which, of course, is still in service, and scads of pickups with crepe paper draped about them. And my personal favorite, the newest John Deere tractor models."

"With or without crepe paper?" Howard asked.

"It used to be without, but I've been gone a while—things could have changed."

I was already at the door. "Why don't we meet on the southeast corner of the square?" I asked. "Near Henshaw's Hardware. That way we can all park at the radio station if things are really crowded."

"I suppose you shall be bringing lawn chairs?" Cecily said.

"The parade won't last that long," I said. "I really need to run. Bye," I called, slipping out the door with one last wave.

Every delay in finding Matt was sending my adrenaline a notch higher, and it took all my self-will not to break the speed laws on the way to the ranch. Still, within five minutes I was driving up to the house; Jeremy was outside the gate, pacing.

"Where have you been?" he demanded, pulling open the car door and jumping in. "And where's Matt? I've been trapped out here."

"Don't start with me, Jeremy. I thought you went riding with Cecily and Howard."

"That was hours ago. Do you know you've been gone all afternoon? Like you always tell me, 'you could have called.'"

I was already on the Farm to Market Road, willing the car to hurry. "I could have, except that I was busy. Look, something's happened."

"What? Is everyone okay?"

"I think so."

Normally I try not to dump on Jeremy. When there was just the two of us, before I married Matt, I had made an effort to treat Jeremy like a little boy, rather than a confidant. According to my sister, Elise, who has done lots of therapy, that would give Jeremy a chance to have a real childhood. It worked well for a while, except as Jeremy grew older he wanted to know what was going on. Naturally I started telling him. Then he turned into a teenager, and I married Matt, and all the rules changed, again. As far as I could tell, they were always changing.

"Well?" Jeremy said.

"It's about Matt."

"Matt?" There was real fear in Jeremy's voice.

"He's fine. Really."

Jeremy's biological father, Steve, had walked out of our apartment some fifteen years ago, taking with him our new car, to meet his new girlfriend, Candy. Apparently he'd never looked back, so he never knew that he had damaged two lives.

When I got married over three years ago, Jeremy had a dad for the first time in his life, and he'd taken to Matt with love and pride. It didn't seem fair to keep things from him. Besides, I needed a friend to understand. Someone who loved Matt as much as I did.

I blurted out the whole story of Matt's "questioning."

"But what about Sheriff Donelly?" Jeremy asked when I was finished. "What's he going to say about Ed? And where was he?"

"That's another story," I said. "Mac Donelly was shot—but he's in stable condition." And I explained all that to Jeremy as well.

Jeremy was outraged. "And how long were you going to hide this from me?" he wanted to know. "I am fifteen."

"That's true. And certainly old enough to listen to the radio."

"Oh. Well, first thing we have to do is find Matt." He looked at the speedometer; we were doing nine miles over the speed limit. "Maybe I'd better drive."

"No. We'll get there," I said, pushing the accelerator a little harder.

"Wait a minute! We passed the Hammond place. Aren't you going to pick everyone up?"

"I just left there—they're coming in their own car."

"Good, they won't slow us down."

We became quiet, and I could almost hear his brain humming with the efficiency of a hard drive as he thought over everything I'd told him.

We didn't speak again until we arrived in Purple Sage. The traffic was now as much foot traffic as cars; there were people everywhere. A family cut across the street in front of us, a little girl riding on her daddy's shoulders. His wife was holding the hand of another child, and they gave us broad smiles as they sauntered out of the way. I wanted them to hurry.

"Hey, look!" Jeremy was pointing up the street toward the court-house. "Matt's Explorer!"

It was indeed. "Damn. That's where I left it parked."

Jeremy stared. "You think he's still being questioned?"

"I don't know."

"I'm going to find out."

He unsnapped his seat belt and was reaching for the door handle when a car behind me honked and a policeman in front of me blew his whistle, waving me forward. Miraculously the traffic opened up, so that I could see the radio station parking lot just two relatively clear blocks away.

"Stay in the car," I said, stepping on the gas at the same time.

"Okay," he said. "But hurry up and park this thing."

"Exactly what I had in mind."

I pulled into the station lot, locked the car, and then we

were practically running for the square. As the crowds thickened I took the lead, dodging around people like a Roller Derby queen. We had to pause at the street surrounding the square, but I needed the moment to breathe. The parade was still a few minutes away. The judges' stand was filled with officials, and the parade chairwoman was introducing them on a PA system.

"On my right is someone I'm sure many of you remember. He served as our mayor from the years nineteen seventy-two through nineteen—"

"Come on." Jeremy had my elbow and was guiding me across the street.

A row of cars and trucks filled every parking space around the square. People had set their lawn chairs in the beds of their pickups and were settled back to view the festivities. We cut through the line of vehicles, across the nearly empty lawn surrounding the court-house, up the steps to the front door, and found ourselves stopped dead. The door was locked.

"Well, shit." Jeremy said.

I grabbed his arm. "This way." I led him to a side door that is unlocked more often than not. One good push and it swung open.

"All right!"

We raced up the old wooden stairs, our pounding footsteps reverberating through the building. When we reached the second floor I headed straight into the Sheriff's Department.

True to form, when Trina saw me she scowled.

"Trina," I said, puffing for air. "I need to see Matt."

She stared at me with her large, dull brown eyes and said, "Can't." Then slowly, and with exquisite rudeness, she turned back to some filing.

"Excuse me! I need to see Matt Wyatt, my husband." I was being concise and clear, in case language was the barrier between us. "Tell Ed Presnell that I'm here."

Her heavy shoulders shrugged as she grunted something I couldn't understand.

"I'm not leaving until I see my husband. Or Ed. Or what about Linc Draper?"

She scratched her arm with nails that were bitten to the quick, and finally said, "No one's here." After a few more seconds, she moved her mouth in a way that might have passed for a smile on another human being.

She said, "If I was you, I'd try the jail."

TWELVE

THE JAIL was located in the Police Department building, a squat, gray-and-white box just a few blocks from the square. Jeremy and I ran all the way there, and paused outside the double glass doors.

"Ed Presnell is a jerk," Jeremy said before I'd caught my breath. He reached for the metal rod that served as a door handle. "We could sue him for false arrest."

"We don't know that Matt's been arrested," I wheezed.

Jeremy opened the door and we entered the small anteroom. It was lit by overhead fluorescent lights, and one was flickering, which gave the place the feeling of an overly lit disco. To our left, the dispatcher sat behind bullet-proof glass. On our right were two plastic chairs for visitors, and in front of us was a four-inch-thick door protecting the rest of the department, and the jail inmates, from unwanted guests. That would certainly be us if we didn't get our way.

The dispatcher, Carl Fedders, had moussed blond hair and a tattoo of a snake on his arm. "Hey, Miz Wyatt. Yo, Jeremy," he said. Someone who spoke our language.

"Hey, Carl," Jeremy said. "Ed Presnell didn't by any chance bring my dad in here, did he?"

"Mr. Wyatt here? No way. The cells are empty, except for some guy they're transferring to TDOC." Texas Department of Corrections—I was learning the jargon.

"Wait," I said. "Matt's not here?"

"No, ma'am."

I looked at Jeremy. So where was Matt? The only cells in the entire county were in this building, which gave me hope that Matt was free. Maybe.

"What about Ed Presnell?" I asked.

Carl grinned and rolled his eyes. His opinion of Ed agrees with mine. "Ah, yes, Deputy Presnell is in the building. He's in the office that the sheriff's officers use at night. Left of Andy Sawyer's. Help yourself."

The heavy door clicked, letting us know it had been unlocked. Jeremy and I hurried through it. Even before we made the final turn toward the cell block we could hear Ed's voice.

"It's going to get me promoted," he was saying. "I might even get elected sheriff once this case gets settled."

Jeremy and I exchanged glances and stopped several feet away from the partially opened door.

After a pause Ed went on in a tone of voice that caused me to suspect he was talking to a woman. "That's real sweet of you to say that. And I know how you feel, but don't you go saying anything yet. When Mr. Bigshot Wyatt is headed for Huntsville is when we can really celebrate." He paused, then giggled, a high, effete sound. "'Course we don't have to wait that long. Just let me get him in custody. I have lots of suspicions, but I'm going to have to collect a tad more evidence before I bring him in for good and final. Oh, wait, hold on a minute, I got me another call." After a quick pause he said, "Presnell here. Who? Carl, you tell him that I'm not in. What do you mean by that? You listen to me, you hear? You are a dispatcher; you answer phones and transmit information. I am a deputy who is acting sheriff of Wilmot County and I sure as hell don't take no orders from you." There was another break and finally, "Hey, baby, I'm back. Now, what were you sayin'? You hold that thought, you hear? In the meantime, I got to go. I don't know when I'll get by there—I'm figuring on following this Wyatt character as long as it takes to bring him down." He sounded like someone in an old B movie, and it might have been amusing if my husband weren't the unwitting star of that film. "I'm headed out now and I'm going to track him like a shadow, but I'll call first chance I get." ·

I grabbed Jeremy's arm and we started backpedaling the way we'd come. The last we heard of Ed's voice was cooing sounds.

"Big dumb..." Jeremy was muttering as he opened the door to the anteroom.

I waved at Carl. "Thanks—see you later." He waved back while Jeremy and I headed out to the sidewalk.

"Now for sure we have to do something about this," Jeremy said as the glass door closed behind us.

My head was whirling in a way that didn't feel healthy. I held up my hand to stop my own thoughts. "Wait. First things first. What we have to do now is find Matt. He's probably with his parents on the corner of the square." Yes, that sounded right. Logical. And I needed to see for myself that he was okay.

"You go meet them," Jeremy said. "I'll run by Matt's Explorer and leave a note, just in case—"

"I already did. I stuffed it into the steering wheel; you could see if it's still there."

He slid an arm around my shoulder, which he can do now that he's six inches taller than I am. "I'll meet you in fifteen minutes. Don't worry, we'll find Matt."

"Of course we will."

As Jeremy watched the traffic, waiting for a break to cross the street, he said, "And then we should find whoever murdered Vera Meece."

I GOT TO THE EDGE of the crowd and stopped. The tension fled my body: Matt was there. His light hair was shining in the sunlight, his broad shoulders were turned slightly so that I could see the cellular phone he was holding. That's when I remembered that I was supposed to keep it so he could call me.

I hurried forward. "Matt—" I started to slide my arms around him, but he turned and stepped out of my reach.

"Where have you been all afternoon?" He kept his voice low, but the fury was unmistakable as he moved us back away from the street and the bulk of the people. The parade had already started.

"I went with Diane to the POW camp," I said as we edged our way through the crowd. "You weren't around so—"

"Not now."

He kept moving until we were behind the building, and when he stopped and looked at me I felt the full force of his fury. "Damn it, Jolie, my parents come out maybe twice a year—I don't think it's asking too much to expect you to spend a little time with them. This was their first day here and you knew I was tied up and couldn't get away!"

Matt doesn't blow up at waiters who bring the wrong order, or at dry cleaners who ruin a good shirt. Usually he only raises his voice when he has to in order to be heard. Like when he's working cattle, or when I'm yelling.

It's rare that he gets really mad, but when he does it's so powerful I sometimes think the planets shift in their orbits.

"Matt, I'm sorry," I said. "I wasn't thinking."

"That is quite obvious." As he snapped the words I could almost feel the planets jerking out of rotation.

"That's not fair! I'm not comfortable around Cecily. She is your ex-wife, and everyone oohs and aahs over her like she's something really special."

"No one has done anything like that."

"Oh, sure. How about your mom? And all that 'Mumsie' crap?"

"That's what she calls my mother." Matt's words were precise, stiff, and vibrating with anger. "You're always saying that you don't have a good relationship with my parents, well, maybe it's your fault. Maybe if you behaved like an adult instead of whining about other people, things would be different." He held out the phone and shook it, as if it were visual proof of my wrongdoing. "And you were going to keep the phone so I could call you."

His brown eyes had grown even darker. I could almost feel the sparks shooting out from them and singeing my skin.

"I forgot," I said. "Look, Matt, I was—"

"I don't want to hear about it!" He whipped around and

left me. Presumably to join his parents. And Cecily and Howard.

In the meantime, I discovered there was a decorative hay bale behind me; I sat down hard on it. I didn't know whether to cry or start hitting someone.

Matt has an older sister as well as his adoring mother. He'd once told me that, when he was a child and he got angry the two would try to tease him out of it. That infuriated him even more, especially as he got older. Now when he's good and mad he doesn't want discussion until he's calmed down. The fact that he had stalked off meant that I was in deep shit and I wasn't getting out anytime soon.

"Mom?"

I looked up to find Jeremy standing over me.

"Hi."

"Are you okay?" he asked.

"Fine. Matt's up there with his parents," I said, pointing.

"I know, I saw him. So why are you here?"

"I'm resting."

He didn't believe it, and who could blame him. "Did you tell him about Ed?" he asked.

"No, and I don't think now is a good time."

"Why is he mad at you?" My son the psychic.

"Because I didn't keep the phone, because I didn't go see his parents, and because I'm unworthy."

Jeremy made a face. "So you're just going to let him get arrested?"

I smiled sweetly, showing off my dimples. "What a grand idea. Cecily can take him a cake with a file in it. I'll bet she makes glorious cakes. Maybe his parents could move in with him. It would be a little crowded, but then they'd all be together."

"Self-pity is really unattractive."

I was up off my hay bale. I grabbed Jeremy by the arm and hissed, "This has been one crummy day for me, and if I were you, I wouldn't say or do anything to make it worse."

He shook off my hand, and said mildly, "Mom, we're missing the parade. I think I'll go watch it."

"DIDN'T I TELL YOU how quaint it would be?" Cecily laughed, looking up at Howard. She was in linen, a sleeveless, sage green top with natural-colored slacks that made her look cool, sleek, and very beautiful.

The parade was winding down, and I had moved to the fringes of the Wyatt group. Everyone had said hello, but there wasn't a lot of conversation. Matt hadn't spoken to me or anyone else that I had heard.

"Wait, I think the best part is coming now," Howard said. "How charming."

Ten five-year-olds were vying for the title of Little Miss Purple Sage. They were passing us now, each one on the back of a Shetland pony on loan for the parade from the Tandy Ranch and their bed-and-breakfast, Das Keller Haus. Some of the girls were in frilly dresses, riding sidesaddle. Others were in cowboy regalia, one swinging a rope like a little Annie Oakley. Even the ponies were decorated. One wore a straw hat with his ears poking through and a denim cape around his shoulders. Another was covered in velvet and lace. The applause was enthusiastic, but subdued so as not to frighten the ponies.

"That's a lovely little addition," Cecily said.

"I knew we'd get you to like something about the parade," Will said to her.

"Oh, Will, you're such a wicked thing; always picking on me."

He was about to respond when a woman stepped into the middle of our group, exclaiming loudly, "My God, I don't believe it! The Wyatts! The whole fam damily, all at once."

She grabbed Edith and they hugged enthusiastically. I'd never seen Edith grin like that before. "Myrna Applegate," she said, "how in the world did you find your way back here?"

"Just luck. It's so good to see you! Is your family here?" She spun around, spotted Will, and grabbed him. "Will Wyatt, you wascally wabbit! Oh, I've missed all of you."

Will laughed as he gave her a quick hug. "You're too ornery to miss anyone. And where's that husband of yours? I haven't seen Sam since y'all left.''

"And what about your boys?" Edith added. "Where are they now?"

"They're all here for the Celebration, except those boys are men now, Edith. Luke and his wife just left. They took their two kids on up to Mother and Daddy's house to get things going. Would you believe that Luke is getting gray hair? And Terry, well, he's got five boys, and they're all little carbon copies of him! Sam is at Mother and Daddy's barbecuing.'' She suddenly recognized Matt. "Matthew Wyatt, I swear you are *still* the best-looking thing I've ever seen. When you were in high school I told your mama she ought to send you off to a monastery to keep you out of trouble.''

Matt grinned and hugged her solidly. "Miss Myrna, that's your story and I don't think it has anything to do with the truth.''

"Yeah, well, I don't know—" She broke off as she recognized Cecily. "And here's your beautiful wife!" Myrna grabbed Cecily by the shoulders and gave her a squeeze. "My, you just get prettier and prettier. I always said you and Matt would make beautiful babies. Or have you already?''

"Actually—" Cecily began, but Myrna cut her off.

"I have this great idea," she said, releasing Cecily to address the whole group better. "I want y'all to come up to Mother and Daddy's. Sam's had three goats on the barbecue all day, so there's plenty for everyone. We've got some other friends coming, and we'll have us a high old time, just like we used to. I won't take no for an answer.''

Matt took ahold of my arm and nudged me forward. "Myrna, I'd like you to meet someone. Myrna Applegate, this is my wife, Jolie Wyatt. Cecily and I are divorced.''

"I see," Myrna said, hardly letting it slow her down. "Well, I imagine we've all got a lot of catching up to do.

"Now, I mean it, you're all coming on up to the house for barbecue and we'll just talk all night." She smiled at me. "And I'm looking forward to gettin' to know you, too, Josey.''

THIRTEEN

THE HOME OF Myrna Applegate's mother and daddy was on Willow, a street of stately old houses separated from the road by acres of lush green lawn, profusely blooming flower beds, and magnificently spreading trees. Some also had sweeping driveways, yard statuary, porticos, and cupolas, as well as wraparound porches. Moving to Willow Street is my idea of dying and going to heaven.

My favorite home is a peach-colored Victorian with white trim that Jeremy and I call Pollyanna's house. The Applegates didn't live in it, but they were right next door, separated by a six-foot hedge of gleaming, dark green, wax leaf legustrum. Theirs was a massive white structure with Doric columns, probably genuine, and deep blue awnings. A huge deck extended from the back of the house for a good twenty feet before the actual ground was visible, and then there was plenty of it. Massive oaks shaded much of the yard as it rolled down to a creek behind the house.

"Now, we've got sodas in the fridge, and beer in the tub over there, and ice tea in the cooler out on the far picnic table," Myrna said to me as soon as I arrived in the backyard. "There's cups on the table, too, and some chips and such for munching, although I know we're not supposed to be eating chips these days, but hey, that's what vacations are for, aren't they?" she added, snatching up a three-year-old who had tried to run by. The little girl squealed with glee as Myrna tipped her upside down, made some gurgling noises against her bare tummy, and then set her back on the ground again. "Everybody else seems to have themselves a comfortable spot under a tree somewhere, but you just kick one of them real tall, good-looking men out of their seats. It'll be either Luke or

Terry. I'm going to run inside and see where Sam is. I'll be back before you can get something to drink.''

"Grammy, do that again!" the little girl begged.

"You are a glutton for punishment, little missy," Myrna said, picking her up. Then she looked at me. "This is Luke's oldest, Megan Ann."

"Hello, Megan Ann," I said, but she was too busy with her grammy to pay attention to me. So was everyone else.

Edith, Cecily, Howard, and Jeremy had driven over in one car, Will and Matt in another, leaving me to make the trip by myself. I had made the mistake of stopping at the radio station, so the rest of the Wyatt clan was already comfortably ensconced by the time I arrived. I hadn't spotted Jeremy yet, but the others were gathered at a table near the creek. Matt had waved in my direction, but it seemed more to let me know where they were rather than to invite me to join them. Which was why I had allowed myself to be waylaid by our hostess. Matt could have gotten up, he could have come over to get me, or he could have jumped in the creek. Any would have been satisfactory to me.

I headed for a far table; it was less crowded and nearer the barbecue cooker, which was a big metal monstrosity made out of what looked like an oil drum.

"Excuse me," I said to an older man as I reached past him to get a plastic cup from the table. I filled it with ice from an oblong ice chest on the ground.

"I'm John Schussler," the man said, holding out his hand.

"Jolie Wyatt." We shook. His hand was soft, but the grip was firm, warm.

John appeared to be in his seventies, and was still slender, only a little taller than me, but certainly attractive. His casual clothes, khaki slacks and white knit shirt, weren't as casual as everyone else's. Something about this man said executive. Or maybe it was money.

"You don't live here, do you?" I asked.

His vivid blue eyes reflected his smile as he said, "Very observant. I'm just here for the Celebration."

It's not that I know everyone in Purple Sage, but I do recognize most of the residents, or at least the names. Schussler wasn't one I'd heard before. "Do you have family here?" I asked.

"No, no. It was actually Myrna and Sam who insisted I come."

That didn't surprise me a bit; Myrna seemed the kind who rushed in and began arranging people's lives without ever realizing she was overstepping the boundaries of friendship. It would all be done with exuberance and love, a deadly combination that left most people helpless. The reason I recognized this form of misguided management so quickly is that my mother does the same sort of thing. I counted myself lucky that she wasn't part of my everyday life. "Where are you from?" I asked John, filling my cup with tea from an orange and white watercooler.

"I live in the Seattle area. Redmond, actually. And what about you?" he asked. "Are you a Purple Sage-ite?"

"As a matter of fact, I am. Transplanted. I've been here for almost four years. That's my husband over there," I said, pointing. "And the rest of those people are his family. Or in-laws. Or outlaws, or something."

"I'd like to hear the story that goes with that," he said. He must have picked up on something in my voice, although I'd tried not to let any irony color it.

"Oh, you know," I said airily. "Just the usual extended family of the nineties." I took a sip of the tea. "Gross!" I almost spit it out. Disgustingly sweet tea is the drink of choice in much of Texas, and that, along with scotch, is something I loathe.

John smiled, probably because I'd sounded more like a kid than an adult. "Sorry," I said. "I just don't like overly sweetened tea. Or sweet tea, at all."

"I think it's terrible, too. Even worse when they put that artificial sweetener in it." He took the plastic cup from my hand. "Here, let me; I know my way around the kitchen."

"You must be staying here."

"Actually, I'm at Das Keller Haus, but Myrna has insisted

that I spend much of my time here. I'll get you some tea that hasn't been polluted."

"That would be wonderful," I said.

"I'll be right back."

As John moved off, Jeremy came slinking over to the picnic bench and said, "Mom."

"Jeremy."

He sat down, leaned over, and said quietly, "Have you told Matt about Ed Presnell?"

"No."

"Mom! Don't you think you better?" he asked. At his outraged tone several people turned to look in our direction.

"You might want to hold your voice down," I said softly.

"Sorry. But what do you mean, you didn't tell Matt?"

"I mean I didn't tell Matt."

"What about Ed?"

"What about him?" I asked.

"Oh, that's a great attitude. And after everything Matts's done for us. For you." I expected him to break into song. *M is for the many things he gave us....*

"It doesn't matter whether we tell him or not," I said. "Matt isn't guilty of anything, so he's not going to change his behavior."

"He could at least be prepared. How would you like to be grabbed by some dweeb like Ed Presnell without expecting it?"

"I wouldn't, but knowing about it in advance, and dreading it, wouldn't make it any better."

"So I'll tell him."

"Fine."

Jeremy stared at me for a good thirty seconds before he said, "You know, I didn't do anything wrong, and neither did Matt's parents. I don't see why you're being rude to all of us."

His words struck the blow that brought me around. A mental review of the last twenty-four hours, as seen from their point of view, did make my behavior appear rude. It wasn't a pleasant realization; I pride myself on caring about people and obviously I hadn't been. That made Matt right, although it didn't give him liberty to behave rudely in return.

"You're right," I said, patting Jeremy's knee. "I'm sorry I've been snappy, and as soon as John comes back with my tea, I'll go and join the family."

"Is John that old guy with the bleached blond hair?"

Jeremy's indignant look almost made me laugh. "Honey, I think his hair has just gone white. The blond is left over. Come on," I said, standing up and taking him by the arm. "We don't have to wait; John will find us."

We moved over to the group gathered under a massive oak, and somehow Jeremy found a spare lawn chair for me, which he placed strategically close to Matt. By this time Myrna was there, too, as well as one of her sons, who I later learned was Terry.

It was still bright daylight at seven-thirty, but the tree's shade afforded a cooling effect and the ripple of the stream not far away added to the illusion of comfort.

"Well, there's Miss Jolie," Will said as I sat down. "Jeremy, where you going to park yourself?"

"Oh, I think I'll just get comfortable right here," Jeremy said, lowering himself to the ground in front of Matt and me. He leaned back against my chair, reminding me of a human Dog of Fo. "Did we miss anything?" he asked.

"We were telling old stories," Cecily said. "I can't believe how Texans lie. Oh, I suppose I should just say 'exaggerate the truth.'"

"Tall Texas tales," Howard added. "Isn't that what they call them?"

"Not in this case," Will said. "I'm telling the truth, the whole truth, and nothing but the truth, so help me God. And Edith, don't go frowning at me for swearing."

"I wasn't even looking at you, Will Wyatt, so don't flatter yourself."

Myrna laughed. "Cecily was going to tell us about when a skunk got Matt out at the little barn—"

"A skunk did not 'get' me, Myrna. It was Cecily who got me."

Cecily laughed. "Oh, and you deserved it. You'd been wretched, and if anyone was in danger, I should think it was the skunk."

"I agree with you one hundred percent," Edith said, a grin on her face. She leaned toward Jeremy. "You see, what happened was that Matt's *business interests,* as he calls them, weren't doing too well, and he still got stuck with a big tax bill, so he was in about as ornery a mood as I've ever seen. He was swearing at the livestock, and snarling at the fence posts—"

"Edith, you're making him sound like some kind of lunatic," Myrna said.

Cecily snorted delicately through her patrician nostrils. "She's being kind. He was actually far worse." When she'd gotten nods of agreement from both Edith and Will, and a half smile from Matt, she went on. "Being a very bright person, I decided not to stay around. Instead I went for a walk to what we called the little barn. I liked to go there and do my thinking, except when I arrived that particular time it was already occupied. By a skunk. Of course I tried to shoo him out, but he wasn't having any of it. In fact, it seemed to make him thoroughly annoyed."

Matt sat forward. "So when I showed up, trying to make amends..."

"To pick a fight is more like it."

"She insists we talk in the little barn. And as soon as I got inside, she slammed the door and barred it from the outside," Matt said. He finished simply. "Leaving me inside with a skunk who had no social graces."

Everyone started laughing.

"Lordy, did he stink," Edith said. "Matt, I mean."

"And he didn't look no better with you and Cecily throwing ketchup and tomato sauce on him," Will said, laughing up a storm.

Edith slapped her thigh with glee. "That was the best part. And Matt deserved it!" She laughed some more, while Matt took it all with a smile and a shake of his head.

Howard stood up. "I think I shall have another beer. Can I get anything for anyone?"

Everyone declined so he moved off toward the house. I watched him for a moment, and noticed that John was standing in the middle of the lawn, peering around as if looking for me. I waved my hand at him, and he came over and handed me the ice tea.

"There you go, Jolie." He'd gotten me a real glass, one that was only slightly smaller than a quart pitcher.

"John. Thank you." I held it carefully and took a sip. "Ah, that's great. Do you know everyone?"

It was Myrna who did the introductions, then finally urged John down onto a picnic bench. "You won't believe this, Edith, but we met John up in Washington," Myrna said. "No kidding. Can you imagine having that many people from Purple Sage in the town of Redmond? Still amazes me."

"I'm not actually from Purple Sage," John said. "But I am a neighbor of Myrna and Sam. We live just around the corner."

"We met while I was out walkin' Fipster, our dog." Myrna patted John on the arm as she enthused, "We love walkin' by John's house because this man can raise just anything! I mean, his place looks like it belongs on a magazine cover. The grass is always perfect; I swear to you, a weed wouldn't dare come up. He grows peonies...you can't believe how big they are." She smiled at John. "And then there's those roses."

"Sounds like you come from good farming stock," Will said, which is high praise from him. "But I don't remember any Schusslers around here. Where exactly were you raised?"

John turned to him. "I wasn't raised here. In fact, I was only in Purple Sage for a day or two."

Howard returned and stopped just on the edge of the group, a long-necked bottle of beer in his hand.

"John was at Camp Seybold," Myrna said. "He was being shipped here when the war ended, and nobody changed the orders, so he and about ten others just kept on coming."

"I don't believe we've met," Howard said, wiping the hand that had been holding the beer. He held it out and shook with

John. "I'm Howard Bremerton. A friend of the family's, if you will."

"John Schussler."

As he said the name, Howard became stone still. "I don't believe it! From Friedlehausen, Germany?" he asked.

John looked surprised and a little wary. "Yes. Do I know you?"

"Oh, no. Sorry, but I've heard your name a hundred times! My uncle talks about you when he tells stories of the camp. About your arrival on the very last day, and how you opted to move to this country. Then how he lost you in the jumble closing the camp. Wasn't there a funeral during all of that, too?"

"Why, yes. You do know all the old stories, don't you?" John was looking curious now. "And your name is Howard Bremerton? I'm sorry, it doesn't ring any bells. Who is your uncle?"

"Oh, I should have said, earlier. It's Friedrich Linzer. He went to school with you."

"Of course!" John said. "In Friedlehausen! What a small world it is. And how is your uncle? Is he here?"

"No, no. He's at home. In Dover, actually. But he told me that if I were to find you, I was to be sure and get an address so he could contact you. He'll be quite amazed that I actually saw you."

"He's well? But wait, you're British."

"Yes," Howard said, and then went into the family history again with the rest of us looking on.

As the two men talked, their conversation became more specific, naming family members and asking if "you've ever heard of so and so." To me it didn't sound as if there was much of a match, but then Howard was of a different generation, and John remembered mostly childhood friends from Germany, many dead in the war before Howard was even born. John did relate a funny story about Friedlehausen that had to do with a hay cart. Howard added one about his uncle driving on the wrong side of the road when he moved to Britain.

"Oh, Lordy," Myrna said. "You want to talk about driving! What about the time that Edith couldn't get to church because of the mud or something."

Cecily jumped in. "It was during that wretched flood," she said. "I don't see how anyone could ever forget. We started calling it the monsoon season and we weren't able to get the cars out of the driveway for days. Cabin fever was rampant; we were all crazy with it."

"I just wanted to go to church," Edith said, with some spirit. "There is nothing crazy about wanting to go to church on a Sunday."

Will turned to Edith and said, "In that kind of rain it *was* crazy. And gettin' on a tractor and thinkin' you were going to church was even crazier."

"I would have made it if this one hadn't started chasing me." Edith pointed to Cecily with a new level of affection in her voice. "Running after me in the mud. And then when you fell down and came up again, I liked to died laughing. If you could have seen yourself…" her words trailed off as she was overcome with laughter.

They were having a wonderful time, playing off each other, swapping looks and expressions. I was the one outside the circle of family and friends, and my chest had constricted so that I could hardly breathe.

"It all might have been worth it," Cecily said, "if you had gone back home, Mumsie. And as for seeing oneself," she added with a laugh, "your face was something to behold, too, when you were stopped by those troopers!"

"I was on a farm vehicle, going to a town that was our nearest market. Tractors are legal on a *farm to market* road, so they had no business stoppin' me for going too slow. Besides, you are the one nearly got us thrown in jail, Cecily Wyatt."

"It wasn't me," Cecily argued, still grinning. "It was you. You're the one who scraped the mud off my arm and slung it at the officer."

"That time. But do you remember when…"

I couldn't take another "do you remember when" story.

"Matt taught Jeremy to drive a tractor...." I began.

"But I'll bet he hasn't taught you to race them," Cecily said with a laugh to Jeremy. "That's what we used to do. And I always won."

"That's not true," Matt began.

I felt a hard little knot of pain beginning near my breastbone.

I'm not sure whether I planned what happened, but as I raised my glass I felt it begin to slip through my fingers. I didn't try to get a better grip, just let it go. The entire glass of cold liquid fell, spilling all down the front of my blouse and in my lap. "Oh, no," I said, leaping to my feet.

"Mo-om," Jeremy said, jumping out of the way of the splash.

Myrna grabbed a napkin and rushed over to start brushing ineffectually at my slacks. "Oh, dear, you're soaked through. My goodness, that was a lot of tea."

"Well, the good news is that in this heat you'll dry out real quick," Edith said, picking up the glass, still unbroken, off the ground.

"How clumsy of me," I said.

Cecily was watching me. "That's twice. Doesn't seem to be your week for tea."

I smiled, already reaching for my purse. "I guess not," I said. "The bad part is that this time it's *sweet* tea. I'll be inundated with mosquitoes any minute; they like me even without a sugar coating." I shot John a quick glance. As I'd suspected, the man was sharp. His sympathetic eyes showed he'd caught my untruth but wasn't going to give me away. "I think I'd better run home and change," I said. I could always come back later.

"Oh, are you sure?" Myrna asked. "You haven't even had any barbecue and Sam's goat is the next best thing to chocolate. You'll love it, Josey."

I forced a smile. "I'm sorry to miss that, but it's my own fault," I said, already backing out of the circle of chairs and people. "It was great meeting you, Myrna, and I'm sure I'll see you again before the Celebration is over." Everyone was saying good-bye to me, and I didn't detect any great real regret. I gave them one final wave. "I'll visit with the rest of you tomorrow. Good night."

Before I was halfway across the lawn Matt caught up with me. "Jolie," he said, "wait a minute."

I stopped near the gate where there was a semblance of privacy created by thick bushes. "What, Matt?"

"I think this is damn rude of you."

"What?"

"Leaving like this."

"I'm covered with sticky, sweet tea, and I need to go home to shower and change," I said, clinging to the lie with only a twinge of guilt. "Nobody seems to mind but you."

"My parents are too polite to say anything."

"This has nothing to do with social graces. And I'm really very sorry that I don't seem to have enough of them. Anything else?"

Matt continued to glare at me silently.

"No? Well I have something to add." I lowered my voice, just in case there was anyone nearby. "Jeremy and I went to the jail to look for you earlier...."

"This afternoon?"

"Something like that. And we overheard Ed Presnell say he was going to be following you. He's looking for proof that you killed Vera Meece."

"What!" That jarred Matt out of his stiff anger. "Ed is delusional. I told him at least half a dozen times that Vera was alive and well at about fifteen after ten last night. That's when I saw her and left the money with her."

"Did you talk with her?"

"Of course I talked to her. It wasn't brilliant conversation. I said 'Hi, Vera,' and she said, 'I'll take that,' and she took the bank bag. She seemed to be in a big hurry and I hardly got out of the Explorer." He stopped and frowned. "I waited until she was back in the building, then I drove off."

"Were there any other cars there?"

He stared at me. "No."

"What about the money you left? Is it missing?"

"What?" He thought about it briefly. "Not that I've heard. Damn. Now, is there a reason for all these questions?"

"I was just curious. I mean, I haven't had a chance to talk to you, or anything." I reached for the gate. "Well…"

"You know, people are beginning to wonder about you."

"Which people?"

"Cecily for one. She asked me if there was anything wrong between us."

A devious ploy from dear Cecily, and Matt hadn't recognized it. It left me speechless. Men can be so obtuse at times I wonder why in the hell we continue to let them rule most of the world. I wanted to tell him that his dear ex-wife was playing some kind of game, and that Mumsie was an unwitting participant. For all I knew she was a *voluntary* participant.

"Matt, don't you see why she said that? She's trying to make me look bad. To create a rift."

"What I see is that you've been doing a fine job of that all by yourself."

My mouth dropped open and before I thought I grabbed for the gate and yanked it open. "Stuff it."

"Fine," Matt snapped, moving the gate so that I couldn't get through. "So you're determined to leave. You can't spend any time at all with my family."

In the past I have been called stubborn, even pigheaded, and I certainly can be, especially when I get angry. However, I am not a coward. Most of the time I stand up and fight my battles, ask for what I want, and make honest attempts to communicate. Unfortunately, this situation was beyond me. I didn't have any weapons to fight with, not that I was sure weapons were called for. So when you can't fight, that only leaves flight.

I slapped at my arm. "Ouch. It's the frigging mosquitoes. I have to go," I said. He released the gate and I whipped though it. "I'll see you when you get home."

Matt's voice was casual as he said, "Okay. Don't wait up; I'm not sure what time it will be."

"No problem." I whirled around and hurried down the street to my car.

I had lied to Matt and, in a roundabout way, I had lied to his family. My guilt was balanced with fury at Cecily, and at Matt for not seeing the game she was playing. I needed to put it behind me; action was called for, and luckily, I had some in mind.

FOURTEEN

BY THE TIME I reached my car two blocks away, the early evening heat had taken most of the moisture out of my clothes. My anger was also dissipating, making more room for guilt. When I heard footsteps behind me, I swung around apprehensively.

Jeremy came sauntering up.

"What are you doing here?" I asked.

"I'm going with you."

"You want to go home?"

He raised one eyebrow. "Mother, you don't drink sweet tea. Ever. So you're not going home to change. You're up to something, and I want to go with you."

Clever kid.

"Fine," I said, climbing into the car and starting the engine. "But I should warn you that if you try to tell me one more story about Cecily and the family, I'll have to kill you. It's nothing personal, but a human being can only take so much, and I have taken too much. I feel like I am going to explode in some socially unacceptable manner."

The passenger door opened and Jeremy climbed in, slamming it behind him. "Where are we headed?" he asked. He had missed my entire diatribe—probably a good thing.

"Here's the deal," I said. "I think we need to find the sheriff and I'm not sure where to start looking. Got any ideas?"

"The hospital."

"Good choice, except that Doc Baxter said he was going to move Mac."

"If you were ragging on me I'd say that, too, just to get rid of you." He grinned.

"I never said that I ragged on—"

"Mom, I've known you my whole life. Trust me, when you're stressed, you stress other people."

So I drove to the hospital and Jeremy went in the side door on his own reconnaissance mission. He knows Wilmot County Hospital almost as well as I do. I waited in the car, tapping my fingers on the steering wheel, imagining the places he might be looking.

There were rooms I hadn't gotten to. Like the spare operating theater that didn't have enough equipment to be functional—yet. And there were several empty offices I hadn't needed to check. Any one of them could have been set up as a patient room and most visitors would never think to look there. One was in the back of the administrative suite, and that would be doubly safe because of the office staff housed between Mac and the general public.

After a little thought, I had to admit that Jeremy's idea hadn't been such a bad one.

But even if we found Mac he couldn't tell us who killed Vera. We'd have to figure that out for ourselves. My instinct was that it had something to do with a man. A gentleman caller, like in the Tennessee Williams play. Had she been dating someone? Did she have some secret admirer?

It was interesting that I'd only spent a couple of hours in Vera's domain, the POW camp, and three different men had shown up: Howard Bremerton, Bill Tieman, and Klaus Braune.

Beyond the *who,* there was another question about Vera's death that bothered me. It was *how.* How did the murderer get to the camp? Obviously the person arrived in some kind of vehicle—they had to. Who would walk four miles out of town to kill someone? And four miles back? That was a long way, and would give the killer a lot of time to be noticed. But where had he hidden a vehicle?

Jeremy returned, hurrying across the asphalt. "He's not there; I checked everywhere, but I have some big news; that's what took me so long."

I started the car, but before I pulled out I reached over and wiped some chocolate pudding off Jeremy's chin. "Now tell me again what took you so long."

"I was starved, Mom. I haven't had dinner, remember? Besides, what really took the time was Miz Carlson. She came in, and then I had to stick around and waste time with her."

"Jeremy. That's no way to talk about Miz Carlson."

"I know she's a nice lady, but would you listen? Something weird happened at the hospital this morning and she told me about it. Do you know Mr. Jeffers? Karen Jeffers's grandfather?"

"Vaguely." He worked maintenance at the hospital, and took a great deal of personal pride in its appearance and operation. We always said hello when we saw each other, and sometimes I'd ask about one of the plants in a flower bed, but that was the extent of our relationship. "What about him?"

"Well, he was working on the outside air-conditioning unit today and got kind of sick, heatstroke or something, so one of the nurses told him to lie down and take it easy for a while. She put him in an empty patient room. Only while he was napping someone came in and tried to hit him with a crowbar."

"Oh my God! Is he okay?"

"They said he was. He grabbed the call button and rolled off the bed to get out of the way. He started yelling, too, so whoever it was ran out the door."

"Did they catch the attacker? Or call the police?" I asked.

"He got away, but Andy Sawyer was there investigating. Mr. Jeffers couldn't describe the person because the curtains were closed and the room was dark. But you know, I keep thinking maybe it was someone after the sheriff, only he got the wrong person." Jeremy was watching me, and when I didn't say anything he added, "Think about it, Mom. Mr. Jeffers and Mac are about the same size, and they both have gray hair. And the room was dark when this guy snuck in. Mac could have been killed.''

I'd almost convinced myself that pushing Dr. Baxter into moving him had been an overreaction. But I'd been right. Sometimes being right isn't good.

I took a breath and said, ''At least Mac is safe. They did move him.''

''Yeah, good timing.''

Timing?

I puzzled over that as we sat in the car. Everything in life is timing, that's what my grandmother used to say. And we had two crucial times to think about. Mac and Vera had been shot sometime between 10:20 and 11:15. I knew for a fact that Howard had no alibi during that time. I didn't know about Bill Tieman or Klaus Braune, but no one could be ruled out yet. It was help of a sort. Then there was the attack at the hospital. I could rule out Bill for the hour or so of the committee meeting, which started at noon, as well as half an hour when he was at Camp John Seybold with Diane and me. That had been somewhere around two o'clock or so, and Howard had been there as well.

''Jeremy, what time was Mr. Jeffers attacked? Do you know?''

''Miz Carlson said it was a little before she left for lunch.''

And having spent so much time at the hospital, we both knew that her schedule was inflexible; she left for lunch at 11:30 every day, except Friday when she had her hair done. Then she snacked at her desk and left work an hour early. It meant the assault on Mr. Jeffers had probably been around 11:15 in the morning.

Jeremy was talking, and I focused back on him. ''Miz Carlson started quizzing me about my back, and my horse, and my grades, and all that other stuff.''

''It's summer—you don't have grades,'' I said distractedly.

''Oh, she's too old to keep track of—'' He sat up straighter. ''That's it!''

"What? What are you talking about?"

Jeremy looked excited as he said, "I know where the sheriff is."

"I WANT a promise from you, Jeremy," I said as I parked the car under a stand of trees. "When I get old I do not want you to put me in this place. Ever. Even if Dr. Baxter is one of the owners, I don't want to stay here."

When we were on the sidewalk I noticed it was cracked, littered with tiny twigs, and stained with bird droppings and pecans that had fallen in years gone by. "It's just the name that's terrible," Jeremy said.

"So if you have to bring me here, make them change it."

To me the name Peaceful Rest Retirement Home conjures up pictures of a stopover spot where you wait while they finish the paperwork so you can go on to a cemetery. It's a disgusting mental image, and I try not to dwell on it.

I know both the administrator and the assistant administrator, Florence Williams, who is the heart of peaceful rest. She brought me in to give a mystery class once; it was fun, but I still don't care for such places. No matter how many people are bright and quick in a nursing home, there's always someone who's ill or senile, a reminder that life is a one-way journey and that, regardless of what we do—or don't do—there is never any turning back. From birth on, we're always going forward, and for each of us the ending is the same.

The thought caused me to shudder.

"What's the matter?" Jeremy asked.

"A goose walking over my grave." And what an apropos image that was. "So, do you have a plan?" I asked.

By now the sun was going down and we were being treated to a magnificent sunset of purples, blues, and reds. I caught myself looking over my shoulder, wondering again about the man who'd tried to kill Mr. Jeffers.

"Can't we just go up to the door?" Jeremy asked.

"If this is like it used to be, they lock the door at eight-thirty, and right now it's"—I glanced at my watch—"exactly eight-thirty."

"They'd still let us in."

"They're not going to tell us if Mac is here. He's in hiding, remember? I think we're going to have to be sneaky about the whole thing."

"How sneaky?" he asked.

"Well, it's going to be a dark night; the moon isn't supposed to come up until three twenty-seven, which should help us."

Jeremy gave me one of those looks that teenagers do so well. "Mother, why would you say something like that? No, why would you *know* something like that?"

"Because I read it on the weather wire this morning. I only said it to be funny."

"But you really *do* want to break into a rest home. That's perverted."

"Probably, but that's not what I want to do. What I have in mind is even worse. Come on," I said. "Stay close to me, and don't make any noise."

We started forward, remaining as near as possible to the trees and shrubbery. Luckily, Peaceful Rest was not one of those modern wonders with acres of barren parking lot and a four-foot chain-link fence around a gravel yard. Here there were lots of trees and overgrown bushes. While the building had been gutted completely during a remodeling to meet new licensing codes, Dr. Baxter had tried to keep some of the charm of the original structure. The vinyl siding on the outside could almost pass for shiplap wood. He'd added dark green shutters on every single window. Most important, he'd kept the huge lawn intact on three sides, along with the flower beds, and even a small garden.

And while I disliked the name, the place won momentary favor because the asphalt parking area and ambulance entrance were on the side away from us, so we didn't have to worry about being seen crossing them.

With the sun gone the sky was getting darker, and it was easier for us to disappear among the foliage. I kept looking over my shoulder to make sure no one was watching us. When I reached the gate I discovered that there was a simple combination lock that had been put up high, at almost the six-foot level.

"Great," Jeremy said softly but with feeling. "How are we going to get that open?"

"Faith," I said. He had a good six inches on me, not to mention being twenty-odd years younger, so I decided he should be the one to deal with it. I added some practical instruction. "Can you see the combination? What numbers are showing?"

Jeremy reached up and shifted the lock until he could read them. "Seven, nine, five, one."

"Seventy-nine, fifty-one. Okay. Now, start changing the first two numbers, slowly. Try opening it after each time. Then go back to the start, reset it at seventy-nine, fifty-one, and change the third number."

"Are you serious? That could take forever."

"Luckily you're young."

As he started fiddling with the lock I began scouting around, searching for another way in. I worked myself between two oleanders, and then sidled along the fence. Lo and behold there was another gate, hidden behind a huge and prickly juniper. As soon as I saw it I began inching forward through the tree-sized shrub. When I got close to the gate I realized that there was no lock; as inaccessible as it was, apparently no one had thought there was a need for one. They hadn't counted on me.

I headed back to Jeremy.

He was diligently turning numbers, muttering the whole time.

"You can stop," I whispered. "I found a better way."

"My arm was falling asleep," he mumbled, letting it drop limply before massaging some circulation back in it. "I suppose we can just walk in somewhere."

"Sort of. Come on."

I took a slightly different route, but within two minutes we were inside the fence. No huge outside lights had come on yet, but I knew they would soon. We went straight to the building, and I discovered that by standing on my toes I could peer inside the window closest to the front.

"This is really gross," Jeremy said as we looked into the reception/sitting area that I remembered from my previous visits. It had only three people in it. All appeared to be residents, all at least ten years older than the person we were searching for. A big poster for the Centennial Celebration had been put on one wall, and a festive draping of ribbon was around it. Somehow it made me sad.

"I feel like some kind of weirdo in a trench coat," Jeremy continued. "We'll probably end up in jail—"

I nudged him sharply with my elbow. "If they hear us we damn sure will!"

He muttered some phrase that contained the word *ladylike*, but much more quietly.

Methodically we crept down the row, poking up our heads just enough to peer inside each room. We found a television room and several patient rooms that had three beds each. We didn't spend much time on those: Mac wouldn't be in a ward. Next was a high window that had steam coming from it, as well as the sound of voices and running water. Since it had to be a bathroom we moved on. Then there was a closet followed by a couple of single rooms.

The back of the building had the kitchens, dining room, and then a sunporch, and I was dreading the thought of having to get past them. Luckily we didn't have to. Just as I was about to give up, Jeremy said, "It's him."

I stuck my head up and discovered a dimly lit private room with the television on. Lying on his side, not a foot from us, was Sheriff Mac Donelly. I tapped on the screen lightly, feeling as if I'd been plunged back into high school, when my friends and I would do the tap-on-the-window, sneak-out-of-the-house routine.

Mac turned over slowly, and saw us. One look at his face and I was firmly in the present. He looked older and grayer than I'd ever seen him.

"What in the hell..." I heard dimly through the glass.

He finally got the window open, leaving just the metal

screen between us. The exertion of unlocking the window had brought out a coating of sweat on Mac's pale face.

"Mac, I'm sorry; we shouldn't have—"

"No need for apologizing. I'm not dying or anything. Actually, it feels pretty good to see someone who isn't treating me like I've got one foot in the grave." His words were hearty, but his voice didn't match. He sounded tired, as I should have expected. "How you doing, Jeremy?"

"I'm fine."

"That's good," Mac said.

"You're pale," I said.

"If somebody put three bullets in your back you'd look pale, too. Besides, it's the light from the TV. Makes people look blue." He moved around to see us better, grimacing when he put too much pressure on his back. Eventually he found a more comfortable position and said, "So, what can I do for you, Jolie? It's too early for Halloween so you can't be trick-or-treating."

I moved closer to the window, wondering what in the world I thought Mac could do from a rest home. The man was obviously not well, and I wasn't going to tell him about the break-in at the hospital; he didn't need any additional worries. As for what I thought I could do to help the situation, I hadn't any idea. "Mac, I'm sorry I bothered you; I guess we just needed to see that you were okay."

Mac stared at me in silence for a good twenty seconds before a slow grin stretched across his face. "Jolie, no offense meant, but you are a terrible liar. If I was you, I'd lead a righteous life, cuz unless it's true, you aren't going to be convincing Saint Peter of your good deeds." He was still grinning as he said, "So now, what's really on your mind?"

I was ready to hedge some more, but Jeremy wasn't. "Someone broke into the hospital, probably looking for you."

"Don't say. Well, guess I'm better off here than I thought." He grew somber. "I thought this was a damn fool idea, moving me here, and I heard it was yours, Jolie, but maybe it's not dumb after all." He shook his head. "What else is going on out there?"

"Ed Presnell took my dad in for questioning. Ed seems to think he's running the place right now."

Mac's eyelids blinked twice. The brief animation we'd seen was gone, and he looked tired. "Deputy Presnell has a might overblown opinion of his own position," Mac said, a furrow forming between his eyebrows. "I called him, but he wasn't around. I was going to call again, but then my phone disappeared." He glanced around, as I did. From my vantage point I couldn't see a phone.

"That's odd," I said.

Wearily Mac ran his hand over his face; there was a scratchy sound when he reached the one-day stubble on his chin. "I don't dare fire Ed now, because I need any kind of manpower just for regular patrol."

Somehow I had believed that once I got to Mac he could solve our problems, but now I regretted disturbing him. "We shouldn't have come," I said. "Why don't I go by your office and have Linc call you tomorrow."

"Can't do that. Not with Linc in a hospital in Waco."

"What?" Jeremy and I said it together.

"Car wreck. Driver of a tractor-trailer rig fell asleep and ran Linc off the road. Trina said he won't be back on the job much before I am."

It was a frightening thought, having both Linc and Mac out at the same time. "Is there some way I could help?" I asked.

Mac looked at me for a moment before he said, "Jolie, I appreciate it. I think you'd make a real fine deputy if you put your mind to it, but I need someone with training right now." He yawned.

That wasn't what I'd meant, but I thanked him anyway. Then asked, "Mac, where was Vera killed? Not inside the headquarters building?"

"No, no. Out on the side of the front gravel. I didn't see her body until I come to."

"Did you see another car? Truck?"

"Not a thing. Sure wish I had," Mac said. The arm propping him up began to shake and he sank back into the pillows.

"I'm sorry we bothered you," I said, reaching up to touch the screen. "Maybe we'll check on you tomorrow."

"If you do, try the front door," he said, closing his eyes. "They let most anybody in."

FIFTEEN

I WENT STRAIGHT home and straight to bed, so I didn't hear Matt come in. The following morning, even after I'd dressed and was ready to face the world, he was still sound asleep, looking more vulnerable than I'd seen him in a long time. The problem was that if I woke him, and if he wasn't over his anger, he'd be about as sweet and yielding as a rattlesnake in full strike.

Rather than chance it, I tiptoed downstairs, made some tea, and prepared vegetables to cook later. I'd fallen asleep thinking alternately about murder and Matt, but I'd woken with a brilliant plan to get myself back into everyone's good graces. My mother always told me that people can't resist a good home-cooked meal—and this would be one of the best. I'd make biscuits from scratch, I'd serve one of our own WW Ranch roasts, and I'd think up some flamboyant dessert if I had to dig through every back issue of *Good Housekeeping* I had. Or better still, I'd call Diane; she's a whiz at such things.

Even though I stayed long enough for two cups of ginger-peach tea, Matt didn't wake up, or if he did, he didn't move around or come downstairs. That was fine; I could call him later and tell him about the dinner.

Next I drove over to Edith and Will's, a cordial invitation to dinner right on the tip of my tongue, except when I stepped onto the porch the house was silent. It had the kind of quiet you only find when everyone is still asleep.

It must have been one helluva party the night before.

So I wrote my invitation on a sticky note from the glove

compartment of the car, put it on the window at the top of their front door, and started toward town.

It was a beautiful morning with the sun a radiant ball of red creeping up over the horizon in the east; the air was warm but fresh feeling. Most of the time I liked the solitude of my morning drive to the station. It gave me a chance simply to enjoy my surroundings without having to do anything. There was no one to talk to, no one expecting anything of me, no one even to listen to. I'd keep the radio off and just drive with a mindless pleasure.

That particular morning I'd already had a full dose of solitude because of the long and empty evening before. After visiting with Mac, my rat-fink son had requested I drop him back by the party with the rest of the family. At the curb I waved him good-bye and headed home to put in some writing time at my computer. When that hadn't been satisfactory, I'd started making long-distance calls. That's always my last defense against loneliness, and one I've rarely had to resort to since moving to Purple Sage.

My first call was to my mom, but I got her answering machine, which could have meant she'd dashed out to the convenience store, or was sailing the Nile in a felucca. With my mom I never knew.

I'd also tried my sister, Elise, but she was in the middle of wrapping presents for her daughter's birthday party and couldn't quite get her mind on me. Not that I was telling her my problems. Mostly I'd just wanted a friendly voice and I'd had no luck in finding one. Even my brother, the high school football coach, was out at some preseason event, according to his twelve-year-old, Bernie. I was actually going through my address book looking for people to call, when I began feeling pathetic. I wasn't that desperate, I'd told myself, and in the end I reread part of an early China Bayles mystery and went to bed.

By the time I got to the station I was actually looking forward to seeing Rory. My voice was brighter than usual as I said, "Good morning, how's it going?"

He didn't even glance at me. "Hey, Jolie," he said. Not exactly an opening for conversation.

I put my purse in a drawer and pulled out my chair. "Anything exciting happen overnight?" I asked.

"That depends. Do you consider six DWIs and a trespassing call exciting?" he asked, still focused on the computer.

"Could be, I suppose. Were the trespassers aliens? Was it someone from 'America's Most Wanted'? Was it Elvis Presley?"

He finally looked at me. "D. None of the above." His hazel eyes grew bright in his round face. "Actually, though, one of them was pretty good. The call was placed by some lady on Willow. You know that street with all the fancy houses?"

I perked up a little. "I've been there," I said.

"Well, it seems there was someone lurking in this lady's bushes, peeking over the fence at her neighbors, so she called the police."

"Wait, let me get this straight. The trespasser was in her yard, spying on the neighbors?"

"Yes. You see, the neighbors were having a party." He referred to the notes on his desk, a grin in place when he looked up. "The neighbors were the Petermans."

This was beginning to sound more than a little familiar. "Did the Petermans by any chance have their daughter, Myrna Applegate, and her family in town?"

"I don't know anything about the Applegates, but it was the big white house with the blue awnings. Why?"

"No reason. Go on."

"Well, when the police arrived, they found a trespasser all right. None other than Deputy Ed Presnell." He began to read from his notes. "'Deputy Presnell was taken to the jail where, out of professional courtesy, he was released on his own recognizance.'"

THE STORIES waiting to be aired on the noon newscast were almost identical to those we'd used at 8 a.m. The bulk of them related to the Celebration, which was happening on a timely schedule, just as the press releases had said. And since we had that schedule in advance, the news copy was already written and ready to go; all we had to do was pull it out of the file.

"I feel like a PR flak," Rory said to me as I returned from the police station. It was a little before eleven, and all was well in Purple Sage. It was well to the point of boring, which is not how newspeople like it. "All we do is tout some event for the Celebration," he went on. "Big deal. I don't suppose you dug up anything exciting?"

"Depends on what you call exciting."

"Right. What have we got now? Jaywalking? Illegal parking?"

"A false alarm at the fire station."

"Oh yeah, that's a big deal." He slumped back in his chair. On his computer screen I could see a layout of cards. Rory had been playing solitaire. "You'd think the crowd would get rowdy, start a riot. Something," he said.

I sat down opposite him. "Actually, we had a shooting just two nights ago. And if it's all the same to you, I'd prefer we didn't have any more of those."

"What good is a shooting if the idiots at the Sheriff's Department won't give us any information? They probably aren't even investigating." He pushed his computer mouse around, punched a few keys, and the solitaire game disappeared, to be replaced by a blank word-processing screen. Then he turned around to face me. "Ed Presnell's so dumb I'll bet his family had a party when his IQ hit double digits. And it was probably last week."

I smiled. "That's such a good line I may have to put it in a book sometime."

"As long as you give me credit."

Rory is young, and still on the lookout for the road to the big time and overnight success. To me, Purple Sage seems pretty far back on the road to start out, but he once confided to me that if something really big happened in town he could send news feeds to the networks. Maybe get noticed and be offered a job. I think the odds of it happening are about the same as the odds of winning for those who plunk down a dollar for a lottery ticket.

Still, I know about dreams, the kind that keep us going when life isn't offering much pleasure elsewhere. I'd spent a long time with mine. Before I'd met Matt I had always dreamed of more. Whatever more was. When Matt had come into my life my dreams had lost their desperate quality and I had learned to enjoy life as it was. I still had some dreams, but I was no longer frantic about them. My hope was that I never would be again, except that with Cecily in town and things going the way they were...

"So, what else is happening?" I asked.

"You've got some messages."

Rory doesn't take phone messages for me, but he does bring them back from the front desk when he retrieves his own. I suspect he does it because he likes to read them.

Rory handed me four hot pink slips of paper with our receptionist's big, looping writing.

According to the first message, my son was going with the senior Wyatts and would be home by nine tonight at the latest. That didn't bode well for the missive from Edith, which was next in the stack. She and Will were taking Cecily and Howard, along with Jeremy, to spend the day with friends in Mason. They were very sorry they couldn't make dinner, but this rock-hunting expedition had been scheduled weeks ago.

Mason is one of the most likely places to find the Texas blue topaz, our official state gem. I've heard it's a real thrill to hunt for the stones, and an even bigger thrill to find one. Unfortunately, it meant that my plan to get back into everyone's good graces was a bust and I was still the Wyatt family black sheep.

It has always sounded daring and romantic to be the black sheep, something like Greta Garbo going off into solitude. Now it felt like being left out. I would have loved to go off searching for blue topaz with Matt's parents. It would have been great fun to be teased by Will, and I could just imagine how Edith would respond if I actually found one of the gems and gave it to her. Cecily would probably stumble across the mother lode.

Even if she didn't find a thing, she was there, part of the family, building even more memories.

My morning wasn't going much better than Rory's.

At least Matt had thought of me, so his anger must be wearing off. The third message slip was from him, stating that he wouldn't be home for lunch. Now that he was the Celebration chair, he had a million things to handle, but he'd call the house and let me know when he would be arriving.

I was batting three for three; luckily it wasn't baseball or I'd be out.

The last note was from Diane, and I scanned it quickly. She was at the POW camp, and why didn't I come see her after I left KSGE?

Why, indeed?

I couldn't believe what I was seeing inside the POW camp headquarters. Instead of the nice neat little room that I had left yesterday, the place was in shambles. The pictures that we had so carefully hung were now scattered on the floor, with a few on the display cases. A large fern rested in the corner, its leaves already dripping on the carpet. Diane was sitting on the floor, while Klaus Braune, our German visitor, was standing at the wall rehanging a photo. It was one of three in their rightful places.

"What happened?" I demanded.

Diane looked around. "Hi. We're redecorating."

"Jeez! It looks more like undecorating. You did this on purpose?"

"Of course."

The room's condition was planned carnage rather than random violence. "I thought maybe someone had broken in and, well, you know," I said.

Klaus turned his oversized, cherubic face to Diane. "She is maybe exaggerating a little," he said, with a nod in my direction.

"She does that. Klaus, you remember my friend Jolie Wyatt."

"Yah. Of course."

"Nice to see you, Klaus." I stepped forward and shook his big beefy hand. "So, I don't understand why you're undecorating. Did we do it wrong?"

"No, no," Diane said. "It's just that Klaus started telling me about the various pictures, and we decided that they ought to be in chronological order."

"Here, you see this?" Klaus pointed to the first of the three pictures already on the wall. "This was the start of the camp."

It was a photo of several buildings that were under construction. One, a tin building, was completely erected, while several men were working on another wooden structure beside it. Nowadays on construction sites you see the crew in jeans and tennis shoes. In this picture the men were mostly in overalls, while others wore dark pants, of a uniform nature. Some were wearing heavy boots, others what looked like dress shoes.

The most arresting thing about the photo was a man standing at the side of the actual work. He was in a sleeveless undershirt and slacks, his dark hair slicked back from a widow's peak, a stub of a cigarette in his sensual mouth. He appeared to be on a break, or perhaps he was the foreman. His pose was casual, one leg resting on the running board of an old car, as he watched the others labor.

"Is that anyone I know?" I asked, pointing.

Diane laughed. "I asked the same question. Klaus says he thinks it was a man who lived nearby. Harley something, but he doesn't remember the last name."

"And he lived around here? Wait, not Harley Tandy! Is that possible?"

"Are you serious?" Diane jumped up for a closer look. She took the photo off the wall and moved to the window to study it.

Harley was Liz Street's father, a very nice man who was now in his seventies, grayed, paunchy, his skin spotted and wrinkled from years in the sun.

"What do you think?" I asked.

"Doesn't look like him, but then this was fifty years ago. My, my, my!"

"More proof that God is not a woman. She wouldn't take away our beauty and youth like that," I said.

Klaus tapped his temple. "At least we still have the brain."

"Small consolation," I said. "Isn't there any information on the pictures? Maybe on the back?" I took the photo from her, turned it over, and discovered only the number one lightly penciled in the upper right-hand corner. "Well, rats. Guess we'll just have to let Liz take a look at it and decide." I handed the picture back to Klaus, who hung it while Diane returned to her sorting on the floor.

I picked up a picture from the display case. "Numbering these was a good idea. It will be a snap to move them to a permanent location in the old jail."

"We aren't doing the numbering," Diane said. "Apparently Vera did, and you and I missed it yesterday. Makes the job a whole lot easier; I've already got most of them in order. Here, would you hand these to Klaus?"

She gave me a stack of pictures, and Klaus took them from me, carefully putting the photos in their proper places. We repeated the steps, so that we had an assembly line going. The pictures began to tell a story. There was the construction of the camp, then a group of men standing at the front gates with a new American flag waving above them. Next came the arrival of the prisoners, disembarking from the train, marching through town, and finally arriving at the newly opened installation.

The camp began to change, as did the mood of the photos. They went from somber to relaxed, and some even touched on playful. There was one photograph of two men in Carmen Miranda costumes, complete with fruit on their heads.

"What in the world?"

Klaus was frowning, but he looked up long enough to take a quick glance at the picture. "Oh, a talent show. But we soon learned there was not too much talent. We had school, though. I learned my English in the camp." He turned back to his work, his expression changing to one of puzzlement. He held out two pictures, turned them over, then gestured with them.

"There is one missing; I have number thirty-five and thirty-seven, but no thirty-six."

"It probably got broken," Diane said. "There are four that I haven't found."

I headed for the little office, saying, "I'll look for them. We could probably get new glass from Henshaw's. I'll bet Joan would cut it for us this afternoon, if we asked."

Today there were some new boxes in the office with napkins, plastic cups, and serving utensils. I peeked into the small refrigerator and discovered it was jammed to the limit with trays of cold cuts, cheeses, vegetables, and small sandwiches, all stacked on top of cases of beer. Beside the refrigerator were the soft drinks, and on the desk was a long, flat box from the bakery. While I didn't open it, I did lean close enough to get a whiff of one of IdaMae's sheet cakes.

After a bit of searching I found the empty boxes that had contained the pictures. There were three photos left in them, the glass broken on each one.

"I've got number forty-one, forty-two, and fifty-eight. No thirty-six," I called out. As carefully as possible I removed the pictures from their frames and took them out to Diane and Klaus. "Here. What do you think? Are they worth reframing?"

To me they weren't anything special. One was of a young man reading a book in front of a tent, another of several men squirting each other with a water hose, and the third showed a young girl leading two horses beside a small wooden building.

"I think that's Vera," Diane said. "Klaus, am I right?"

He moved beside her and looked at the photo; I did, too. The girl, probably in her early teens, had blond hair in a soft pageboy. On her face was a bright, satisfied smile.

Klaus began to laugh. "That was Vera. Always the little troublemaker! I sent this picture; she was stealing the guards' horses while the men ate breakfast."

"You sent it?"

"We all sent pictures. Vera asked us to so we could bring back the memories. She made copies and returned the photos, and she promised us a surprise." His big body heaved with a sigh. "It is not a good surprise that she is dead." He shook his head, as if in disbelief. "It has made us sad. Even Minna, who only knew Vera from her letters, was not happy."

"Where is Minna?" Diane asked.

"She discovered all the little shops around the square, and now she is busy buying presents to take home." He handed the pictures back to Diane. "These are all special to someone; we should put them up. I will leave spaces for them."

He turned back to his chore.

I was beginning to see what a monumental task Vera had taken on. She had overseen the entire Celebration as well as being personally responsible for the POW camp. I knew of two flyers that she'd had printed and distributed, but there must have been hundreds of letters that went out as well. Beyond that she'd planned events for the returning POWs. A cocktail party to be held this afternoon accounted for the food and such already in the office. A second event, "Memories of the Mess Tent," was scheduled for Saturday. It was an outdoor barbecue with a slide show. Vera had labored hard to make the men from the camp part of the festivities.

Since the war had ended over fifty years ago, I was puzzled by how she'd found the men. I asked Klaus that very question.

He stopped what he was doing and said, "That was easy for her, I think. We have a Camp Seybold reunion every five years in Germany, and the men come from all over the world. She must have gotten the list from someone."

"Oh. That makes sense." Yet I never would have guessed that men who had been together in what was literally a prison would want to see each other again, much less have regular reunions. Certainly our American POWs had few fond memories of their years of internment. I'd interviewed a local man who'd come home from a German prison camp weighing just eighty-five pounds. All the time he'd talked about the war years, he'd never smiled. Bitterness and anger had tinged his words, as if the scars wouldn't heal.

"Jolie, are you going to help or what?" Diane asked, handing out several photos.

"Oh, right. Sorry."

By the time the pictures were all in place, Diane had more little chores for us. Klaus put a hook in the ceiling for the fern, while I swept out the fallen leaves. When we were done Klaus looked at his watch. "I must go," he said. "I have promised Minna that I would pick her up."

"Don't forget the cocktail party," Diane said.

For the first time since we'd found Vera's picture, Klaus smiled. "Yes, and that is why I must get Minna now. It can take a long time for her to get ready."

"WHAT AM I missing here?" I asked, staring at a color photo. It was one of Diane's, and while I was sure it was technically very good I couldn't make out why it was so important. "This just looks like the ground."

"Mac said there wasn't another vehicle parked here the night that he found Vera dead. And we know that only an idiot would walk out here, right?"

"Right."

"So there had to be another mode of transportation, and now we know what it was. This is the proof."

I took a closer look. It was still just a picture of the ground with some leaves. I tilted it to remove the glare, and for the first time I noticed a slight depression in the dirt. Two depressions. "Wait, are those hoofprints?"

"Exactly! Clever, isn't it? I took the picture yesterday, outside here. Now let me show you the real thing," she said, taking the picture from my hand and leading me outside. "This will put it all in context."

I followed her back to the edge of the cleared area, where the narrow track I'd seen the day before went off into the brush. Staying on the side of it, we made our way ten feet farther down the pathway. When we stopped there was a small depression, and the ground looked as if it had been muddy and then dried out. Diane leaned down carefully to brush away some leaves and twigs so I could clearly see the hoofprints.

"Interesting," I said, "So what does this prove?"

"I think it proves the killer was on horseback. If you look

at it logically, that's how it pans out. It rained Sunday, remember?"

"It poured," I said. The dire prediction had been that the Celebration would be rained out. "And Monday was even worse," I added. Luckily, after dumping a great deal of water, the clouds had dissipated before causing any permanent damage to either the landscape or the nerves of the Celebration Committee.

"Right. Until about ten o'clock that night, if I remember correctly. Trey called me into the den to watch the weather report on TV, while Randy was yelling from outside that the rain had stopped."

"That sounds about right."

"Okay. So our horseman—horseperson—had to have come through here after that time. My guess is late Tuesday after the ground dried up some; if it had been any earlier the prints would be deeper." She took a breath. "Vera was killed Tuesday night."

It all made sense. "Good job, Great White Tracker," I said. "So, where does this trail go? And could just anybody get on it, or only the person who lives at the end of it? And who is that?"

Diane gently replaced the leaves and twigs on top of the prints and stood up. "I don't have any idea," she said, brushing off her hands. "Obviously, we still have some research to do, but I think we've at least got a starting place."

SIXTEEN

THE BAKERY on Main Street is owned by IdaMae Dorfman, and is without equal in the quality of cakes, cookies, and cream pies it sells.

The bakery is peerless in other ways, too. For example, when it sells out of most of its goods, whether that's at noon or 5 p.m., it closes. The reason is that IdaMae refuses to be the slave of her public's sweet tooth. On the flip side of that coin, she also doesn't believe in wasting a golden opportunity, which is why she had doubled the volume of her baking during the Celebration.

When I arrived at a little past two, a heavenly calorie-laden aroma surrounded me. I stopped to indulge in a few deep breaths before slipping around the eight or so women who were jockeying for position in front of the glass display cases. Two young girls worked quickly to fill orders, as well as the familiar white bags adorned with the words *The Bakery*.

"Is IdaMae here?" I asked one of the girls.

She looked up to see who I was, then nodded toward a door behind her. "Back there."

"Thanks."

I found IdaMae in her tiny office. A frizz of white hair framed her face and her feet were resting on the open bottom drawer of her battered desk. Her eyes were closed, and in her gnarled left hand was a cigarette. The room was hazy with smoke, despite the open window above her.

"Hi," I said.

IdaMae jumped, banging her knee against the desk. "Jolie Wyatt, you liked to scared me to death," she said, rubbing her knee. "Don't you be sneaking up on me like that."

"I wasn't sneaking. You wouldn't have hurt yourself if you hadn't been feeling guilty." I looked at the cigarette but didn't say anything. Just the week before, Dr. Baxter had told her to quit smoking, the same instructions he'd given her at least fifty times over the years. IdaMae is at an age where she does what she damn well pleases. I know this for a fact, because she's told me so herself in no uncertain terms.

"You could set down," she said, gesturing to the avocado green plastic chairs that were crowded between the front of the desk and the wall. I wedged my body down into one of them, and she took another puff of her cigarette before she said, "So, Jolie, to what do I owe the pleasure?"

"Oh, I just thought I'd stop by and say hi. You know, see how you were doing...."

IdaMae let out a laugh that verged on a cackle. "Now, that's a good one. Who writes these speeches for you? Hope your books is better." She sat up a little straighter. "You're wantin' something, so you might as well tell me up front what it is. I'm old; I don't have time for pussyfootin'."

Apparently my acting skills had fled me completely of late. "Okay, we'll do it your way," I said. "I do want something. What do you know about Vera Meece? Who was she dating? Anybody special?"

"That's what I like—cut to the chase, just like them Bruce Willis movies!" she said. "So, you're pokin' around Vera's murder. I expect you have to, though, what with Ed Presnell out there stalking your husband."

I didn't ask how she knew. "So?" I said. "Can you tell me who Vera was seeing?"

She eyed me for a minute, thinking about my question. And her answer. IdaMae has scruples about passing along gossip; in most cases she has to decide if telling something is going to worry her enough to interrupt her sleep at night.

"Matter of fact," she said, apparently deciding in my favor, "I been hearing some stories, and I reckon they're true. I heard that Bill Tieman was sniffing around her." She leaned forward. "I also heard that she wasn't having any of it, but Bill, he just kept on coming."

I wasn't a bit surprised. "I should have figured that out from the way he's been acting. Wait a minute, I think I remember seeing them together. At a supper, or someplace." Purple Sage, like many small towns, has pancake suppers, craft shows, and other mini events that bring people together and raise money for worthy causes. In this case I couldn't place either the event or the cause. "Am I making this up?" I asked.

"You don't sound like you're lyin'," and usually I could tell."

"Why, thank you," I said, but IdaMae only grinned. "Okay, so Vera wasn't interested. But Bill's the chief of police, not a likely candidate to do murder."

"That's certainly what he'd say."

"What I meant," I said, "is that I have suspected our law

enforcement people of less than honorable behavior in the past. More than once. I can't keep doing that.''

"Why not? Eventually you're bound to be right. Them are the odds.''

I couldn't help but laugh. "Then I'll keep Bill in mind, but what about any other men? Past, present, or future. Was she dating anyone else, or did she want to? And what about her husband? I heard that he died, is that right?''

IdaMae nodded, her expression turning somber. "Of a heart attack, and there weren't a nicer man on this earth than Jim Meece. Real nice man, at least from what I knew of him. Grew up over to Hedwig Hills, but they lived here for maybe a year before they moved on off.''

"Do you know of any other men?''

"Don't go sexist on me, Jolie, it coulda been a woman killed Vera.''

I had my doubts. "I haven't heard about Vera having any female friends.''

"Come to think of it, I don't know of none, either. She liked the men.''

From what I'd seen, Vera Meece was open about her flirting; it was just her way with males of all ages, and she seemed to adore each one. Although Matt had said she'd been a slave driver when she wanted something accomplished. So where was the motive in any of that?

"But why would someone kill her? Jealousy?'' I shook my head. "That doesn't work. Vera dated older men, and lust and such should be gone by that age.''

IdaMae grinned. "Jolie, lust ain't exclusive to the young, I can promise you.'' She picked up her almost full pack of cigarettes and slid it under some papers in the bottom desk drawer, along with her matches. "You know, Vera could be real bossy, in her way. Especially about this Celebration Committee. I reckon that could be a reason for murder.''

"Most people would quit the committee before they'd take a gun to her.''

"Most people don't kill.'' IdaMae emptied her battered tin ashtray into a big coffee can. When she was finished she put the plastic lid back in place and hid the can and ashtray under her desk. As if no one would guess she'd been smoking. "I think it had to do with men," she said firmly.

"Now who's being sexist?" I asked. "Wait a minute—was Vera after somebody's husband?"

IdaMae shrugged, but she didn't look that innocent or disinterested.

"Ah-ha! She was," I said. "Who was he, IdaMae? Do I know him?"

"I don't have the least idea. I don't know that he was married. I didn't even hear his name." She sighed, her tiny frame giving up the secret. "I just know that Vera Meece was in love with some man from the past."

"Was that bad?"

"I think maybe it was. See, when Vera married Jim Meece it was on the rebound from some other man she couldn't have. I know that happens, but I think Jim spent most of his life knowing he weren't ever number one with her." IdaMae looked angry. "Don't that beat all? Here she had her a real nice man and he weren't ever the right one. Sometimes I think human beings set out to make their lives miserable." IdaMae shook her head, then straightened up. "Anyhow, I don't know who that other man was, but I know she was real excited about the Celebration. When she came in and ordered the cake for tonight's party she was telling me she felt like a girl again; she was gettin' a second chance at her Prince Charming. Ain't that something?"

"The one that got away."

IdaMae watched me a moment before she said, "You got one of them, too, don't ya?"

"Not anymore," I said, lifting my shoulders in a shrug. "I thought so at the time, but I was lucky he left."

"Jeremy's dad?"

"The very one," I said. I had never discussed this with her; she just knows things. "Now, of course, I have the best."

She flashed me a wicked little smile. "That Matt's some hunk," she said. "You ever get tired of him, I reckon there'd be a line to take your place."

That wasn't something I wanted, or needed, to be reminded of. The line appeared to be forming already, and dear Cecily was right at the front.

IdaMae was watching me with her bright, curious eyes, so I did the only smart thing I could. I stood up. "I guess I'd better get going."

"You got something you want to talk about?"

"No. Besides, you've got customers."

IdaMae pushed herself up off the chair. "More'n I care to deal with."

"Well, thanks for the info," I said, easing my way out from behind the chairs. "Can I use your phone before I go?"

"Sure. Just leave your dime beside it." With a last wave, she left me alone in the little office.

I tried the cellular phone first, but Matt didn't answer. Then I called the ranch, and there were four rings before the machine picked up. Instead of leaving a message, I dialed the code to see who had called us, and got Matt's recorded voice. He sounded rushed. The carnival had arrived and there was some problem with the permits. Bill Tieman was being hard-nosed, and before the carnival could set up in the park it had to be straightened out. Matt was currently at the courthouse trying to accomplish just that. He was planning on attending the reception at the POW camp. Would I be there?

I would indeed—at seven on the dot. Or a little later, if I wanted to make an entrance.

First, though, I had another stop.

MAC DONELLY was right: They do let almost anybody in the front door of Peaceful Rest. They certainly let me in, and no one challenged me when I went straight down the hall looking for Mac's room. I was grateful for that personally, but it made me more concerned about Mac's safety. What if someone else figured out where he was? What if someone had already gotten to him?

I quickened my pace, hurrying past open and closed doors alike. I hardly noticed the distinctive Lysol smell that characterized the rest home, or the pervasive sound of too many televisions all a bit too loud. I made a beeline for Mac's room, and after just one wrong turn I found him.

I saw immediately that he looked better. His skin was more pink, his eyes more alert, and that eased one of my concerns.

"Loretta," he was saying, "you tell that little ass-wipe that if he isn't around next time I call he's going to have a hard time getting another paycheck from the county. And I'll see to it." Mac was trying to hold his voice down, which only made him sound more furious. "I *know* it's not your fault, but I have got to talk to somebody, and I don't much care what I have to do to get it done. No, I told you before, I can't leave a number. Wait a minute, I know what let's do. You tell Wiley that I'll be callin' at exactly five o'clock, and somebody best be there with some answers for me. Thank you, I miss you too and I'm feelin' just fine." With that he put down the receiver and almost threw the old princess-style phone back on his tray table. As he did, he saw me still in the doorway, content to stay out of firing range. "Jolie Wyatt."

"Hey, Mac. How are you doing?"

"I been a great deal better." He lay back and groaned involuntarily as his skin touched the bed. After he'd rolled on his side, he said, "What time is it?"

"Three-fifteen."

"Damn. I can't even find my watch," he snapped. "And if you've come to see if I'm alive, you got your proof—I am! So, what else?"

"Nice mood," I said, crossing my arms against my chest as I leaned against the doorjamb. "You want to yell at me some more or are you done?"

He glared fiercely at me before shaking his head and closing his eyes. When he finally reopened them, he said, "I'm sorry, Jolie. This has got to be the most frustratin' day of my life, and I don't ever want to watch another daytime television program. I'll tell you what, they pipe that into all hospital rooms and there'd be a big contingent of us that'd never get sick again."

"I know what you mean; I hate being sick unless the house

is clean and I've cooked some great meals in advance. Oh, and have my comfort books stacked up by the bedside.''

"Happen that way often?"

"Never so far, but there's always hope." I smiled.

"I'll tell you what really makes me mad—someone keeps taking my phone and I don't even have a radio."

"So you aren't listening to my newscasts? Now there's gratitude for you."

"I don't have any idea what's going on in town. It's like livin' in some kind of deprivation tank." He shook his head. "I asked Florence for a radio, but she said they don't have one. I think it's part of some plot."

"Communist? Nazi?"

"Doctors. They think I'll get well faster if I don't worry, but what they don't know is that keepin' me uninformed is *really* making me worry."

I moved closer to the bed. "Well, I'd better not bring you a radio until I get Dr. Baxter's permission; so what else can I do to make your day better?"

He snorted. "You can fire two deputies and replace them with highly qualified, exemplary law enforcement officers who don't mind working long hours for peons' wages."

"Why don't you fire them yourself?"

"Because I can't prove they're available when I call and I can't leave a number for them to call back. Besides, I've got to have somebody working. I'd intended to fire—"

A voice interrupted us. "Mac Donelly, you are *supposed* to be resting. Recuperating." Florence Williams stood a few feet from us in the doorway, but her presence crowded the small room. People say she's the heart of Peaceful Rest, and the dearest soul alive, but Flo can also be frightening. At that moment she had drawn up her large frame and reminded me of a vengeful black goddess.

After barely a pause, she swept into the room, pulled up the blanket around Mac's chest, and grabbed his wrist to take his pulse. "This is not what you are supposed to be doin'."

"I can talk and recuperate at the same time," Mac said. He sounded like a kid who was almost sassing back, but not quite.

"I imagine you got lotsa talents, Sheriff, but I don't have time to hear about them just now." She silently checked her watch, and when the time was up, apparently satisfied with what she'd learned, she laid Mac's wrist on the bed and looked at me. "Jolie, what are you doing here? Nobody is supposed to know where he is."

"Jolie's the one who talked Doc Baxter into hiding me," Mac said. "If it weren't for her, I might not be here. Or anywhere."

Flo looked me over. "I see. So what are you doin' sneakin' in now?"

Before I could think of an answer, Mac spoke up. "She's my spy," he said.

"Covert activities, huh?"

"Something like that," Mac said.

Florence looked at me quite seriously. "I hope you made sure no one followed you."

"I was very careful." And I had been. My car was three blocks away and I'd cut through an alley for good measure.

"I heard about what happened at the hospital, and I'll tell you something flat out," Flo said. "I intend to see that this man gets well right here at Peaceful Rest. I won't truck with anybody tryin' to do him harm." She reminded me of a school principal giving the evil eye. After I nodded dumbly, she turned her focus from me to Mac. "And I'll tell you something else, too. You best not be havin' any more visitors without asking me first, because I don't know that I trust anyone. Half the people in this town could've shot you."

Mac sounded unconcerned. "There has to be a motive, a reason to want to harm me."

"Don't flatter yourself; you aren't that much of a joy to be around."

"You are one tough woman, Florence."

"That's right, and if you ever have any doubts about it, you just ask my no-count ex-brother-in-law. He won't be comin' around my sister's house again." She straightened the bed-covers as she said, "I'm real serious; I want you safe, Mac Donelly, and I intend to keep you that way. And by the way, you are not supposed to be makin' phone calls, so I'll just take this.'' With that she unplugged the telephone and snatched it up. Then she patted me on the arm. ''If you hear of anyone plannin' to harm Mac, you call me and I'll be waitin' for them with a shotgun. And I can use it, too.''

''I doubt that will happen, but if it does, you'll be the first to know.''

She left, clutching the phone to her side like a running back with a football. I turned to Mac. ''I just came to ask you a quick question.''

''I reckon I could answer one or two.''

''This is an easy one. Did you see a horse at the POW camp that night?''

''A horse? No, I sure didn't. Why? What do you know?''

''Oh, nothing really.''

''Jolie, Gordon Onstott should be down here any minute to investigate. If you know something, I expect you to tell him.''

I felt a flicker of disappointment, which I realized was childish. Along with it came relief that a real professional was taking over. ''Of course I will.''

Gordon Onstott was a Texas Ranger, a group known as the toughest law enforcement officers in the West. Legend has it that once a riot broke out, and the Rangers got a call to come stop it. They sent one man. One riot, one Ranger.

Now there are only a hundred and four Rangers to cover the entire state of Texas. Although they can legally investigate any crime, they primarily cover violations allegedly involving law enforcement people, or police shootings. Ours was exactly the type of situation that called for the Rangers' expertise and impartial judgment. Gordon would put both Ed and Wiley back in their places.

Except I'd heard no mention of the Texas Ranger coming to Purple Sage.

''When is he getting here?'' I asked.

''No idea,'' Mac said, resting his head back on the pillows. I'd tired him out again. ''Nobody is tellin' me a thing. Probably within the hour.''

So why wasn't I as confident of Gordon's imminent arrival

as Mac? Maybe because I didn't understand the chain of command in such situations. "Between Flo and Gordon it sounds like you're pretty well taken care of," I said.

Mac tried a smile, but it wasn't an enthusiastic effort. "I reckon you could go by my office and get the DPS lab report on the shooting. I'd at least like to know what they picked up on Vera's murder, and I suspect that Gordon ain't going to tell me much more than the rest of them have been."

"Actually, I could do that," I said.

He shook his head. "I was kidding. It's probably locked up tight in Deputy Presnell's office and you'd have to break in and steal it."

"I can do that, too."

"What?" He lifted his head from the pillow an inch or so to look at me more closely. Finally a real smile touched Mac's face. A satisfied smile. "Really? You'd do that?"

"I said I would."

He rested his head back. "You know, Jolie, if I don't hear from Gordon by this evening, I reckon you could help," he said, then turned to me. "You got any plans for this evening?"

"A cocktail party at the POW camp, but I can stop by afterward."

"I'll look forward to it."

SEVENTEEN

WHEN I GOT HOME I told myself that it was like getting ready for a date, a big date in high school when you were pretty sure the guy liked you, but you didn't know how much.

In truth, it didn't matter what I told myself because I knew I was lying. This was far more important than anything I'd done in my teens, and the consequences were more far-reaching. My stomach knew it, too; it was rumbling constantly with butterflies that had turned ugly.

Couples do fight and it can be healthy, but there is also a time to be a team, a unit that stands together against all comers. Matt and I should have been together when we told his parents about the Hammond house. And we should have stayed together during their visit, instead of going off in different directions. It was just that so much was happening with the Celebration, and Vera's murder, and that damn Cecily. I had spent much of the last twenty-four hours trying not to think about any of it, and I'd done pretty well. Now that I was focusing on the problem it really frightened me. What if Matt's withdrawal was based on more than just my social blunders? What if our relationship was in real trouble?

Most of my adult life had been spent looking for someone like Matt. He wasn't perfect, but he was a lot closer to it than I was, and he'd filled an empty space in my existence. He was also a crucial part of Jeremy's life. And Matt had never tried to disrupt the relationship between Jeremy and me, either. Instead he'd made a spot for himself so naturally that I couldn't help but wonder how we'd lived without him for so long.

As I stepped into the shower the warm water hit my body and I shivered.

My first marriage had ended disastrously. It had happened almost sixteen years before, when Jeremy had been just over a month old. Before that moment I had seen myself as a modern version of the *Madonna with Child,* rocking Jeremy, feeding him, absolutely glowing with love and happiness. I had envisioned the years ahead for all three of us—Jeremy, Steve, and myself—as an endless series of happy days with family picnics, trips to the mountains, and Christmases filled with sugar cookies and presents—a happily-ever-after life.

One night it had all changed, and that night remains vivid in my memory, perhaps because I've played it over so often. Steve had worked even later than usual, and while all the overtime had bothered me slightly, it hadn't added up sufficiently to crack my euphoric state. Then, a little after ten, Steve had come in the door of our tiny apartment; he hadn't greeted me with a kiss or even a hello. Instead, he had stood across the room saying words that at first I couldn't believe.

He was leaving. Parenthood wasn't for him and neither was I. There was someone new in his life. Her name was Candy; she was beautiful, she made him happy. She was fun. She was also waiting for him in our new car.

"Hey, I'm sorry, Jolie, but having a kid, being tied down like this, it just isn't for me, you know?"

In retrospect it was all so seventies, but however you labeled it, Steve's departure had ripped apart my cotton candy world, leaving me frightened in a way that I had never been before. For three days I stayed in the apartment, holding the tiny Jeremy, sometimes crying, sometimes expecting Steve to come back. When the rent was due and I didn't have the money to pay it, I'd had to call my parents. There was little discussion—they simply drove down from Dallas with a small truck, helped me pack, and moved me back with them. My father remained jovial the entire time, as if I were moving home at the end of a semester and it was the right and natural order of things. My mother had been filled with silent recrimination, as if it were all my fault. I certainly believed it was. If I'd been a better wife, smarter, prettier, a better cook, better in bed, Steve wouldn't have left. I didn't know what my specific sins were, but I was sure I'd committed them.

Afterward, there had been many nights when I had sat alone in the darkened living room of my parents' house, clutching a sofa pillow to my stomach, staring out at the black night sky. I'd probably recounted every minute of my life with Steve, looking for my flaws that had driven him away. Even though I was in the place where I'd grown up, those months were the loneliest I've ever known and Jeremy had become part of my isolation. After a while it became apparent to me that the major thing Steve had left behind was a belief I held about myself. That I was unlovable. Not only did my husband not love me, but no one else would either. Except for Jeremy, thank God.

It had taken a long time to move beyond that. Eventually I had let myself care about other men, men who were around. Some were probably much better people than Steve, and one or two were just as irresponsible and self-centered as he was.

But all that was a long time ago. Now, of course, I had the best in Matt and it was time I let him know that.

I finished my shower, washed and dried my hair, and avoided looking at my face until my hair was down and curled the way Matt likes it best. Makeup was easy: heavy on the mascara, light on the foundation and blush, and lips as sumptuous as they would get. I outlined them in a geranium color, and filled them in with pink.

Standing there in my best underwear, I wondered how many other women had set out to win their husbands back through seduction. I also wondered how many of them had succeeded, and if the odds were in my favor.

I hardly looked at the clothes in my closet, just reached in and chose the dress that Matt had pulled out the day of his parents' arrival. It did look like something out of the fifties, probably because the material was a print with geraniums and leaves. I stared at it critically for a minute and decided it would do fine for drapes. Maybe sheets.

And it didn't matter. It was off the shoulder, had a swirl of full skirt, and Matt loved it, which was really the only criterion I was interested in.

Finally, I slipped into some high heels, made some final adjustments to my hair, and grabbed my purse. As I stopped by the full-length mirror for one last look, I gave myself a smile and a high sign. I didn't look like Cecily. I never would, but the good news was that I looked pretty, in a friendly way. And I looked a lot more confident than I felt.

WHEN I PULLED UP to the camp the gravel parking area was filled with cars, and five or six more lined the side of the highway. It was just after seven-thirty and the cocktail party was a success if you based it on sheer attendance. We had actually worried that no one might show up.

I maneuvered my car into an empty space not far from the entrance, and got out, my high heels sinking into the dirt. The music drifted on the still evening air as I walked toward the camp. It was the big band sound of "String of Pearls" that wafted toward me, pulling me in. I couldn't wait to find Matt.

I had my plan worked out. I was going to make eye contact with him from across a crowded room, keeping a secretive and seductive smile on my face. And pray that he even noticed.

The large cement slab was covered with a tent from Jackson's Funeral Home. Not terribly festive, but very practical, especially since there was a big commercial fan at one end to keep the air circulating. Up front was a table where visitors were being given name tags by Liz Street. I stopped long enough to pick one up, then moved to the bar behind her, where I paid for a diet Coke. The music was louder now, coming from speakers at each end of the building. It certainly set a mood, the swaying rhythm seductively surrounding us all.

Eight long banquet tables gave people a place to sit. This seemed wise, since most of the attendees were in their seventies and probably not up to a long night of standing around in the heat. Nor was I. I could feel my cheeks beginning to turn pink, and my hair starting to droop. I scouted the area looking for Matt.

There were only ten or so people in the tent and I only recognized a few. Klaus Braune and Minna were deep in conversation with another couple I'd not met. Liz Street's dad, Harley, and his new wife were there, picking their way through the hors d'oeuvres. I also spotted Bill Tieman, but there was no sign of my husband. I hadn't noticed his truck parked on the highway, but then I hadn't really looked. I didn't go look since it could be quite some distance away.

I turned toward the small headquarters building. I could only assume that Matt would be inside where it was cooler. It seemed most of the other guests thought it would be cooler inside, too. I could barely get through the door, and then it took a lot of smiling, nudging, and just plain elbowing to get across the room. After several minutes of slow progress through the press of bodies, I found myself near the visitors' book. I scanned the page quickly, and besides the names of the few people I'd recognized outside, I didn't seem to know a single one. And there was no Matt Wyatt.

After I scribbled my name, I flipped back to the first page, glancing at the entries as I went. An international crowd had gathered at the site of the old POW camp. I saw two entries from Friedlehausen, Germany, another from Amsterdam, one from Dallas, and one from Cairo. Someone had come in from New York, and another from Beirut. Finally I spotted Matt's name, so I knew he was there.

Next to me several men were enjoying the wall of pictures, pointing and exclaiming. There was conversation in at least three languages swirling through the tiny building, which the window air-conditioning unit wasn't quite cooling.

The music had shifted now to "In the Mood," and it added a frenetic energy to the crowd. People were snapping their fingers to the beat, smiling, talking faster. This made it even more difficult for me to get back to the office of the small museum. When I got there, I didn't see Matt, but I did find Diane. In the midst of the chaos she was calmly refilling vegetable trays. Somehow she managed it with the grace of royalty.

I edged in her direction, and when she spotted me she smiled. "Hey, Jolie. Welcome."

"Have you seen Matt?" I asked.

Her eyes took in my dress and high heels, both appropriate for the occasion, if slightly more sweet than my usual style. She smiled and went back to her vegetables. "Well, Matt *was* here, but you just missed him."

She'd seen the effort I'd made to impress Matt.

"Let me guess. Cecily kidnapped him and they're on their way to the Casbah."

"No," Diane said, adding a swirl of carrots to the tray. "His cellular phone rang and it was Edith and Will. They were on their way back from Mason when they had car trouble; Matt went to see if he could help. Or at least bring them home."

"And Cecily is with Edith and Will."

"He didn't say anything about her," Diane said. "Anyway, if she is, then Howard is there, too."

"The charming, but ineffectual, Mr. Bremerton."

Diane took my arm and pulled me back from the crowd so no one else could hear us. "Jolie, what's wrong? Is there something going on that you haven't told me about?"

I glanced around. Everyone seemed far enough away that they couldn't hear our conversation. I said, "Unfortunately, there is. My entire family is in love with Cecily."

Diane shook my arm lightly. "Oh, right."

"But it's true. She calls Edith Mumsie, and Edith loves it. And I can't get Edith to come to dinner, or smile at me, or anything, and she's my mother-in-law. Then there's Will. He and Cecily spend most of their time teasing each other like junior high kids."

"They've always had that kind of relationship."

"Yeah, well, try being the odd man out. And that's exactly how it feels." I picked up a carrot stick and put it in my mouth. I had quit smoking years before, and didn't normally even think of cigarettes when I was under stress, but for some reason this time I wanted one. "And Matt is hardly talking at all, at least not to me. Just to the rest of the Wyatts."

Diane's brown eyes began to reflect concern. "You two had a fight?"

"He fought; I just stood there and felt stupid."

"Oh, dear. What about?"

With all the people moving around us, I told the story in bits and pieces, never quite making a whole. It made my worries a little less real because I couldn't focus on them.

Neither could Diane. "Jolie, don't let this upset you. You know Matt gets this way. He always has." She studied me to see how her advice was registering. "And it doesn't mean he loves you any less."

"On some level I think I know that."

"That's a start. The timing is just off right now, what with all the things Matt has on his plate. The Celebration and all. And maybe he's dealing with his own issues."

"Issues," I said with a brittle smile. "You sound like Dr. Laura on the radio."

"Who makes very good sense, and so do I. Just give Matt a little time."

"Jeremy is even wearing clean T-shirts when Cecily is around. Maybe we should give her a self-help book for Christmas. You know, 'Women Who Are too Perfect and the Men who Love Them.'" I heard the hitch in my voice and it gave away how much I really cared about all of this.

Diane slid an arm around me. "Jolie, whatever Cecily is, or isn't, is no reflection on who you are. You are wonderful." Her dark brown eyes were on me, intensely so, as if she could will me to believe what she was saying. "You are loyal, beautiful, talented, and my friend. That alone should be enough to give you some self-confidence. I do not choose my friends lightly."

I nodded and Diane went on. "You usually have more self-confidence than this…. Maybe it's hormones."

"Now I'm menopausal?"

"Quick-witted, too." She paused, watching me. "Are you going to be okay?"

I took a deep breath and nodded. That was the one thing I could assure her of, and myself. No matter what happened in life, no matter how much I hurt, or regretted, I would always come out the other side. Maybe not happy, but I would always make it. "I'll be fine," I said.

"I knew that." Diane nodded. "I just wanted to make sure you did." She adjusted a few things on the tray, then looked back at me. "You know, this is really simple to fix; when everyone gets home, kiss up to Edith and Will. Better still, kiss up to Matt. In the meantime, let it go. Worrying won't help you or them, so do something useful. Go out there and mingle." She gestured toward the party and lowered her voice. "Eavesdrop. Whatever it takes; you might learn something valuable."

"I can't stay very long."

"You just got here."

"I know, but I have something to do for Mac Donelly."

"Oh?"

"He needs someone to pick up some things for him from the sheriff's office."

Diane's eyes narrowed. "That doesn't sound so important

that you can't put it off until after the party. I mean, if you're going to just wander in, gather a few things, and wander out.''

"Well…it might be a bit more complicated than that. Oh, and Mac told me that Gordon Onstott is supposed to take over the investigation of the shooting and the murder. Have you heard anything about that?''

"No. Who was supposed to phone him?''

"Larry, Moe, or Curly. Mac didn't make the call.''

For a moment she looked pensive, then said, ''Maybe he's just been tied up with something.'' It made no sense and we both knew it. ''Maybe he's arriving tonight.''

"I hope so. In a few days the Celebration will be over and all these people will be gone! Doesn't anyone realize they have to get moving?''

"Get a grip,'' she said, looking out toward the guests, smiling blandly as if we were discussing computer paper. She reached down and handed me the tray. ''Take this outside and talk to some of these people. Maybe you can learn something important. It will save Gordon some time when he does show up.''

"If he shows up.''

"And if you need me tonight, let me know,'' she said. ''I should be finished here around eleven-thirty.''

"I hope I'm home by then, but in case I get thrown in jail or anything, it's nice to know that someone cares enough to bail me out.''

"Jail? Ah-ha, I thought your little midnight foray sounded illicit.'' She glanced around. ''Seriously, if I can help…I do have some experience.'' She cocked her head.

"I've heard that,'' I said. There was one more thing I had to know. ''Matt didn't mention when he'd be back, did he?''

She looked at her watch. ''No, but figure at least an hour there, a half hour to mess with the car, depending on how easy it is to fix—or how macho-stubborn he's feeling—and an hour back. Then he has to drop everyone off at the Hammond place. I'd say ten at the earliest, but I bet it's more like ten-thirty or eleven.''

More hours to wait. Too many hours, but it wasn't Diane's

fault. I tried to sound as if it didn't matter. "Thanks," I said with a wave. Then I made my way toward the door through the crowd of strangers, moving to the rhythm of a Glenn Miller hit.

EIGHTEEN

"MORE VEGETABLES? You girls got any desserts hidden away?" The speaker was none other than Harley Tandy, Liz Street's father. I set down my tray carefully on the table, but before I could respond, the woman beside him reached over and took his hand.

"Harley, you have diabetes, remember? Dr. Baxter said you're to stay off sweets until we get your blood sugar under control." She rolled her eyes, then looked at me. "Good evening, Jolie. It's nice to see you. Seems like Diane got things going in the right direction out here at the camp, not that I ever doubted she would."

"Marge. Hi."

Marge was Harley's new wife. They hadn't been married more than a year, and I remember Liz's great relief when her father announced their matrimonial plans.

"Thank God," she'd said dramatically at a Tuesday night meeting of our writers' group. We'd all been gathered around the antique table in the old jail, which now serves as a museum.

"Were you worried they'd live in sin and embarrass you?" Diane had asked.

Liz, for once, had very practical reasons for her reactions. "I don't personally care if they have sex on the square at noon. I'm concerned about my father getting old and not having someone there for him. He won't be alone now, which leads me to believe he'll be happier, and will probably eat better. It relieves me of a great deal of worry, so I can expend my energy on my own life.''

As I looked at Marge, I realized this was only the second or third time I'd actually spoken to her, although I'd seen her around town. From what Liz had said, Marge had grown up in Purple Sage, but had lived in Conroe most of her adult life. She'd only moved back to town after a cousin of Harley's introduced them and they began to date seriously.

''Men are sometimes worse than babies,'' she was saying to me as her husband continued to pick around the cheese tray.

''Easy for you to talk that way,'' Harley responded. ''Besides, if you're not careful, I'll have to stay away from you, because you're the sweetest thing I ever did see.'' He pinched her on the bottom and she let out a giggle.

''You naughty boy!''

Marge Tandy was a fairly large woman, about five-eight, attractive, with a flair for dressing that was eye-catching. It was nothing like Liz's, with her bizarre outfits; Marge had a more conventional, yet artistic, look. This evening she had on a long, beautifully patterned Indian matchstick skirt in shades of green, brown and ochre, with a green scoop-necked blouse. Her dangling earrings were made of matching beads and brass monkeys that glinted when they caught the sunlight. A tortoiseshell comb pulled back one side of her curly gray hair.

I felt like a voyeur watching their play, and I looked around quickly to see if there was anyone else I knew. Liz was still at the front table, Bill Tieman was talking to a group I didn't recognize, and Minna and Klaus were just entering the museum.

''Don't mind us, Jolie,'' Marge said, lightly touching my arm. ''He used to be the sexiest thing in seven counties and he thinks he still is.''

''I am.'' The lazy, seductive smirk he flashed at her echoed the one he'd worn in the picture Diane and I had oohed and aahed over the day before. It was nice to know that even the long years between now and then had left something untouched.

''Ignore him, Jolie,'' Marge said. ''Come and sit down with

us. Very smart of Diane to get a tent. And a fan.'' She chose
a spot just a few feet away and Harley sat -on her left. She
indicated a chair for me on the other side of her.

The music shifted again. Marge began swinging her foot
with the music as "Don't Sit under the Apple Tree" began.
A faraway look touched her face, making it softer and gentler.
"Camp Seybold has been part of my life almost since I can
remember," she said, then smiled at me. "Did you know that
Harley's family and mine were neighbors when we were kids?
And Harley helped build the camp?"

"Helped tear it down when they auctioned off the buildings
after the war, too," he added. "That was in nineteen and forty-
seven. Didn't take them long after the war was over to move
on. I was living in town back then."

I asked Marge, "What was your involvement with the
camp?"

"Mostly proximity. I lived right across the road from the
back gate. Boy, did my daddy hate that." She laughed. "I was
only thirteen, and believe it or not, just a little bit of a thing.
That was before I got my height, but my sister was seventeen
and my daddy was just sure that all those men were going to
storm the house and compromise us. We were forbidden even
to look at the place." She gave me a coy smile.

"But you did," I guessed.

"What daddy wanted us girls to do, and what we did, were
usually two different things! It was like forbidden fruit, and
you know how kids are when you tell them no. At first I used
to ride my bicycle down the road and get just as close to the
fence as I could. Then if one of the men said anything to me
I'd pedal ninety-to-nothing to get away from there!" She
laughed again. "That was the most fun game we had, living
so far out of town."

Harley leaned around his wife to say, "What Marge isn't
telling you is that when she turned sixteen she worked for the
government and became a translator at the camp."

Marge put down her empty plate and wiped her hands with
her napkin. They were pretty hands, big, like Marge, with
peach-colored polish on her longish nails, and four or five

exotic rings on her fingers. "We'd had a German neighbor who used to baby-sit us when I was little, so I grew up speaking the language. The job was a natural for me."

"And they needed her," Harley added. "I remember sittin' in the cafe in town with my daddy, listenin' to the guards complain about how the POWs were always playing tricks on them because they didn't speak German. They'd switch identities and do each other's chores, pulling stunts like kids in school. But Marge caught 'em out." To me he added, "Marge can do most anything."

Marge winked. "I've got him well trained, don't you think?"

I laughed with her, but my mind was on figuring out where exactly she'd lived, and where the Tandys had lived. If Marge's home had been across the road from the back of the camp, then the property the Tandys owned now must have been *part* of the camp.

When I asked Harley if that was correct, he nodded. "After the war the government auctioned off 'most every piece of tin and board, then they sold off the land. I bought a big chunk of it because it attached to our home place. They kept back this portion"—he indicated the ground we were on, along with the tiny headquarters building—"but they never did anything with it."

"Which is why Liz could tell us about the camp," I said, finally understanding how she'd been able to give Howard and me a tour of Camp John Seybold.

"She grew up playing all around here." Although this expansive gesture pointed toward the back of the tent where the fan was, I knew he meant beyond that. He was speaking of the rough pasture land behind us with the tiny path where Diane had found hoofprints.

"Some kids have an imaginary friend, but Elizabeth, she had thousands. She used to have colonels in for tea at her playhouse, and she'd march the soldiers up and down, shouting commands." Harley shook his head, smiling as the memory took hold of him.

"And now you have Das Keller Haus?" I asked. "The new bed-and-breakfast?"

"That was Marge's doing," Harley said. "It was supposed to be little, just one bedroom we let out. Something we could keep up with easily that would bring in a little cash for our retirement. Now, though, we're up to two bedrooms, and two more to go, so there's plenty to do to keep me out of trouble. No rest for the wicked."

I smiled, then Marge asked in a somber tone, "Have you heard any more on Vera's murder? Have they caught whoever did it?"

"Not yet," I said. Since I've been with K-SAGE people often ask me questions about the goings-on in Purple Sage. Most of the time, unless they haven't heard the latest newscast, I don't know any more than they do. Sometimes, when someone's been hanging out at the Sage Cafe, they're even ahead of me. "The sheriff's office hasn't released much information yet," I said, feeling apologetic because I couldn't help.

Harley said slowly, "We knew Vera some. Not much."

"We were so busy getting the B-and-B ready in time for the Celebration that Harley and I didn't do much socializing." Marge spoke quickly, and I detected a note of guilt, the kind we all feel when someone dies and we haven't spent as much time with them as we think we should have. "I meant to get together with Vera, I really did. You know how that is, though; we talked once or twice on the phone, but we were just so busy. It's so tragic. You just don't think of things like that happening in Purple Sage."

I made some soothing remarks. Marge nodded, but she didn't appear to be listening to me. She seemed to be back into the music and following her own train of thought. When she saw me watching her, she said, "I'm sorry, this whole place is so full of memories. I was thinking about Vera and her German soldier."

I quickened at that. Was this the old boyfriend IdaMae had mentioned? The one Vera had planned to meet? "Did you know him?" I asked.

"His name was Nicholas something. I can't remember back

that far, but the first name stuck because it was the same as the Russian czar. Nicholas was young and very handsome. A second lieutenant from the Afrika Corps—now, isn't that a strange thing to recall?" She shook her head and added, "And I remember how Vera described him too. 'Eyes like the moons of Saturn and a smile that could melt the snows of the Alps.' I was pretty romantic back then, so I thought her description was pure poetry."

Harley snorted and shook his head, but Marge only smiled.

"That is poetic," I said. Nicholas had all the qualifications to be Vera's officer and gentleman. "What was he like?"

"I didn't really know him well," Marge went on. "I don't imagine anyone did except Vera. He was kind of a loner; he didn't go out on the work parties that went to the farms or anything like that, although he had his own garden here at the camp."

When I feigned surprise she told me that officers lived very differently from the men. They were allowed to keep their enlisted valets and they were paid a salary, an extravagant one by Marge's standards. "I think he made more than I did, although he never volunteered to help with anything. It was a shame because he spoke perfect English. Read it, too. Vera would bring him books by the sackload. I kidded her about spraining her back from lugging so many library books all the way out to the camp, but Vera didn't mind a bit. She was crazy about that boy. She was just sure that when the war was over he wouldn't be gone but a minute and then he'd be back here to marry her." Marge sighed. "He died the night before they closed the camp. There was that flu going around, remember? Half the men were sick, and I guess that's what got him. Is that what he died of, Harley?"

Harley was a few feet away, at the food table again, busy poking around in the recently replenished trays of hors d'oeuvres. "I don't know for sure," he said, only briefly glancing at her. "It was real fast, and they buried him while they were closing the camp. Put a sad end on the whole thing, I always thought."

"Yes, it did," Marge said, in perfect agreement with her

husband. "And we were all so busy trying to get things packed and sent off, and shut down. What a time that was. And then Nicholas dies."

"That is sad," I said. I was remembering IdaMae's story about Vera's lost love. But if he died, why was Vera so happy before the Celebration, talking as if she were going to see him again?

"Well," Marge said, shrugging her shoulders, "he couldn't have come back here after the war, anyway. They wouldn't have let him, you know."

"Oh. Why is that?"

"He was a Nazi."

IT WAS JUST AFTER nine-thirty when I parked my car on a side street and started toward the darkened courthouse. The swishing of my full skirt made me feel as if I were wearing a costume, and a very heavy one at that. Nevertheless, the trickle of sweat that rolled down between my breasts had nothing to do with the bulk of my clothes or the air temperature.

All the Celebration events were taking place in other locations, so here the streets were virtually empty. Out of habit, or more likely nerves, I looked both ways at the dimly lit and barren street that circled the square. When I realized how foolish that was, I hurried across it. The asphalt was still sticky from the long, hot afternoon, making my high heels silent when they hit the pavement. On the sidewalk that bordered the courthouse, it was a different story; my heels seemed to clatter mightily, so as quickly as I could I slipped off into the grass, and ended up tiptoeing to the building to keep my thin heels out of the dirt.

It makes me crazy when the heroine of a movie heads into the house where the bad guys are lurking. Especially when she's in a tight skirt and high heels, or some similar outfit. Those are simply inappropriate for midnight forays into dangerous places. And why is it that it's always dark when she decides to make her move, and she never thinks to carry a weapon? I find myself, probably along with everyone else, mentally screaming, "Don't go in the house!"

So there I was, just like the heroine in one of those silly movies, in a dress with petticoats that was totally inappropriate, wearing high heels, heading for the dark courthouse. And I didn't have a weapon of any kind. Not even my pepper spray.

I told myself there was no comparison, because I was armed with the sheriff's keys in one hand, and directions from the sheriff himself in the other. But what if Wiley Pierce caught me prowling through the courthouse? Worse, what if Ed Presnell himself caught me? Neither one would hesitate to put me in jail for the night, after a booking procedure, which I'm told is both unpleasant and demoralizing. Then by tomorrow morning my name would be on the news. At the Sage Cafe they'd be talking about me and what a despicable person I was for stealing things from law-abiding sheriff's deputies. Wouldn't that be a pleasant thing for Edith and Will to hear over coffee?

I gave myself a mental pinch. I wasn't really breaking and entering a law enforcement office after hours, even if it did feel like it. Besides, no one was going to see me. All calls switched over to a central dispatching unit at the police station after eight o'clock. At night the sheriff's deputies worked out of a tiny office at the PD; it saved the taxpayers money on both personnel and utilities because the courthouse was virtually empty. Someday, when the commissioner's court had sufficient funds, or as IdaMae said, guts, they would build an addition to the police station and the Sheriff's Department would become a full-time resident. In the meantime this arrangement meant I had the courthouse to myself until shortly before 5 a.m. I could look around at my leisure, get what Mac needed, and get out without anyone being aware of what I'd done.

To further assure I wouldn't be seen, Mac and I had decided that even though my errand was legitimate, I wouldn't turn on any lights. There would be sufficient illumination from outside streetlights to help me find what I needed.

Simple. Except that a hoot owl from one of the many pecan trees chose that moment to fly into the night sky, and I jumped a good foot off the ground. I was mentally screaming at myself, "Don't go in the building!"

Yes, well, I was going into that building, regardless.

At the front, it was a simple matter to get the keys from my pocket and slip inside. The door closed with the gentlest movement I could manage, and still, in the silence, the latch clicking into the lock sounded like an explosion. I waited to see if there would be some answering sounds. Footsteps, someone yelling at me, gunshots, whatever. There were none except the creaks and groans of an old building. I took a relieved breath and discovered that the courthouse's usual musty smell was cloying on this dark night.

From there I headed up the staircase. That caused some even louder groans like an old man's complaints as the wooden steps bowed with my weight. I tried staying on the sides of each board, but it didn't help. I took the last several steps at a run, then paused again at the landing, this time to let my eyes adjust.

A small window let in the dim illumination of the distant streetlights and after a moment I could see well enough to maneuver. I went toward the sheriff's office. The old wooden door had a very solid, new dead-bolt lock. Mac had been very specific about which key would serve to open what, and it didn't take me long to hear the click that burglars must find very satisfying. Just as quickly I had the door open; I whisked through but didn't close it—I wanted a getaway path if necessary.

Here it was even darker, but I couldn't miss the old wooden counter. Mac had reminded me about the old-fashioned slide lock that held the wooden gate at the side. I located it, then stepped back into the inner chamber.

Wiley Pierce and Ed Presnell shared a desk in the office that was farthest to my right. Deputy Linc Draper also had a desk in there. As I walked toward the office, even the floorboards were creaking. Their door was wood and still had the original, old-fashioned lock that could only be operated with a skeleton key. Mac had said the key had been lost years before, so the door wouldn't be a problem. He was right—it simply opened when I turned the knob.

Like a swimmer about to take a plunge, I sucked in a huge breath, then slid into the office.

NINETEEN

IT WAS brighter here, mustier, and the two desks were cramped together along with two old filing cabinets. A new computer sat on one of the desks, which I assumed was Linc's, while the other was practically barren. There was only a phone, a lamp, a black plastic in-basket, and a calendar desk blotter. Casually I peered at the calendar, as if someone might see me and accuse me of snooping. Very coy. There were smudges and doodles on the top page of the blotter, but nothing of any significance written there.

Next I tried the center drawer and discovered that it was locked. Mac had anticipated that, too, and so, following his instructions, I slid my hand under the drawer and along both sides of the kneehole. There I found a key taped to the wood. It unlocked the desk, just as promised, so I could begin my search.

By this time my senses were heightened. I could hear every car that passed the courthouse and even imagined that I could hear the conversations taking place inside them. When I thought I heard a car stop and its door slam I almost broke my neck tripping over the desk chair to get to the window.

Below me was a surrealistic scene in shades of blues and blacks with layers of shadows, and even darker shadows. A car made its way slowly around the square, the headlights a muted yellow that flowed from one building front to the next. Through the foliage of the pecan trees I could barely make out the window of Henshaw's Hardware Store across the street. Nothing seemed unusual, nothing frightening.

With my willpower in high gear I turned back to Ed and Wiley's desk and began searching diligently. It's surprising what accumulates in desk drawers, and this desk was no exception. Besides the usual supplies I also discovered a playbill from a community theater in San Angelo. It was dated two years before. I found Wiley's checkbook and learned that he was careful with his money and regularly made deposits to a savings account. Small ones, but steady. There was even a wrinkled *Hustler* magazine buried under several file folders; I was careful not to touch it. And while Mac had been very detailed in his description of the report from the DPS lab, I didn't find anything like that.

After the desk, I went through the file cabinets. There was absolutely nothing on the shooting at the POW camp. I didn't find the report, a file, or even one scrap of paper that mentioned the incident.

So, what next? I straightened up and thought about that. Linc's desk was also in the room, but I couldn't see Ed stashing information in it. Linc was older, gruff, and didn't seem the type to put up with any nonsense. Yes, he was in a Waco hospital, but even the slimmest chance of his reappearing would be a deterrent. Then I decided that Linc's desk might be the perfect temporary place for Gordon Onstott to rest his Rangers hat. I opened the top drawer and several others. Squeaky neat and clean with no sign of any new presence. Interesting.

Ed could have taken the file home with him, or kept it with him on patrol; if he had, then Mac was out of luck. Or he could have given it to Gordon Onstott, but so far, I seriously doubted that Gordon had arrived. I glanced at my watch. I hadn't planned on spending this much time, but I was getting stubborn. I decided to try the dispatch area. As soon as I was outside the office I heard something. A creak, or soft footsteps that melted into a quiet shuffle. I quit moving—almost quit breathing.

It wasn't a cleaning crew coming, because they would turn on lights and make noise. This sounded like someone afraid to walk openly in the hall. I knew it wasn't Mac because he was at the rest home waiting for me. Which is why I decided to hide in his office.

I whipped across the floor in a soundless glide and grabbed the old metal doorknob. It opened easily. For another second I paused, listening as hard as I could, but I was farther away now, and from here I couldn't detect even a rustling in the outer building. No matter; I pushed open the door and closed it tight as soon as I was inside. The large, old-fashioned desk faced me, the three windows behind it letting in enough light to put everything in silhouette. I whirled around. Behind me were two metal file cabinets and a hat rack, but no hiding places. On my right were three low bookcases, and a couple of boxes on the floor that I would have to avoid. Mac's chair was a new executive style and it was pushed tightly into the kneehole of the desk.

That was my spot.

As gently and carefully as I could, I repositioned the chair so I could crawl in front of it. The desk would hide me from whoever was out there.

By now the blood pounding in my head was distorting even normal sounds. A car on the street below sounded like a bellowing train. My own breathing vibrated raucously like an asthmatic's. When my head touched the drawer above me, the wood slammed into the metal slides like a rumble of thunder. But no definable sounds came from the outer office.

I waited.

After an excruciatingly painful passage of time, I crept out from under the desk. I didn't rise at first, just waited, breathing fresher air while my cramped legs began to tingle. More minutes passed, and still I didn't hear any other sounds. I rose slowly, the blood prickling as it coursed through my stiff limbs. When I was upright I waited again, but there was nothing.

My aching body screamed for release; either I had to move normally or I had to sit down and relax. I glanced at the chair. On the seat were some folders, and I reached for them. The label said: MEECE-DONELLY SHOOTING.

I had actually found what I came for. I couldn't help smiling. This detective work wasn't so tough—all you had to have was a little persistence.

Then the overhead light burst on and I was momentarily blinded.

The voice that broke the silence was equally shattering. "Don't move, don't talk, don't even breathe. I've got my gun on you and if you make one wrong move I will shoot. Do you understand?"

"Ed," I said, my mouth suddenly dry. "How nice to see you."

"Put the files down, then put your hands up, and come on out from behind the desk."

"You don't understand—this is just a mistake. I have a key, see? That's how I got in." I held it out to show him.

"Come out from behind the desk and move slowly."

He was still in the doorway, his booted feet spread and planted, his outstretched arms holding a gun. The gun was pointed at me.

I put the folders on the desk. "I wasn't stealing anything—I was just moving these. They were on the chair." I sidled around the corner of the desk and stopped. "Ed, this is all a mistake. If you'll just let me explain, you'll see—"

"Turn around and put your hands up. Now."

I put my hands up. "Ed, you're not listening. If you'd just give me a minute—"

"You ain't listening. I said turn around, and do it now."

I did as he said, but it was very uncomfortable turning my back on an obvious madman who was wielding a gun. "Look, I came here because Sheriff Donelly asked me to. I have his key. I have a note from him. I—" My words stopped as I was shoved forward and my hands were grabbed. "What in the—" He kicked my feet farther apart and shoved me down over the desk. I gasped, "You—damn it—get away from me!" My head hit the wood and suddenly my right arm was pulled back; a handcuff was clamped over it. "You can't do this."

"You are under arrest for breaking and entering." My left arm was pulled back and pinched into the cuff. "You have the right to remain silent. Anything you say can and will be used against you in a court of law. You have the right to call

an attorney and to have an attorney present during questioning...."

"Yes, and I have the right to sue you, and the county, and
I intend to do both!" He let go me of me and I jerked my
body up straight. "Mac Donelly sent me here. If you'd stop
and—"

"If you cannot afford an attorney one will be appointed for
you. Do you understand these rights as I have explained
them?"

"I understand that *you* are going to be looking for a job in
the very near future."

He turned me around so that I was facing him. He had
moved back a few feet and the gun was holstered but still very
available. "Do you understand your rights?"

"Of course I understand my rights." My forehead was
throbbing from its collision with the desk and I wanted to call
him foul names. I knew better, but I couldn't stop all my
anger. "Do you think I'm stupid? Do *you* understand that—"

"Now you can explain what it is you been babbling about."

I would have put even money on the outcome of a fight
between us. Despite the fact that Ed Presnell was a good eight
inches taller than me and at least seventy pounds heavier, all
that would have been negated by my fury. It was only the
handcuffs, and maybe some last shred of good sense, that
stopped me from butting him with my head and stomping him
into a quivering pulp.

With a pretense of calm and civility I took a deep breath
and said, "Deputy Presnell, I am Jolie Wyatt. I work for K-
SAGE Radio. I know you know who I am." He actually responded to my words, even if it was with just the tiniest nod
of his head. "Good," I went on. "Now, I talked with Mac
Donelly earlier today. He said he needed some things from his
office and he sent me to get them. I have his key. Here it is."
But I couldn't bring my hands around to give it to Ed, so I
dropped the key on the desk behind me. I shifted over slightly
so he could see it. It was on a worn leather strap that Mac had
taken from his own key ring. "You see, that is Mac's."

"It looks like his. I seen it before."

"I thought you had." Finally. "I also have a note in my pocket. It's in my right-hand pocket, and it's from Mac. It gives me permission to come up here and get a report for him." I shifted my body slightly, sticking out my hip so that he could get the note.

Instead he backed farther away. "You need to get the note out," he instructed.

"Oh, right! Are you—" The look on his face stopped me.

Whatever he was, I wasn't in any position to question it. It was the last bit of evidence I needed to realize that the regular pattern of my life had been interrupted. An hour before I had been telling Mac to hurry so I could leave Peaceful Rest, get his report, and get back to the ranch to see my husband. My real focus had been on smoothing over the bump in my relationship with Matt. However, that had been shunted aside by the appearance of Deputy Presnell. If I wanted to get out of this bizarre detour in any reasonable period of time, I was going to have to be very cooperative and very rational. It wasn't going to be easy.

It took several minutes of twisting and grunting to get the note out of the pocket. When I did, it slipped from my fingers and fell on the floor. "There," I said. "That's the note he gave me."

"Pick it up and hand it to me."

I stared at Presnell in disbelief. His answering look, with one corner of his mouth lifted slightly, convinced me that he was not only serious, but that he was enjoying this very much. He was probably getting even for the news story we'd done about his arrest. I, personally, hadn't had anything to do with it; that had been Rory's story, and thank God he'd left out the name of the officer involved. If he hadn't Ed would probably have used his gun to pistol-whip me.

Fine. Let Ed have his little moment of fun. In ten minutes I'd be out of here, and then I would tell Mac about the behavior of his fine deputy. I would call Gordon Onstott myself. I would call the governor and anyone else I could think of. In the South they say that revenge is a dish best served up cold.

Perhaps this time I'd make an exception and serve it very hot. But I *was* going to get my revenge.

With an answering smile at Presnell I carefully bent down, turned, and reached for the note. Without the agility of a Russian dancer there was no way I was going to put my hands on it from that position. I suspected he wouldn't consider my kicking it to him the same as handing it. With every ounce of grace I could muster I went down until my knees were on the floor, sat back as far as I could, leaned around, and got the paper. Ha.

I stood up, turned, and handed it to him.

"Thank you," he said politely, as if I'd just passed him tea at a particularly charming party. He cleared his throat. "Now, I want you back up against the desk so I can read this."

The blood was again pulsing through my brain, but it wasn't due to fear. That's okay, I told myself, my time is coming. With freedom so close I did exactly what he ordered.

He read the note to himself, his lips moving so that I could follow every word. The note said:

To whom it may concern:
I have requested that Jolie Wyatt enter the courthouse in order to retrieve materials that I need. Those materials will include, but not be limited to, the DPS report on the shooting of Vera Meece and myself, MacDonald Donelly, at Camp John Seybold this past week. Mrs. Wyatt is also authorized to get any files that pertain to the case and bring them to me.
Signed,
MacDonald Donelly, Sheriff
Wilmot County, Texas.

Ed looked up at me. There was something odd about his expression, but I put it down to annoyance over his loss. He'd been wrong about me, and I'd proved it.

"Are them the files you had?" he asked, pointing to the ones I'd placed on the desk.

I nodded and said, "Yes. They are."

He moved to the desk and, without touching the folders, he read the labels. When he was finished he looked up at me. "You got exactly what the note says you was supposed to get."

"Yes, I did. Now can we end this? Unlock me and let me out of here." I had considered asking for an apology, but decided that wasn't a wise move until I was actually out the door, or better still, safe in my own car. I turned around and held out my handcuffed wrists to Ed. "And I'm late, so if you'd hurry…"

"Well, seems we got us a problem." I'd heard Mac say exactly the same thing a dozen times before. Usually it had to do with a story I was writing, and he wanted me to reword some part of it. We'd always negotiate and there was never much of a problem at all. Those same words coming out of Ed's mouth seemed a much bigger obstacle. I tried to make light of it, probably for my own benefit.

"Let me guess," I said. "You forgot the key."

"A bit worse 'n' that." He waited until I'd turned to face him before he said, "You see, while this note is signed with the sheriff's name, it don't look like his handwriting to me. Now see, here on his calendar"—he moved to the desk and pointed without touching—"I know for a fact that Sheriff Donelly wrote that cuz I was standing right here when he did. But the writin' on this note don't look the same."

I leaned over. The note was a reminder to call Burl Johnson at the Texas State Law Enforcement Agency, and it had a number. Admittedly the handwritings weren't much alike. The note on the calendar was penned with a thick black ink and the strokes were firm, with a slight left-hand slant. The note in Ed Presnell's hand was written while Mac was lying on his stomach, and the cursive scrawl was lighter, and sloppier.

"Mac had been shot when he wrote the note he gave me. He wasn't feeling well."

"Yes, ma'am, or someone else coulda written it. Like you, maybe."

"I didn't write that.…" I slowed down. I was winning, even

if it didn't feel like it. With exaggerated calm, I said, "Mac wrote the note today. When he gave me the keys. The keys are the proof, remember? You recognized them."

He nodded, the prissy little grin still in place. "Proof you seen the sheriff, but not of anythin' else. 'Sides, I believe that you seen him. Sometime. Maybe a couple of nights ago. You coulda forced him to write the note after you shot him. Coulda been when you took the keys, too."

"What? Are you crazy? I didn't shoot anyone! And if I did, why would I be so stupid as to come back here and get those ridiculous files?"

Ed grew somber. "Those files got my reports. They point a finger at your husband, but maybe I was pointin' at the wrong Wyatt."

TWENTY

ED MARCHED ME out of the courthouse, down the stairs, and out onto the street. I walked the short distance to the police station with my hands cuffed behind my back. A few cars passed us, but it was too dark to see who was in them. They got a very clear view of me. And of Ed, who had his gun out and pointed at me the entire time.

He took me through a back door of the police station, into an area I'd rarely been in. It all seemed suddenly foreign, as if he'd walked me through some door into a different city. It made me nervous, seeing what seemed like the dark side of the police department.

Ed left me in a temporary holding cell while he made a few phone calls. I asked repeatedly for the same courtesy but he ignored me; he didn't even bother to act as if I'd spoken. After he was off the phone he led me out. He was whistling. He kept it up the entire time he removed the handcuffs, finger-printed me with an old-fashioned black ink pad, and took my picture. By that time we had company. Trina Elson, the morning dispatcher, had arrived to finish the process of putting me in jail. Having been called away from her home, or cave, or tree, or whatever place she roosts in, she was even more sullen than usual. I clung to the fact that Mac had said Trina had brains.

"Trina, look, you know me," I began. "I'm not a criminal. This is a stupid move on the part of Ed Presnell, and we all know he isn't bright." I could say those things because he was gone. "You know this is a mistake."

Trina snapped on a pair of rubber gloves.

"Come on," I said, holding my voice at a calm level. "Just let me make a call and let me get out of here, okay? I'll phone Mac and he can explain the whole thing—"

"Please take off your shoes and hand them to me, one at a time."

"Trina. Just listen. I don't know what Ed wrote on the report, but I had a note from Sheriff Donelly. Mac sent me to the courthouse. This is a false arrest. I could sue the county for—"

"Please take off your shoes and hand them to me, one at a time. Do not kick them, throw them, or attempt to come any closer to me."

We were locked in a barren six-by-six room and I had no desire to get any closer. I took off my right high heel and handed it to her. I reminded myself her gruffness was not directed at me personally, merely at mankind in general and I was the closest. She took the shoe without a word, gave it a cursory glance, then grasped it firmly in both hands and twisted it. I could hear the spine break.

"Why in the world did you do that?" I demanded. "You just ruined my shoes!"

"Please hand me your other shoe. Do not kick it, throw it, or attempt to come any closer to me."

"Oh, right. So you can trash that one too?" When she remained in silent, unyielding rudeness I handed over the shoe, which she proceeded to destroy, then place neatly beside the other one. "Why are you doing this?" I asked again. "Wanton destruction of property doesn't seem very politically correct to me."

"You could be carrying contraband. Needles. Heroin." She looked at me. "Not that it's any of your business. Now, take off your panty hose. Turn them inside out and hand them to me. Do not kick them, throw them, or attempt to come any closer to me."

I pulled them off under my skirt, and despite the fact that it was obvious there was nothing in them, she eyed them carefully before giving them a well-muscled twist.

How could I have been so stupid as to go to the courthouse at night? I'd known that Ed was looking for an excuse to harass the Wyatts, and I'd handed him one. What could I possibly have been thinking, showing off like some headstrong teenager instead of a mature woman?

"Please hand me your belt. Don't drop it, throw it...."

I had the belt off and in her hands before she could finish. I just wanted all this over with. I wanted to go home, or if I couldn't have that, then I at least wanted to retain some dignity. I hated the sight of Trina manhandling my clothes with her rubber-gloved hands.

"Are you done?" I asked. "Can't you just put me in jail—"

"Hand me your dress...."

Inside I cringed, but nothing I could say would end this until I had done what she wanted. My anger mutated into humiliation. I struggled with the back zipper, considered asking for help, and decided against it. If I could get the damn thing on, I could get it off. Besides, I was in no hurry to stand before her in my underwear.

After some twisting and grunting I got the zipper down and the dress dropped to the floor.

"Please hand it to me. Don't kick it, throw it, or attempt to come any closer."

I stepped out of the dress and handed it to her. When she finished with it she demanded my bra. I withered both physically and psychologically. She pretended not to look at me as she ran the bra through her hands and finally placed it on the pile of my other clothes.

By that time I was prepared for any degradation, but she allowed me to keep my panties on, probably because it was apparent there was no contraband inside them. She did have me hold out my arms and turn around while she eyed my entire body critically. Next I had to stand like a stork, first on one leg, then the other, so she could check the bottoms of my feet.

She told me to kneel. I did so; she stepped close to me and I ducked, expecting her to hit me. Instead she ran her hands through my hair, then quickly pulled off the gloves, as though even they had been soiled.

I was thoroughly demeaned and demoralized. My only response was gratitude when she handed me a large orange jumpsuit with the words WILMOT COUNTY JAIL stenciled on the back. I put it on, zipping the front quickly. Next came a pair of spongy, orange-brown, throwaway slippers. They were too big, and as I looked down at the ridiculous things I discovered that tears had gathered in my eyes and were starting to fall on the slippers. I sniffed as hard as I could and tilted my face up to the ceiling, my eyes closed. Trina may have thought I was praying, and maybe I was.

"You want to call someone?" she asked.

My head came down and my eyes flew open. I stared at her in shock. I still had some rights, slim though they were.

"Yes. I certainly do. I do want to make a phone call."

"This way." She led me out the door and into the next room. Anyone could see me standing there in my jail suit, including two tourists who'd apparently lost something, from the bits of their conversation I overheard. They gave me accusatory stares. I didn't have the fight left to do anything more than turn away from them as I snatched up the phone and the phone book.

My first thought was to call the ranch, but I hesitated. What if there was no one there? Car trouble doesn't have time limits, and there was a possibility that I would just get the answering machine. It seemed much safer to get the sheriff's assistance, then I could phone Matt.

"I'm calling Mac," I told Trina. "He'll explain everything; you'll see."

I punched out the numbers so rapidly that the phone misdialed and I had to slow down the second time to get the call through. When I heard Florence's voice offer a sleepy "Peaceful Rest," I wanted to cry.

"Oh, thank God. Would you put the sheriff on the phone? I need to talk to him right away."

"Who is this? It's the middle of the night."

"It's me, Jolie Wyatt. They've arrested me. I'm in the jail."

"My Lord, Jolie! How in the world? No, don't you worry, I'll take care of it. Oh, but wait." She stopped completely and I was terrified that she'd hung up before I finally heard her voice again. This time it was hesitant, probing. "Jolie, are you there?"

"Yes, of course."

"You say they have arrested you?"

"Yes. Ed Presnell arrested me, and now Trina is here. I've been handcuffed, and they're going to put me—"

"I see." Again there was a heart-stopping pause before she said, "I hear what you're tellin' me, and I understand." She cleared her throat, then said more loudly, "There's no one here by the last name of Sheriff, and I don't know why you're callin' this late, but you musta got the wrong number. I'm gettin' out my shotgun, too." And then she hung up.

I stared at the phone in disbelief. How could she have done that to me? Unless she thought I was talking in code, delivering some warning.

After a moment of mind-numbing silence I pressed down on the hook and closed my eyes. I was getting hit from too many sides by too many blows. I couldn't assimilate them. I couldn't even think.

Whatever Florence had assumed was irrelevant now. I needed someone who could get me out of here just as quickly as possible. I opened my eyes and began dialing the very familiar number of the ranch, but Trina stopped me.

"That's all, Miz Wyatt. You don't get any more calls."

"But I didn't get to talk to anyone."

"Please walk out the door." I had been allowed one call, I had made one call. Period. It was the way things were done because of the rules. "Start moving now. I will be right behind you. Don't stop until I tell you to, don't try to reach back and grab me...." She marched me down the hall.

My anger and frustration hit levels too high to calculate. It's good I didn't know martial arts, or I could have seriously hurt someone. Instead I decided to fight back with the only weapon I had. As I entered a small interrogation room and sat down on the hard wooden chair, I clamped my mouth shut. I knew a few rules myself and I decided to use them.

Ed Presnell returned and tried to question me. I said not one word. No attorney, no talkee.

My silence got me many disgusted looks, much exasperation, and finally a speech from Ed.

"I know that criminals got rights, too, Miz Wyatt, but I want you to know that you aren't helping yourself any!" He got up, swung his body around behind the chair, and gripped the back of it with white knuckles while he pinned me with his beady eyes. "This kind of behavior ain't proper. You need to tell me why you broke into the courthouse and what you were trying to steal. And you better do it now, you got that?" He glared at me; I looked at him quizzically, as if his words were in some foreign language. "Damn it!" he snapped. "The system would work a whole lot faster if you'd stop acting like some kind of smug Buddha and cooperate. It would save taxpayer money, and that's your money, too. Don't you understand nothin'? Speak up! What do you have to say for yourself?"

I have never wanted to flip someone off quite so much as I did Ed Presnell. It took great willpower, but I remained aloof. Raising one eyebrow, I shook my head. All without uttering a word.

"That's it, lady, you're goin' to a cell!"

That had been inevitable, and it was not a threat, but a relief. When we'd gone down two halls and turned a couple of corners, Ed stopped me while he opened a heavy metal door with a medium-sized, double-thick wire window. It reminded me of the backside of a security zoo exhibit. Once inside I learned that the Wilmot County Jail cells are built for two—at least the women's are—with two bunks, a sink, a toilet, a metal table that comes out of the wall, and a door that closes with a whoosh and a clang. Mattresses are provided, but you have to carry your own. When Ed handed mine to me, I took it the way Linus would take his blanket, hugging it to my body as if for protection. As soon as Ed closed and locked the door from the outside, I put the skinny pad on the farthest of the two empty bunks and stretched out. The mattress was uncomfortable, more like something for a pet to rest on than a human being, but I wasn't looking for comfort, merely a place to lay my head while I worried, and perhaps had a good cry.

I closed my eyes, took a few deep breaths, and surprised myself by drifting off to sleep.

SOMETIME DURING the night a man was put in a nearby cell, and even though the conversation between him and the police officer sounded amicable, their voices woke me. I sat up.

I knew exactly where I was, and I knew the voice outside my cell. "Andy?" I called out. It was Andy Sawyer, the assistant chief of police. I ran over to the door. "Andy? Is that you?"

As he moved into my line of sight I watched the expression on his handsome face show surprise. His dark eyes narrowed. "Jolie?" he said. "I always figured you'd get caught eventually."

"I haven't done anything. Ever," I said, and Andy gave me his slow grin.

This is a man who could haunt a woman's sexier dreams, and probably has. He's a little over six feet tall, has dark eyes and hair, and muscular shoulders that shift when he gets anxious.

Waking up in a jail cell suddenly didn't seem so horrific. "I haven't done anything wrong," I said again. This time my voice was without the shrill note that had been so obvious earlier. "Ed Presnell has gone berserk and is rounding up innocent citizens. He must have gotten lonely."

Andy laughed. "I don't have any idea why you're here, but I'd bet my paycheck that you're guilty of whatever it is."

I waved away his words. "I was in the courthouse after hours," I began, and went on to explain, without too many details, what had happened. "So you see," I finished up, "I really didn't do anything. I was simply on a mission for a friend."

"Jolie, has it ever occurred to you that you don't operate the way normal human beings do?"

Back when Matt and I had been separated, I had gotten the distinct impression that Andy was interested in dating me. A murder in Purple Sage and a few other technicalities, such as Matt himself, had put a stop to Andy's interest. Still, I always saw a spark of pleasure in his eyes whenever we ran into each other. Or maybe I invented that to bolster my own ego. I thought I saw that spark there now, and I had never needed it more.

"I'm not like normal people," I said. "I'm far from your average, ordinary, human being, but at the moment, I'm also stuck in a jail cell. I'd prefer to be home like the rest of the world."

"I'll bet you would."

"Andy, this is ridiculous and you know it. Just get me out of here, okay?"

His eyes searched the floor for a moment before he could look at me again. "I'd like to help, Jolie, I really would, but there's nothing I can do."

"Sure you can. You can open this damn door and let me loose."

"That sounds real simple, but there are laws and rules, and it's my job to uphold them. You know that."

"Ed Presnell is an idiot. I could sue him. I could sue the county."

"But I work for the *city*," he said, his muscular shoulders twitching uncomfortably. "The two don't mix, kind of like oil and water. There's no way I could step in and take over his arrest.''

''But it's wrong! Besides, the courthouse is within the city limits.''

''The courthouse is owned and maintained by the county; it's considered county property. Jolie, I'm real sorry, but even if I worked for the Sheriff's Department I couldn't do anything. If we see something that's out of line, unless it's life threatening to a civilian or another officer, all we can do is report it to someone higher up.''

''That creed of silence,'' I said bitterly. My earlier fears were returning, along with a tightness around my heart. I wanted to go home.

''It's nothing like that,'' Andy said. ''It's a creed to support your fellow officers, that's all. And it works.''

''Right.'' I had run up against it before, this wall of stone and righteousness that sometimes surrounded law enforcement people. They seemed to cut themselves off from the rest of humanity, some say because it would be too painful to get involved, but to me, an outsider, it sometimes made them bullies who put themselves above the rest of us and exercised their power in a most ruthless way.

I've discussed this with Mac before, and he claimed that only bad cops didn't listen, cops who bared their teeth like wild dogs and snapped at the people they had sworn to protect. Usually, too, you found it in law enforcement people who worked in large cities with a higher stress level. And a higher fear level. I wasn't sure I bought all of Mac's beliefs. There was a fine line and I'd seen it crossed even in small towns. I believe it comes with the job.

Andy was still watching me, then he shrugged. ''I'm real sorry,'' he said and started to turn away.

''Wait, Andy!'' I changed to a softer tone, not even caring if he heard the desperation I was feeling. ''Andy, I didn't get to make a call. Matt doesn't know where I am; he probably thinks I've been kidnapped or killed in a car wreck. Could you at least phone him and tell him where I am?''

Andy rubbed his hand along his jaw.

I couldn't seem to stop myself from pushing harder. "Several people saw me being walked across the square; you could call anonymously if you want. It wouldn't have to be official."

He shook his head. "No. I'll call, and I'll tell Matt it's me. But this is between the three of us. If anyone in the sheriff's office finds out, I'll deny I ever did it." The stone wall was still there, but at least he'd peered around it.

I nodded. "Thank you. I wouldn't admit it, either." Then I gave him the number and watched him walk away.

I was hoping very hard that Andy would call right away, and that Matt could do something to get me home.

TWENTY-ONE

IT'S A CLICHÉ that you have a lot of time to think in jail. Well, it's true. Maybe because the lights never seem to go away, nor do the sounds of people moving around just outside your line of vision.

The things I was learning.

I sat on the bunk, wishing I'd asked Andy what time it was. As if that were important, but it would have given me something solid to hold on to. I was so completely out of my element, and so completely without control over anything.

My entire life had gone haywire.

In the dim recesses of the cell, I found some distance from the events of the last few hours and even the last few days. I discovered that I no longer cared so much that Edith and Will didn't like the Hammond house. I was pretty sure they would come to like it, eventually. My bet was, now that they had it, they'd be in Purple Sage more often, and for longer periods of time. They could get back to the close relationship they'd had with Matt. And they could develop one with Jeremy. At least that was my opinion.

And maybe my opinion was nothing more than self-righteous justification. Another jailhouse truth.

Well, it was a situation I could do nothing about. They would decide in their own good time if the Hammond house would work for them. What I did have a bit of control over was my relationship with Matt. I intended to get that straightened out first thing. As soon as I was sprung from the slammer. I shook my head at my own inanity, but didn't rein in that bizarre portion of my mind that goes off on tangents. I might even get Cecily straightened out. The hard way. I could put her in a book, make her the evil ex-wife, and reveal her wretched soul. Not a bad idea. Being a mystery writer is so satisfying sometimes. You can do terrible things to people and never go to jail.

What irony—I *was* in jail.

I lay back on the pad, twitched around to get comfortable, and started thinking about murder. Not Cecily's; even on paper I wouldn't stoop to that, at least not now. No, I was thinking about the murder of Vera Meece, and it sobered me up. There is nothing amusing about real-life murder. The sheriff's being shot brought the crime closer to home for me. It also added an element of urgency because Mac wouldn't be safe until whoever had done the shooting was caught. Mac could be located by the murderer at any time, even at Peaceful Rest.

And I had called Peaceful Rest from the jail.

Oh, damn. Who'd been close enough to hear my conversation? Trina, for one. Those tourists, whoever they were. And who else? Had I said Florence's name? I went over the conversation in my mind, trying to remember each word. I decided that no, I hadn't used Flo's name. But the phone. Could someone hit the Redial and find out about Peaceful Rest that way? I let the phone call play back through my mind again. At the end Florence had hung up on me—and I had tried to call the ranch. I was sure I'd dialed two numbers, at least two, and that would cancel the redial.

For the moment, I hadn't endangered Mac, but his safety wasn't assured until the murderer was caught. And it followed as the night the day that Ed Presnell wasn't going to catch him. And where the hell was Gordon Onstott?

I quit worrying about that and focused on the murder. It was all the tangle of the camp and the war that added confusion. Vera had said an officer and a gentleman was coming to see her, and that had conjured up visions of someone who had been at the camp during the war. IdaMae's story about a long-lost love had clinched it. Probably Nicholas, but he was dead. If only we knew more about him.

I thought back. Vera could have been talking about a police officer just as easily. Like Bill Tieman. Or an American army officer. I hadn't seen any in Purple Sage during the Celebration, but that didn't mean there weren't any. Another possibility was someone who had been an American army officer during the war. There had been several of them running the camp.

Ideas were whizzing through my brain like quasars. Someone like Vera could have had dozens of old flames. And I was being sexist, because Vera could just as easily have been murdered by a woman. Maybe someone who felt Vera was after her husband. A vision of Marge Tandy popped up. Das Keller Haus was at the end of the little path. She could have done the killing; it didn't require premeditation. Say Vera was arguing with her murderer. The murderer reaches up, grabs the gun, loads it, and walks outside to shoot Vera. While Vera was doing what? Running away?

So where was that damn gun now?

Harley Tandy was just as close by physically, and for all I knew the man was some kind of an officer. Maybe in the National Guard. Or maybe it wasn't Vera's gentleman caller who had shot her. He could have been long gone by the time the killer showed up.

If only I had read the DPS report and whatever other information Ed Presnell had gathered. What lousy timing that just as I found the report, he'd found me. And what was his problem with the Wyatts, anyway? Was it his usual overzealous behavior or was there another reason?

I couldn't think of any past history that would justify Ed's dislike of the Wyatt family. Maybe he had his own agenda here and the Wyatts looked like handy scapegoats. If he was trying to get a fast promotion, he'd picked the wrong people to go after. I'd make sure of that.

My eyes didn't want to stay open and my body was heavy with exhaustion. I needed more sleep; tomorrow Diane and I could figure it out. I closed my eyes and let my brain slow its frenzied pace. Tomorrow would be soon enough. Maybe Matt would be willing to help; Matt was good at such things.

IN JAIL, room service doesn't knock.

That would make a great title, I thought, as I rolled over and stared at the grin of Wiley Pierce. He was carrying a tray in front of him, holding it out enticingly.

"Mornin', Miz Wyatt. I got your breakfast. Mary Maggie, over to the Sage Cafe, told me you liked your eggs scrambled, your bacon crisp, and your toast with butter on the side, so that's how I got it for you."

I momentarily considered my two-day diet and decided to hell with it. Since I was still in jail, I should be allowed some indulgences.

"Thanks, Wiley," I said, sitting up and running my fingers through my hair. I remembered just in time not to rub my eyes. I didn't need mascara all over my face. "My husband isn't here by any chance, is he?"

"No, ma'am, but he was here."

"He was? Where'd he go? Why didn't you tell me?"

"Miz Wyatt, this is a jail," he said with precise pronunciation. Like I hadn't figured that out. "Your husband's out finding Ellis Kramer, and then he said he's goin' to go wake up some judge. I expect it will be Judge Patterson, and I don't figure he's going to like it much." He put the tray on the small table, took the metal cover off the plate, and used my napkin to mop up a spill of orange juice. "Hope you're hungry, I got the big breakfast with three eggs."

Actually, I was. "Thank you, I'm starved." I moved over to the table, picked up the fork, and took a couple of bites before I said, "So where's Ed Presnell this morning? Out tor-turing small animals?"

"Now, Miz Wyatt, Ed's not like that." Wiley straightened up, and even in someone so young I could see the beginnings of the stone wall.

"He *is* like that," I said. "And I may have to sue the county."

"Yes, ma'am. I'll be back to get the tray when you're done."

He left me alone while I ate, and then while I waited, and finally while I paced. I didn't have a watch, so I didn't know how long it actually was, but I know I felt an incredible surge of relief when the door opened. Relief switched to joy when I saw Matt.

"Oh, thank God." I flew across the room in those spongy slippers and went straight into his arms. "Oh, Matt."

"It's okay, sweetheart." His arms went tightly around me. "Are you all right?"

"I am now."

"Your forehead—there's a bruise."

"Yes, well, Mr. Presnell gets a little overzealous."

Matt held me at arm's length to look at my face. His voice was stiff as he said, "Did he hit you?"

"No, no. He just pushed me down on the desk. The ass-hole."

"We'll deal with him after we get you out of here." He hugged me again and then kissed me.

A polite throat-clearing interrupted us. We looked up to discover Wiley Pierce.

"I reckon you two want to get on home," he said, "so I won't hold you up none." He was blushing. "If you'll come this way, we'll get your things, Miz Wyatt, and sign you out."

Matt nodded, but his arm was still firmly around my shoulders. "I think it's checkout time, Miz Wyatt," he said, kissing me lightly on the forehead.

"Yes," I said, moving in sync with him out the door, "and this is a terrible hotel. Let's never come back here, okay? I mean, the bed was uncomfortable, I never got my luggage, and I suspect they don't even have a hot tub." I was hanging on to Matt, keeping the conversation light in order not to think about the night before.

"If I had my way, you wouldn't have been here in the first place," Matt said.

"If you'd been at the reception like you were supposed to be, I wouldn't have had to go to the courthouse alone. And I wouldn't have ended up here alone." As soon as I said it, I realized that we were close to talking about our real-life problems.

Matt nodded, his arm still wrapped around me. "You're saying jail is an experience best shared by two."

"Life is an experience best shared by two," I said firmly. "Us two. You and me. Together. And your family. And mine."

Wiley had led us to a small room where he went behind a counter; Matt and I waited just inside the door.

"Is that an apology?" Matt asked, turning to face me directly, his dark eyes locked onto mine.

I could feel myself slipping into his gaze, drifting like a woman lost. "Yes." Earlier I might have explained that my behavior, my distance from his parents, had been unintentional. I might have said a lot of stupid things. I was beyond all that. "I'm really very sorry. And I love you."

He put his hand under my chin and tilted my head up. "I'm sorry, too." He kissed me lightly. "I love you." Then he kissed me not so lightly.

WILEY GOT US out of there in record time, probably because he couldn't take any more. Matt grinned when I walked out of the rest room wearing my dress, and he kept the smile all the way home. I made sure he had good reason to be wearing the grin when he left the house, too.

Unfortunately, we were going our separate ways again. He and his father, along with Howard and Jeremy, were going out to the show barns for a special auction. I was spending the day with Edith and Cecily. I'd already called the station and had a brief yet satisfying discussion with Rory. I was scheduled to be off for the next three days, anyway; I'd planned to spend the time with Matt's family during the Celebration, and Rory could fill in with a part-timer. That wasn't my concern when I called, though. I had another little problem.

"I do not want to hear my name mentioned on KSGE today. Not at all. Never. Not *ever*," I said. "Okay?"

There was a titter in Rory's voice as he said, "I don't know, Jolie, it's pretty standard to say, 'I'm F. Rory Stone filling in for Jolie Wyatt.' Or something like 'Jolie Wyatt has the day off,' etcetera. I mean, is that going to bother you?"

"No."

"How about if we add, 'because she was in jail last night....'" Then he laughed outright.

"Keep it up, Rory," I said. "I know your dark secrets, too." Rory laughed again. "I mean it, I don't want a story about me. Please. It was a false arrest; I'll have to sue the county. I'll have to sue you. And KSGE."

"You want me to suppress the news? I don't know...."

"Like I said, Rory, I know the truth about you. And you owe me, remember?" What I know is that Rory has a younger sister and brother: One is in prison, the other on probation. He owes me because I've never told the whole truth about a misadventure his brother got into. And because I went to the judge and went to bat for both his siblings. I didn't do it for Rory; I did it because I believed it was right. Still, I'd use whatever weapons I had to keep my own misadventure quiet.

"Well?" I asked.

"Yeah, yeah, sure." There was still a streak of humor in his voice. "But if you get arrested again, I will report it."

"If I get arrested again, I will kill Ed Presnell, and then you'll have some big news." I added, "By the way, do you want to know what really happened?"

"Andy Sawyer told me your version. That is, if you trust Andy."

"Obviously not. The man is a blabbermouth."

"Then I'll see you on Monday," he said. "If you're not in jail—"

I hung up, and started pulling out clothes to wear. Now that one worry had been put to rest, I had to deal with others. How was I going to spend my day with Edith and Cecily and enjoy myself, with my mind racing ahead, fighting the clock? I pulled out the phone book and put in a call to Texas Rangers headquarters in Austin. After some transferring I was given another number, this one of Gordon's office in San Angelo.

I looked at the number long and hard, wondering if I ought to call it. I've met Gordon Onstott twice. He is humorless, and sometimes beyond imposing to the verge of terrifying. I picked up the phone and called anyway. I got a dispatcher at the law enforcement office who told me that Gordon had left just an hour before. He wasn't expected back for several days as he was going to be working on a case. Did I want to leave a message? I said no and hung up, a sigh of relief escaping from me. Gordon was on the job, headed for Wilmot County.

I put on Bermuda shorts, a short-sleeved red blouse, tennis shoes and socks, and pulled my hair back into a French braid that took me a full two minutes to do. There was so much I needed to accomplish. I ran out and jumped into my car, putting on a little more speed than necessary as I headed up the drive.

I quickly realized two important facts. Number one, Gordon Onstott might not be coming here at all; he could be on his way anywhere. I had never asked and the dispatcher had never specified.

Second, even if he did arrive soon, it would be Ed who would be briefing him, bringing him up to speed, as it were. He would be reading Ed's files and seeing things from Ed's point of view. By the time Gordon got beyond all that nonsense, the Celebration could be over and the murderer long gone.

Damn!

At the gate I stopped, turned the car around, and drove back to the house. I had to go to the Hammond place—there was no way around it—but maybe Diane could get started on some things. I phoned her.

"Slow down," Diane said. "You've been where?"

"Jail. But that's not important. Before that I went through the sheriff's office and I didn't find any of the old records from the camp."

"You got arrested? Are you okay? Was it on that little mission for Mac?"

"Yes, and I'm fine. About the records—"

"The ones you said Vera had?"

"Exactly. They've got to be at her house, and we've got to go through them. Can you get in there on some excuse? Say you need something for the exhibit? Wiley might let you in, but don't try Ed."

She didn't even hesitate. "Don't worry, I'll get in. And I'm not going to get arrested for it. So, you think her murder had something to do with the war years. Could be. If I do find something, where can I reach you?"

"I'll be at the Hammond house. Kissing up."

"Good girl."

Within minutes I was back at the highway, looking both ways before I turned. I hoped that Diane could get Wiley to help her. And I hoped that Ed didn't find out what she was doing. We didn't need more people in jail.

Something tucked away in the trees across the highway glinted in the morning light. I eased the car forward to lessen the glare. It was something white, something fairly large. I pulled out a little more and recognized a sheriff's car almost hidden by the mesquites.

With my heart pounding I drove a quarter of a mile down the highway, my eyes trained on the rearview mirror. Even though I was only traveling about twenty miles an hour, no other car appeared behind me. I stopped completely and waited, periodically digging in my purse like I was trying to find something.

Still the sheriff's car didn't show up.

I jumped out of my car, ran across the road, and then hustled back almost to the spot where I'd seen the other car. I took

quiet, careful footsteps until I could peer between some
bushes. A sound coming from the vehicle caught my attention.
I ducked, waited, then slowly rose up again.

It was a sheriff's car, all right. Ed Presnell was asleep behind the wheel. Snoring.

So dear Ed was still following one of the Wyatts, but his
late night had done him in. Too bad.

My kingdom for a cherry bomb.

TWENTY-TWO

I LEFT the sleeping deputy and drove on to the Hammond
place, resisting the temptation to hide my car. If he wanted
me, he could find me.

I knocked on the front door. Edith had her purse over her
arm when she opened it.

My first thought was that she was going somewhere. When
I asked about that she said, "No, no, I was just looking for
my reading glasses." Which, as she sat down, I noticed were
on the end table. "We're just here and it'd be real fine to have
you join us." Why did I think Matt had been there ahead of
me, telling *them* they had to be nice to me? And why didn't
I just tell these people I had other things that needed doing?
Sometimes the conventions of polite society are beyond my
comprehension, although I'm scared to death not to follow
them.

"Well, well, look who's here," Cecily said, coming out of
the hall. "You don't look so bad, considering your night in
jail. It doesn't appear anyone beat you, except for that tiny
bruise. Why is that?"

"Probably because they didn't." I went to the recliner and
sat down. "It's illegal, you know, and Matt *is* influential in
Purple Sage. I'm assuming they didn't want to piss him off.

Uh, annoy him," I corrected, remembering that Edith was listening, too.

"Oh, but he was quite annoyed. It might be more accurate to say he was distraught over your disappearance." Cecily arched one eyebrow and looked at me. "Isn't that interesting?"

Mac Donelly was at Peaceful Rest with three bullet holes in him and I had to put up with this instead of hunting for his attacker. "Well, he is my husband."

Cecily smiled as she sat on the end of the couch, and leaned forward. "Not really."

"Cecily, why're you being so ugly to Jolie?" Edith peered at Cecily over her reading glasses. "And what in the world would make you say Matt and Jolie aren't married?"

"Simple fact."

"I was at the wedding," Edith said. "I wore that beautiful rose-colored dress that Will complained about my buyin' so much." She went back to her knitting. "I don't know why that man can't understand that nice clothes cost money, which he's got enough of, and it doesn't matter if I never wear the dress again. I wanted it and I bought it. They can bury me in the thing and I'll wear it on into eternity. That ought to make it worthwhile."

"It was really pretty," I said, hoping the conversation had moved on.

"So why did you say that Matt and Jolie aren't married?" Edith asked Cecily again.

Cecily's smile was angelic, a ticket that would get her into heaven at any portal. "Because they are divorced. They separated last year, filed for divorce, and it became final before they smoothed over their little spat."

The woman had gone from mildly annoying to downright abominable. It was destroying my serenity, and I didn't have a great deal to spare.

"Look—" I began.

"Jolie, is that true?" Edith demanded.

"Well, yes, sort of…"

"No 'sort of.' Are you and Matt married or not?"

"Not," Cecily said, delighted with herself.

"I asked Jolie," Edith said. "Well?"

"At the moment, we aren't exactly married. We have been intending to get that handled, but—"

"I should say you are." She shoved her knitting into a big, flowered, vinyl carryall with wooden legs, snapped it shut, and stood up. "I believe we have a wedding to arrange."

"Oh, goody," Cecily said. "May I be the flower girl?"

"Cecily, I have no idea why you are so ornery today, but I think you'd best put a stop to it. Right now."

"Oh, sorry, Mums." Cecily's expression wasn't a bit contrite as she said, "It's just the strain of the trip and all. And then to hear Matt talk about Jolie as if she had the virtues of a saint was really more than I could bear. It was especially too much to take before coffee."

"You walked out on him, in case you don't remember."

"He sent me off, you mean."

My education continued; I'd had no idea that Matt had instigated Cecily's departure. Not that it mattered how their marriage had ended; it had nothing to do with me, because I firmly believe that Matt is not the same person as the man who'd been married to Cecily. I am no longer the same woman who'd been married to Steve, either. We all grow and change; at least I certainly hope we do.

"Now, both of you, let's get around the table and get this wedding planned." Edith bustled up to the table and sat down. "We're flying home on Monday, so I believe we'd best set it for Sunday."

Even as I rose from the recliner I was fighting the idea. I had other very important things to be doing right now. Someone had to figure out who'd killed Vera Meece. And Matt hadn't asked me to marry him again. What if he didn't want to formalize our relationship? And who the hell had told Cecily we were divorced in the first place?

"Wait," I said. "I think Matt has to *want* to marry me. He should ask me."

"I don't see the problem," Edith said.

"Yes, well, there might not be one, but then again, Matt and I should discuss it."

I was wondering if I could use that as an excuse to leave when Cecily leaned forward over the table and whispered, "Ooh, this could be a really grand problem!"

"Good lord," Edith exclaimed, backing up. "Cecily Wyatt, I smell liquor on your breath. You've been drinking!"

I stared at Cecily. Drinking? I began to look for telltale signs of imperfection on the usually perfect Cecily. Part of me was gratified to find them. There was a slight redness around her nose, her hair was mussed just a touch, and her movements were loose-limbed and laconic. The perfect Cecily was, as they say, in her cups.

"I certainly didn't drink much, just a touch," Cecily said to Edith. To me she added, "And don't assume"—she drew out the *s*'s haughtily—"that there is some sort of problem. There is not."

"I thought you'd quit drinking," I said.

"As did everyone else. Including me. It appears we were all wrong, doesn't it?" Cecily stood up and moved away from us. Once she was ensconced on the arm of the recliner she said, "So, are you chomping at the bit? Can't wait to race back to Matt and tell him that his ex is still a lush?"

Chomping at the bit, yes. Wanting to tell Matt, no. "Not really," I said.

"Oh, piffle." Cecily made a very unladylike face and started laughing. "Or bullshit, or whatever the current terminology is. You can't wait to tell Matt.... Not that I wanted to get him back anyway. He's not my type. I require a little more fire."

Personally, I thought Matt had a hell of a lot of fire, but I wasn't going to tell Cecily so. "Then why are you here? In Purple Sage?" I asked.

She cocked her head to the side. "I wanted to let everyone in town, along with Matthew Alan Wyatt, see that I'm just fine. Wonderful, in fact, and not...what I was. And yes, to make sure everyone knew that Matt shouldn't have sent me off. That I was the better choice." She slid into the seat of the chair. "The best choice." She studied me critically. "Yes, I believe I am prettier than you."

"No contest. You've got better hair, better skin, you're taller, and thinner. What the hell more do you want?" The question had been rhetorical, but Cecily answered it seriously.

"From you? Not a thing. Although I must admit I do like your spirit."

"Well, it doesn't come in a bottle." It was a low blow, even though the pun was unintentional.

Cecily didn't take it hard; instead she laughed again. "You see, I knew that you could be a real bitch."

"Cecily, you watch your language," Edith snapped.

"The problem," Cecily went on, again seriously, "is that I have been feeling the pinch of stress, and simply couldn't abstain any longer. Besides that, I adore the taste of gin. Prissy, who is Matt's sister—oh, but of course you know her—got me some gin-flavored toothpaste one year for Christmas and I even liked that. And here I am, a semiconfirmed teetotaler. Another wretched irony of life."

Edith stood up. "Okay, missy, that's enough self-pity. How much did you have to drink and where's the rest of it?"

"I had only a little bit." Cecily tried to wave her away, but it was like trying to hold off the *Queen Mary* with a rubber raft. Edith moved closer to Cecily, who quickly added, "Two swallows. Small swallows."

"And the bottle is…?"

"Oh, for God's sake, it's not like I'm a child—"

"There are times when you act like one. Makes me want to turn you over my knee and paddle your behind," Edith said, towering over her. "You are the most self-destructive woman I ever did meet! Most folks with your looks and your way of talkin' would figure the Lord did them a real good turn. But not you. No, you got to go out of your way to mess up ever' good thing that's ever happened to you." Edith was twitching in her anger, and more than once she reached out as if to grab Cecily and shake her. She stopped each time. "Now, you'd best tell me where that liquor is, and you'd best do it now."

"But—"

"And I mean right now!"

Cecily rolled out of the chair and headed for her bedroom. "Oh, all right. I am sorry, Mums," she said. "I really didn't have but one swallow. And this is the first bit I've had in years."

I hung back in the hall as they went into the middle bedroom that Diane and I had decorated. There was an antique iron bed covered with an old-fashioned friendship quilt. The oak tallboy and a matching three-mirrored dressing table were both scattered with makeup and jewelry. Cecily's carefully understated look was obviously more artful than natural.

The other thing I surmised was that Howard Bremerton was not sleeping with Cecily, at least not in Edith's house.

Cecily went straight to the side of the bed, bent down, and pulled out an open suitcase that was still half packed with clothes. She brought out a pint bottle of gin. As she handed it to Edith her eyes were down. "This was a wretched way to repay your hospitality, Mums," Cecily said. "I'm truly sorry." And for once, I believed her.

Edith took the bottle without comment and held it up to the light. There was very little gone and I wondered if Cecily had put water in the bottle.

"This is it?" Edith asked.

"That's it." Cecily nodded. "I'm out of practice."

"Don't plan on getting back *in* practice, either. Leastways not while I'm around." Edith sailed into the kitchen with Cecily and me in close formation behind her. Once there she unscrewed the lid of the bottle, poured the clear liquid down the drain, and threw the bottle in the trash, carefully covering it with paper towels. For good measure, she used the sprayer to rinse the sink. "Now," she said, turning to us, "we are going to pretend this never happened. We are never going to speak of it, and it will not happen again. Not as long as I got breath in my body."

We both nodded; I was fighting the urge to say "Yes, ma'am" and curtsy.

"Good," Edith said. She took a heavy pottery cup out of

the cupboard and filled it with thick, dark coffee from a pot on the counter. "Now, Cecily, you drink this and sober up. Jolie, you want any?"

"Uh, no, thank you."

"Then we'd best get down to work," Edith said.

I glanced surreptitiously at my watch, but I hadn't been there even half an hour. There was no way I could leave. Edith led us back to the dining table. We pulled out chairs, but before we could sit down she barked more orders. "Cecily, bring the phone on over here. Jolie, there's pencil and paper in the drawer of the sideboard; we'll need that. Bring the *big* wire tablet—we got a wedding to plan."

Which brought us right back to our opening point of contention, and as much as Edith could be intimidating, she couldn't cow me on this one. "Edith, I really appreciate what you want to do, however, this is Matt's decision first. And mine."

She surprised me by not arguing. Edith merely nodded her head, picked up the phone, and headed for her bedroom. "Go ahead without me."

Next thing I knew Edith was back, handing me the receiver. "Hello?" I said cautiously into it.

"Good morning," Matt said.

"Where are you?"

"At the auction. Mother tracked us down." He sounded like he was laughing. "So, my lovely not-quite-wife, would you like to get remarried this weekend?"

"Well…" I let out a sigh. God, what a romantic I was. Even with everything that was going on I wanted Matt on his knees in the moonlight, quoting Byron and telling me how my hair glowed like spun gold. It hadn't been quite that way the first time, but close enough, and I wanted at least that, if not more, the second time around. "I guess I wanted to be asked. Uh, nicely. You know."

"Ah, I see. Okay, how about if we rendezvous this evening in the park? At nine o'clock by the Bowie Oak? I'll ask you then properly, but in the meantime, you can plan the wedding with my mother. Will that work for you?"

That was better. "Yes, it's a deal."

"I don't know when I'll get free," he went on. "I probably won't make it home for dinner." Before he'd left that morning, Matt had told me that being chair of the Celebration was bringing a raft of problems to resolve. There was, along with a ticket insufficiency for the carnival, something about concessions for tomorrow's football game and there were two bank accounts, both requiring Vera's signature. Obviously that situation had to be rectified.

"Wait," I said. "Did you ever find the receipts from the dance?"

"They'd been taken to the sheriff's office for evidence."

"Oh."

"I'll see you tonight," Matt said. "I love you."

"I love you, too."

Then he was gone and I hung up the phone and said to Edith, "It's a go."

"Good," she said with satisfied nod. "Now one more thing. Your last wedding was all your show and you didn't let nobody help. Not even me—"

"You weren't there."

That first wedding had been held in Austin, and Edith and Will had arrived just an hour before the ceremony. The extent of Edith's involvement had been to pin on her corsage and Will's boutonniere.

"I coulda been there, except you didn't want no help. I bet you told me twenty times on the phone how you had everything handled." She put her hands on her hips. "Then when I got there, you were throwin' up in the bathroom because you'd worked yourself into a frazzle. This time why don't we do it a might smarter? You do the picking and choosing, and I'll see that it gets done."

"Well, I—"

"I know that's tough for you, being so almighty independent and all, but it's smarter—don't you think?"

She had stripped me to my soul, in front of Cecily no less. Both women were watching me curiously.

"Okay," I said with a nod. "Okay. That sounds fine. I'd appreciate your help. I'd enjoy it. Let's get started."

Edith was like a horse that finally got the bit in its mouth and took off running. She thought of things to do, and I wrote the list for her. Then she started on the phone, wielding what I called the Wyatt Clout with great finesse.

After a while I started thinking about murder. Edith lined up a minister; I flipped to a blank page and jotted a note to call Diane. Edith arranged for a location, which was to be the courthouse lawn, and I wrote *Picture # 36*. While Edith talked to caterers, I listed possible killers.

Amazing how long that list could be, once I really thought about it. Almost anyone at the Celebration could have killed Vera. It was far more likely, though, that it was someone who'd been out to the camp since. In one of my crime seminars, I'd learned that if you take a picture of the crowd gathered at a murder scene, you will probably get a picture of the killer. Because they come back. They hang around, then lurk. And I had the feeling our killer was lurking around the POW camp.

I could eliminate anyone who'd been at the dance, which meant Liz Street, Cecily, the rest of the Wyatts, and Diane and Trey. Although Liz could have left the dance shortly after I did, and if she had, there would have been time to kill Vera.

Because I would never believe Liz could kill, I wrote her name very lightly along with others I couldn't eliminate: Harley and Marge Tandy, Klaus and Minna Braune, Howard Bremerton, and Bill Tieman. I wasn't forgetting all the other POWs who were in town; I just didn't have their names, although I might be able to get them by this afternoon. Surely there would only be fifteen or so. Maybe less.

An idea kept pulling at me: What if Nicholas weren't dead? What if a very much alive Nicholas had ridden a horse to the POW camp that night to kill Vera?

"Will roses work for the bouquet?" Edith asked me.

"Asphodels," I said. "Blue ones. For the something blue. And put in something cream-colored like..."

"More asphodels?" Cecily asked.

"Fine. Maybe freesias. Oh, and not a big huge round thing of flowers. Something small. Slender. Like a, a…"

"Bouquet," Edith said.

"Right."

Edith went back to the phone and I went back to my notes. We knew a horse came from somewhere behind the camp. And it appeared the path it had been on led to more of the Tandy property. Damn. There was so much I needed to be finding out, and it wasn't getting done.

I wrote on the pad: *1) List of POWs. 2) Follow path.*

If I only had the information that Ed did…if I'd kept my hands on that report. My hindsight wasn't moving me any farther forward, until I realized I knew someone who might have read the police file. Rhonda Hargis, a member of my Tuesday night writers' group, is also a reporter for the Sage *Tribune*. She has employed nefarious means for her fact-gathering when she considers it justified.

I looked up to see where the phone was; Edith had it in use. She was coercing an out-of-town company to deliver, set up, and remove 150 wooden folding chairs for the wedding. She was very insistent they be white and wooden. I started to tell her I didn't want that many people, but I stopped. It was her wedding. Or for her.

Instead I wrote Rhonda's name and her phone number in the notepad, with the notation *DPS report.* I hoped she had read it, as well as anything Ed had gathered.

Edith put down the phone with a brisk and satisfied nod. "That's done. Oh, and Jolie, you can pick out the menu from the country club this afternoon. We'll also order a cake from The Bakery. Right now you need to call Rhonda at the *Tribune* and get a story in tomorrow's paper. I'll start a guest list. We'll just have to call folks and invite them."

Call Rhonda. "An excellent idea," I said.

"Well," Cecily said. "As much as I've enjoyed looking up phone numbers and taking notes for you, Edith, I don't believe there is anything more I can do for my ex-husband's wedding. It simply wouldn't be proper."

The phone rang and Edith pointed to it. "You can answer that."

Cecily did so and after her quick hello she handed the receiver to me. "For you. Such a surprise."

"Hello," I said into the mouthpiece. It was Diane.

"You won't believe it!"

"What? Where are you you?"

"I'm at the POW camp." She cleared her throat. "You have to see this. Can you come over here?"

"Uh, I don't think I can get away, Diane. Especially not now—"

Edith put her hand up and said, "I was just about to propose that we break for some lunch soon anyway. Have her meet us at the country club. Eleven-thirty."

I passed on the information to Diane, who agreed hesitantly. "I guess so. What are you doing that's so crucial?"

"Planning my wedding."

"Now that's a surprise!"

"My thoughts exactly. Want to be my matron of honor?"

"When is the wedding?"

"Sunday. Edith can give you the details when we see you."

"Fine. Eleven-thirty," she said as she hung up.

Edith was jotting down names for the guest list. She had the notebook I'd been using in front of her, one page already half filled. She ripped it out and handed it to Cecily. "More numbers for you to look up. We'll make the calls this afternoon. Oh, and Jolie, do you have a dress?"

"Uh, a dress?"

"Never mind, we'll figure something out," she said. She gave me one quick, pointed look then added, "Now are you going to call the *Tribune* before we go, or not?"

"I'll wear my wedding dress," I said to Edith as I dialed. "Makes sense."

"I reckon you want your own vows?" Edith asked.

"Yes," I said. "I'll find them."

As I spoke I watched Edith rip a second page from the notebook. One more page and she'd be down to the list I'd made, which had nothing to do with the wedding.

I couldn't look. "Rhonda," I said when the phone was finally answered. "It's me, Jolie. I have an item for tomorrow's paper. Society news, I think." As I talked, I stood up and walked into the bedroom. Let Edith wonder what I was up to.

"I'm getting married again, and Edith wants it in this week's paper. Can you do that?"

"If you talk fast."

A keyboard clicked away as I gave her the information. When I finished she said, "Well, congratulations. Or, best wishes, or whatever I'm supposed to say. I thought you were going to give me the inside scoop on your arrest."

"You're running a story on that?"

"No, no," she said. "Professional courtesy. Besides, it was Butthead who did the arresting. He didn't even file a proper report. Or if he did, I couldn't find it."

"You're kidding."

"It's the truth, and when you sue that moron let me know. I want to be in court and stick my tongue out at him. Or maybe we'll make it a class action suit. Is two a class?"

"I have no idea. What did he do to you?"

"Two tickets in three days. Both for speeding on my bike. The dumb—"

Rhonda rides a bicycle around town. The kind that you pedal, nothing motorized. Although, in truth, she does ride it too fast, and she is sometimes a traffic hazard. Ed may have been doing it for her own good. I suppose he'd say all tickets are for our own good, not that I see it that way. "Can he do that?" I asked.

"Well, the first one was just a warning, but as soon as the Celebration is over I intend to find out. Got to run."

"Wait. I need to talk to you. Have you been digging around in the sheriff's office lately?"

"Me?" she demanded. "That's illegal."

"You just told me you couldn't find a report on my arrest," I reminded her. "Bet you found one on Vera's murder, though, didn't you?"

"You're getting really good, you know that?"

Rhonda has no sense of humor, so I took that as a compli-ment.

"Thank you," I said. "Have you read the report? And can you meet me to tell me about it?"

"I'm under deadline, Jolie, and the information is not for publication. Or broadcasting."

"After deadline. And I won't use it on the air. This is for me."

There was a pause, then, "Okay. Three o'clock. My of-fice."

"It's a deal."

When I walked back into the dining room, Edith was wait-ing for me. She gestured to the paper with my list on it—the murder list. "You want to tell me what this is all about?" she asked.

TWENTY-THREE

I STARTED WITH the shooting of Vera and Mac, which Edith already knew about. As we drove to the Sage Country Club I covered the things Diane and I had surmised, and by the time we were seated at a table with Diane I was at the end, talking about Ed Presnell lurking outside our gate that very morning.

After frowning seriously, Edith said, "You know there are some folks in this world that I just don't much care for, and God forgive me, Vera Meece was one of those folks. Every time a man walked up she started simperin' like there weren't a whole bunch of them on the planet. Seemed real silly to me." She took her reading glasses off. "Mac Donelly is a different matter, though. That man's done a lot of good in this world, and a whole lot of it's been for the Wyatts." She looked at Cecily. "No tellin' how many times you'd have landed in jail if Mac hadn't been the one pullin' you over." She shook her head at the memory. "He'd drive her home himself so she didn't kill herself or nobody else. In my book that's one fine man." Her voice grew tough. "And now he's laid up with a killer lookin' for a second chance at him, and some dim bulb is persecutin' my family. And you weren't going to say a word about this?" She frowned at me again. "Is that right?"

"I didn't see any reason to bother you—"

"Like always. Independent. Cussedly so."

Diane laughed. "I've told her that before."

"Then you ought to recognize it in yourself." Edith placed her napkin on her plate and said, "You know, I was here during the war and I know some about Camp Seybold. I believe we ought to get our food to go and head on over there. We can eat in the car, and the wedding plans will just have to wait a bit." She picked up her purse and stood up. "Are y'all coming or not?"

"TAKE A LOOK at these," Diane said, opening a plain cardboard box and pulling out several thin, spiral-bound booklets.

"What are they?" I asked.

"You'll see." She handed one to each of us. Even Cecily seemed interested as she flipped open the cover of olive green card stock. I did the same to mine and discovered that the title page inside called it a memorial annual of Camp John Seybold. On the second page was a dedication to all the men and women who'd played some part in the history of the camp. The third page was a letter from Vera Meece, welcoming the reader to the reunion. It also told how she'd gotten the pictures for the annual, and how she hoped the Celebration would be a homecoming for the men.

I glanced at Diane.

"It's something, isn't it?" she said.

I nodded as I went back to the annual. All the photos on the wall were duplicated in the little booklet; Vera had added a caption under each one. The first photo was the building of the camp; I found the talent show, and the shot of Vera as a young girl stealing the horses.

"We've got these pictures," Edith said, gesturing toward

the wall where the framed ones hung. "What made you so excited about these books?"

"And where did you get them?" I asked.

"They were delivered here this morning from a printer in San Antonio. This is the surprise that Vera promised the men. Each one was going to take home an annual. *Is* going to take one home. Look at the last pages."

I flipped to the back and discovered the names and addresses of all the men Vera had been in contact with. She'd also left several blank pages, I assumed for other addresses and personal notes.

"I agree with Mums," Cecily said. "These are nice, but I don't see what makes them so important."

"When Jolie and I first came out here after Vera's death, we found those pictures in boxes in the office." She explained that some had their glass broken, and one was missing. "We assumed the killer did that, searching for something." Diane took another annual from the box. "We never did find one of the pictures. Remember, Jolie? Number thirty-six—"

I was already flipping pages. "It's in here?"

And there it was. A picture of a young man and a horse, standing in front of one of a row of tents. His hair and his eyes were light colored and, judging his height by the size of the horse, he wasn't very tall.

The caption beneath the photo said simply, *Lt. Nicholas Zandorf.*

I sucked in air. "Lieutenant Nicholas Zandorf. Vera's long-lost love. And his photo was missing."

"I keep having this crazy idea," Diane said. "It's not possible—"

"That maybe he's not really dead?" I had a feeling our crazy ideas matched.

Edith had been studying the picture; now she looked up. "If he wasn't dead, how would that work?"

"I could be all wrong on this," Diane said. "But I keep thinking that Nicholas killed some other soldier and switched identities. I know why he'd do that; Nicholas was a Nazi and he wanted to come back to live in the States. A Nazi wouldn't be allowed.''

My own pet theory had been forming in my subconscious and now it popped out full blown.

"It's possible," I agreed. "Here's what I worked out. This other soldier has the flu; there was a lot of that going around. He's in his barracks, sick, weak, and while the rest of the POWs are out doing something, probably taking down the camp or packing up the place, Nicholas comes in and strangles the man. After the murder Nicholas puts the body in his own bed and pretends to be the other soldier, you know, says he's sick, keeps the covers over his head until it's time to march to the train. Then he slips into the back of the line, away from the other man's friends, and the next thing he's on a boat to Germany."

Diane nodded agreement. "And I'll go you one better. What if he kills someone who just arrived at the camp. Someone the other men didn't know?"

"But they knew Nicholas," Cecily said.

"He was an officer," I explained. "He didn't go out on work parties and he didn't fraternize with the other men, at least that's the impression I got from Marge Tandy. She said he stayed near his tent, read books, and tended to his private garden. Only Vera was close to him. If Nicholas changed uniforms and kept at a distance, who would notice? Who would care? Besides, there was all the confusion and excitement of the men going home, some after years of being prisoners here."

Edith had set down the annual and was all business. "So he kills another soldier and goes on to Germany. I can buy that. I can even buy him coming back to the reunion. It would just be too intriguing to pass up, don't you think?"

"That's what I think," Diane said. "Now the *why* of Vera's murder. Let's assume they correspond and when he arrives they make a date to meet the night of the picnic."

"An officer and a gentleman. That's who Vera said she was meeting," I added.

Diane nodded. "So they meet. Vera shows him the pictures,

she asks what happened to him, how it was that he didn't die—''

"And then she figures it out," Cecily said, yawning daintily. "And, of course, even after fifty years he has to protect himself, so he murders Vera. When the sheriff arrives he shoots him, too. Voilà."

Hearing Cecily say it in her sarcastic way killed the ending. Diane glowered at her. "If you keep going the way you are now, your old age will be miserable," Diane said. "And nobody's going to give a shit."

"Habit," Cecily said airily.

"It's a bad one, and if I were you, I'd break it." Diane took the annual out of Cecily's hand and put it back in the cardboard box.

"Everyone is so sensitive today," Cecily said, and wandered into the office, leaving us alone with our theories.

Edith watched her go, but didn't follow. I personally wondered if Cecily was acting that way to cover something up. Maybe something about Howard?

"I think this is all quite possible," Edith said, "but you don't have one shred of evidence, and last I heard, some of that is needed in a courtroom."

"Ed Presnell probably has scads of evidence," I said. "He just doesn't know what it means."

I stared some more at the picture of Nicholas and wondered what Vera found so magical in this young man. Why two people end up loving each other is a question that fascinates me. I once heard that love occurs when you've done the best you can on the open market. That's the cynical theory, and I prefer to think that love occurs when you find someone who makes up for your weaknesses. Matt is wonderful with numbers, and I've been known to throw IRS forms across the room in frustration. Matt is gentle and listens to reason. I make up my mind on an issue and dare anyone to present evidence to the contrary. He lives by reason and I live by emotion and fiction. A perfect combination. So what was there about this Nicholas that Vera would find attractive?

Vera was flighty on the surface, southern belle style, and

had a streak of steel down her spine. Was Nicholas the kind of man who appeared tough, yet would sway in the breeze of opinion? Is that why he became a Nazi, or did he truly believe in their creed? And who in Purple Sage was like that? It might be one way to distinguish the killer.

"How'd this murderer get out here?" Edith asked. "I heard at the cafe that Mac didn't see another car."

Cecily returned from the other room. "He could have parked in back of this building. There's enough room for a car and it would be quite well hidden."

"We have another theory." Diane told them about the horse.

"Which would mean someone out at the new B-and-B was Nicholas," Edith said.

"John Schussler!" I almost shouted it. Why hadn't I seen it sooner?

Diane frowned. "Who?"

She hadn't been at the party, and hadn't met him. It was Edith who told her about John; everything she said seemed to support our theory. John was short, Nicholas was short. John was blond, or had been fair; Nicholas had been fair-complected. Nicholas was an officer; John carried himself with power and authority. John was staying at Das Keller Haus, which was the start of the murderer's horseback ride, and Nicholas was photographed with a horse. He probably rode, too.

As a final piece of evidence, I added, "Nicholas spent his time on his garden, and guess what? John is a great gardener."

Cecily had more. Once she decided to get involved she was quick. "Didn't John say that he arrived at the camp on the very last day? He met up with Howard's uncle and then they lost touch again. Where? On the boat? When they got back to Europe? It's all so vague. Perhaps some explanation is due."

"They lost touch," I said, the phrase sounding false. "That seems a little odd, don't you think? I mean, after the experience of the war I would want friends around. Wouldn't you?"

"I would, indeed," Edith said, "but John didn't look like the type to get real involved in people's lives. Standoffish."

"Which is exactly how you'd be if you were living an assumed identity," Diane said. "So, why haven't I met the man? Did he come to last night's cocktail party?" She went to the guest book and searched each page. When she reached the end she looked up, shaking her head. "He's not in here. It appears he hasn't been out to the camp at all."

"Hiding out," Cecily said. "Bad sign. Looks guilty to me."

"But so what?" I could feel my frustration level rising. "Even if we have hard-core proof of this and, as Edith pointed out, we don't, we all know that Ed won't listen. And Mac can't do anything from where he is...."

"Consider it handled." Diane raised one eyebrow and grinned. "Trey can make Ed listen. Trust me on this one."

My hackles rose. Small-town Texas is behind the times on equality of the sexes, especially if Diane was suggesting it took a man to get something done. "I do understand why I can't go to Ed Presnell, but why do you think Trey can be more effective than, say, you or Edith?"

"Very simple, Jolie. Because Trey is the mayor pro tem or whatever. Even though Ed works for the county, and Trey will be governing the city, Trey has political clout. Can you keep a secret?" She was looking at all of us.

"Who would I tell?" Cecily asked.

Edith and I both nodded. "Of course," I said.

"Well, last week Ed came to our house. He wanted Trey to appoint him chief of police."

"You're kidding!" I was flabbergasted. "What about Bill Tieman? Doesn't Ed realize there's someone in the job already?"

Diane laughed. "Oh, Ed thinks Trey needs a 'team player' in that position. Someone who's 'like-minded.'"

"Simple-minded is more like it." Bill Tieman had run against Trey in the primary and, obviously, lost, but no one doubted that Bill would follow Trey's lead. Bill wanted to keep his job. "Wait! I forgot about Gordon Onstott!"

"Yes, where is our dear Texas Ranger?" Diane asked.

"He's out of his office investigating a case, but I'm not

positive where. Maybe Trey can do something on that one, too. Find Gordon, get someone down here; preferably someone who will listen to reason, instead of Ed.''

"I believe it's time we made us a plan of action," said Edith, ever the commander. "Here's what I think needs to be done."

Her plan was simple and do-able. First, Cecily would round up Howard and have him call his uncle. Howard was to find out everything he could about the real John Schussler. Height, weight, age, interests, identifying marks, anything that would help us determine if the man in Purple Sage was the genuine article. He would also ask when and how the two men had lost contact.

Since it was already getting late in England, where Howard's uncle lived, Cecily left immediately in Edith's car.

Diane was to locate Trey, who would have Bill Tieman run a background check on John Schussler. Edith would go with Diane, just in case Trey was hesitant. After that the two women would stop back by Vera's house, and, with the key that Diane had gotten this morning from Wiley, they would let themselves in and go through everything they could. Specifically they would look for any correspondence that Vera might have kept, and any record of John Schussler. It was going to be a long, arduous task, and I was glad I didn't have to tackle it.

Because my jobs were going to be quicker, I had three of them. First, I would go to Das Keller Haus and see what else Marge knew about Vera and Nicholas Zandorf. I planned to be far more candid with her than I had been the other night at the cocktail party. Second, I would talk to Rhonda Hargis. Last, I was to talk to Mac to see if he could tell me anything more about the murder.

At seven-thirty the four of us were going to meet at the Hammond house.

"We're in the homestretch now," Edith said. "By that time we ought to just about have this thing done with."

TWENTY-FOUR

THE SAGE *Tribune* is housed in a three-story gray building that has bats in its attic and newsprint over its big windows. Why no one has considered blinds, or tinting the glass, is a question I've never asked. I didn't that day either.

"Did you read both reports or just Ed's?" I asked Rhonda. We were sitting in her boss's office. Rhonda was leaning back in Morris Pratt's old leather swivel chair; her feet, clad in aerobic shoes, were resting on the top of his desk. From what I knew of their relationship, Morris wouldn't mind a bit.

"I never said I read those reports," Rhonda said very seriously. "I may be able to give you some information, though. Quid pro quo." Meaning she wanted as much in return as she gave.

"Okay," I said with a nod. It wasn't like I had much, and she couldn't use it until next week's paper anyway. *"Mi información es su información."*

"Good." She took her feet down and the chair flew upright. Once she was resettled, she said, "They're pretty sure Mac and Vera were shot with the OM1 carbine that Vera had on the wall. The bullets were in the case in front of it."

"I knew that. What about fingerprints?"

"The gun is still missing so that's a bust, and there were none on the display case. Elsewhere they found a dozen different ones, particularly in the office. So far they've identified Vera's, those of Mark Perez, who helped build the place, and Bill Tieman's. Bill was dating Vera, so his are understandable. What else?"

"Wait," I said. "There are dozens of prints that they can't identify?"

"You got it. And they probably never will most of them. If they find a suspect, then they can match his prints to what they have. They can't do it the other way around." She shook her head and her blond ponytail waggled. "If they'd get access to some decent computer equipment, it would be a different story, but no one will spring for that. It looks more impressive to put more cops on the street. Politicians!"

"What about suspects?"

"Oh, that's simple." She grinned, pulling at the leg of her blue biking shorts. "Those are mostly Wyatts. Matt was there at the proper time, and you had a motive."

"Me? Why would I kill Vera Meece?"

"So you could take over Camp John Seybold during the Celebration."

"Are you nuts? Is Ed nuts? I didn't take it over; Diane did. And it was under protest! The man has twelve screws loose." I huffed and puffed for a minute or two. "Damn. It's a wonder we don't have bigger problems than we do." I actually stood up and walked around the chair. "Who else has Ed talked to?"

"He called Vera's cousin in Oklahoma, who hardly kept up with her at all. He, the cousin, didn't even know Vera had moved back to Purple Sage. That's the only relative she still had living." Rhonda clicked the others off on her fingers. "Ed also talked to the McClennans, the Keelings, Clara Winters, and the Bridwells, since they all live on FM Four-forty-four. None of them saw or heard a thing."

Probably not since the closest to the camp was at least a mile away. And with the Celebration, everyone was busy with their own activities.

"Did he do anything on Vera's background?" I asked.

"No warrants, no arrests."

"Ed's thorough, too." I shook my head. This was like a bad joke. "So, what else did the DPS report say?"

"Beats me, I don't understand those things. And this was a preliminary, so it was a handwritten copy and it looked like Greek. I didn't get much off it."

The useful information was coming in slowly. I had gone to Das Keller Haus right after lunch, and since there was no one there, I had walked the path behind their barn. By the time

I'd discovered it really did end at Camp John Seybold, I was hot and sweaty. The walk back to the B-and-B wasn't any better, especially since neither the Tandys nor their guest had shown up. At a little before three I had driven back into town, only to be kept waiting by Rhonda.

"You're failing me badly, Rhonda," I said. "Didn't you learn anything important? Has Ed looked at any of the former POWs? Or guards?"

"No. Should he?"

"I think somebody should. Does he at least know how the murderer got out to the camp?"

"Sure. In his Explorer. Or her Intrepid."

We were back to the Wyatts again, and I wasn't in the mood to defend myself.

"I'm serious," Rhonda said. "He's sure it's one of you two. If I were you, I'd duck that guy for a while."

"At least until Gordon Onstott gets here."

"Gordon?" She all but smacked her forehead. "Of course! The Ranger should be handling this." Already she was reaching for the well-used Rolodex on the desk. "I'll give him a call and see what the deal is."

I stood up. "I'm out of here," I said. "Thanks for talking to me, at least."

"Wait a minute; you owe me some info. Where's Mac?"

I shook my head. "I don't have any idea."

"Liar," she said with hardly a smile. "You got arrested, and you had Mac's keys and a note from him. So where is he?"

I leaned forward over the desk, shaking my head. "Rhonda, I can't tell you. I just can't."

"Why? You think I'd tell someone? Maybe go shoot Mac?"

"No. But it's just too dangerous." I couldn't explain my fears; I only knew that they were real, and I wasn't about to put Mac at risk. Not for anyone, even Rhonda, whom I trusted. "I will tell you this: I think the killer rode to the camp on horseback. I think the motive had something to do with the days when the camp was running during the war. I suspect a former POW, or guard,'' I added out of fairness. "I also think that person came in for the Celebration.''

Rhonda let out a soft whistle. "My, my, isn't that interesting.'' Then she scowled. "That also means that if someone doesn't get their butt in gear, our murderer will be long gone in a few days.''

"Bingo,'' I said, heading for the door and the mean streets of Purple Sage.

"JOHN FLEW IN Tuesday around noon,'' Marge said, confirming her own statement with a nod. "That's right—it was the day of the picnic in the park. Oh, and the shooting at the camp. I still can't get over that. Right here in Purple Sage.'' She shook her head.

"It was terrible,'' I agreed.

We were in the parlor of Das Keller Haus. Two modern overstuffed couches coexisted with a hundred-year-old rocker and side table. No matter where you looked, there was something worth seeing, so the room should have had a soothing effect on me. It didn't.

"More ice tea?'' Marge asked.

"No, no. I can't stay long.'' This had been my third trip that day to Marge's. After leaving the *Tribune* offices I had driven out to the B-and-B again, waited for over a half hour, and then had gone to the library hoping to discover something more about Camp John Seybold. As I had suspected, no new material had magically appeared in the last few months.

Worse, I'd already been at Das Keller Haus for some time, and I was just now getting to the point of my visit. Marge had insisted on giving me a tour first, and I have to admit I learned a few things that might help. "Where did John fly into? San Antonio?'' I asked.

"Our county airport. Didn't you know? He's a pilot with the Confederate Air Force. John showed us around this afternoon and there must be thirty vintage planes in for the air show this weekend. It's something to see.'' She laughed. "Speaking of seeing, you should have seen John when he came in the front door that first time. He was walking like a sailor who hadn't touched land in a year.''

I laughed with her, pretending to find it funny. "Must have been a long flight. I'll bet he had to overnight somewhere. Somebody said he was out on horseback that very evening—is that possible?"

Coy, Jolie, very coy.

"That man is something else, but that would be pushing it, even for him. He did go out for a long walk, though. Said he wanted to see the land from close up instead of from the sky."

"So he rode later that evening?"

"No, I don't believe so. In fact, I know he didn't, because he went to bed real early," Marge said.

"But his room has an outside entrance. He could have left and you wouldn't have known. You wouldn't have cared if he'd borrowed a horse."

She frowned at me. "Jolie, I know there's a point to your visit and this interest in John, I just can't figure out what it is. You want to tell me?"

The answer to that was a simple no. However, having been caught, I felt I owed her some explanation. I made it succinct.

"Marge, there was some talk that John had known Vera, been involved with her, during the war. And that he might have had something to do with her death.''

She gave me the same look a parent gives a child who's said the bogeyman ate the cookies. "That doesn't even touch on reality," she said, adding something that sounded like *tsk*. "John Schussler is a very nice man. He did not kill Vera, if that's what you're insinuating. And another thing you ought to know, back during the war Vera was no better than she had to be. I hate to speak ill of the dead, but it's the God's truth. There are lots more men you ought to be looking at."

That's when I remembered Marge had been a translator at the camp. "You were there!" I said. "Did you know John back then?"

"Never met the man until he came walking up the porch this week. He was only at Camp Seybold for the last few days it was open, maybe only the last day, and I was at home with a bad case of the flu.''

"Then how did he find out about Das Keller Haus? Did you advertise?''

To my own ears I sounded like a Nazi inquisitor, but Marge didn't seem to notice. She smiled. "You might say I did. Accidently. Do know Myrna Applegate? Used to be a Peterman?''

"I met her the other night."

"Myrna and I go way back," Marge said. "Even after she moved off we still kept in touch. In the last year or so we've been writing pretty regular, so of course I told her about this place." She gestured to the house. "Then Myrna told John, who called us that evening. We weren't even planning on being open for the Celebration, but Harley said we could do it if we pushed, so we pushed."

"And did a beautiful job," I added.

"We're real proud of it."

I took a final sip of my ice tea. The paper napkin under it was wet and ripping, a sure sign it was time to go. I reached for my purse. "Well, I appreciate the tour. Thank you again.''

Marge and I both rose and started toward the front door. "Come back anytime," she said when we were on the porch. "And Jolie, I think you're on the wrong track about John. He seems to be a real nice man. Very much the executive."

"He seems to be." That wasn't necessarily in his favor. Not when it was a variation on a trait so prominent in Nicholas. I turned to Marge. "You said you were aware of Nicholas Zandorf during the war, but did you know him enough to, well, recognize him if he came walking up to your front door today?''

She glanced at the seven porch steps, then at me. "That's been years, Jolie. We've all changed a lot. I don't know that I'd recognize anyone from back then.''

"Oh. Of course." It was exactly what I'd thought.

With a last, slow wave, as dictated by southern hospitality, I walked along the path between the front flower beds and over to my car.

"Is that your sidekick?" Marge called, pointing to a spot down the road.

We were miles out in the country without another house in sight. I gazed around at the fields and pasture land surrounded by cedar-post-and-wire fences. I didn't discover what she was seeing until I opened the car door and stood up on the frame. Parked under a shade tree was a sheriff's car, and while I couldn't see inside it yet, I would have bet money it was Ed Presnell.

"Not my sidekick," I said, my stomach muscles tightening.

"Must be a slow day for tickets."

"Well, I hope it doesn't pick up until I'm just a speck on the horizon." I climbed into the car, slammed the door, and started the engine. At the end of the driveway I turned left toward Ed Presnell; that way he had to turn around before he could follow me. Which he did.

Damn.

I kept the car at an even forty-two because I didn't know the speed limit and that seemed safe. Meanwhile I kept my eyes on the rearview mirror.

It's a wonder I didn't run off the road and hit something. Ed stayed right behind me, not quite on my bumper, but much too close on that empty stretch. I could see the sunglasses on his face, and the smirk beneath them. Had it been anyone else I would have pulled off and let them pass. Since it was Ed I was afraid he'd take that as an opportunity to stop and harass me some more, so I kept on going.

Before I went to see Mac I had to lose Ed Presnell, but how in the world was I supposed to do that in Purple Sage? Speeding would get me a ticket, and I couldn't think of a maze of streets where I might shake him; that left me with no alternative but to go inside some building and hope he'd lose interest or be called away to some official duty.

By the time I'd reached that conclusion I was pulling into the park road. On my left the carnival was in full swing; it was Kids' Day and there were children everywhere. My car seemed invisible to them as they ran across the road to the music and the rides. Teenagers were in abundance as well, since they seem to spend a lot of time looking for something to do in Purple Sage. Most of the girls had younger children in tow, and the teenage boys were just following the girls.

At one point I stopped completely to let a group pass and took the opportunity to glance in the rearview mirror. Ed was still there.

I picked up the pace until I was almost on Main.

Ed remained my faithful shadow. After two quick turns I pulled into the Sage Cafe parking lot, squeezed my car in between two minivans, and ran inside. The smell of chicken-fried steak and cream gravy engulfed me.

Talk about a madhouse. It was nearing five-thirty and people were lined up for the privilege of sitting at one of the booths or tables. Only the glassy-eyed deer heads on the wall seemed placid. I edged my way toward the cashier, and when one of the owners whisked past I called her name.

"Mary Maggie! What's going on?"

She was apparently doing double duty, but stopped long enough to put her pencil in the pocket of her pink uniform. "Kids' Day at the carnival is almost ending and the Night-Light parade is on the square tonight." She ticked off the events as if she had them memorized, and she probably did. How else could she answer questions and anticipate the crowds? "Then the pet parade's starting in an hour. Everyone wants to eat first." She snatched four menus off the cashier's stand, then swung back to me. "How are you?" she asked, looking me over.

"What?"

"You know. After your night in, well, you know." She looked around. "Are you okay?"

Ah, yes, Mary Maggie knew about my time in the Wilmot County Jail, since she provided the food for the place. No wonder it was impossible to keep a secret in Purple Sage. "I'm fine. It was all a misunderstanding."

"It was Ed, right?" I nodded and she added, "That boy's not bright." *Boy* being a derogatory term, not to delineate age, but lack of brainpower. "You want something to eat? I'm sorry but it's going to take at least twenty minutes for a table."